UNTETHERED

WANDERER OF WORLDS

BOOK TWO

ACKNOWLEDGEMENTS

The following people are our constant support and sounding posts; Susan Strathdee, Kylie Crase, David Woodward and David Strange. They are the wonderful readers who lovingly pointed out errors both big and small, so that our story could be as interesting and as seamless as possible. We are eternally grateful.

DEDICATION

For David, Sue and Diane

For David

THE STORY SO FAR

Daeson of Cloverlea, Kharltae

Daeson accidentally travels away from his home-world and enters the next world after touching the Wanderer Portal. He is accosted first by the Authorities and then by a group of criminals (led by a man named Nick Logan). Nick takes Daeson to meet his boss, the sophisticated Omerri Backhouse. She owns and operates the Queen of Hearts, a legal brothel with an illegal nightclub and gambling den attached. Omerri understands that Daeson's strange clothing, money and language means he's a Wanderer.

Omerri is the only one that can fluently speak Daeson's language. He reveals to her that he knows when people are lying to him and Omerri identifies him as a Wanderer Intuit. She vows to protect him from the Authorities and assigns him to Nick, who uses Daeson's ability while he interrogates rival criminals. Daeson becomes enamoured with Omerri. When she discovers he's also a Healer, she takes him to a resort-world where they begin an intimate romance.

Synjan Walker of Gredann, Trent

Forced to manipulate an old friend's death, Synjan is left reeling from her actions. She contacts Nick Logan, her sometimes lover, and he remains unaffected. Working past her grief, she goes about her business as usual; picking up contraband from Oceangate (the Authority base), and training with a Unit Commander she affectionately calls Freddie. Her boss, Ellis, sends her to investigate a report of squatters on a property he owns and it leads to an armed confrontation. Synjan is forced to defend herself and kills them. Early the next morning she consoles herself by visiting an old haunt of her late father's. On her return she is summoned by Nick and finds out that he needs her for a mission, one that will have her infiltrating the Authority base, posing as a soldier.

Hawke Aron of Donovan Court, Boronia

Eight year old Hawke is abducted by a group of horse-thieves that turn out to be Wanderers. While on the run, they discover he is a Wanderer Shielder and take him with them to the next world. An Authority unit pursues them and Hawke is sacrificed so the group can escape. He is captured and questioned before being assigned a ward of the organisation—unable to return to his world because they are ignorant of other worlds and their workings.

Hawke is sent to Willets Academy, an Authority run school for boys. He is also required to visit the DOME laboratory for testing, because his Wanderer Shielder bloodline is new to them.

Hawke is beaten by some of the other boys for being a Wanderer in an Authority school. His Authority sponsor—Lieutenant Cayden—goes beyond his duties and takes on a more fatherly role. Hawke spends three years in the Academy environment. When he is eleven, he visits the Oceangate base on a school excursion. While there, he is pulled away from the rest of his group by a Unit Commander, who takes him to a warehouse in the middle of Gredann's dockside neighbourhood. The warehouse is empty except for a peculiar lounge setting and a man on an armchair who introduces himself as Howard Ellis.

The Hunter of the Authorities

The Hunter assassinates a Wanderer couple that he has been tracking for a long time. He reports into the closest base and finds a new trio to go after, choosing them because they will be passing through Baxter—a world where he has some unfinished personal business.

In Baxter, while waiting for a sign of the Wanderer trio, he tracks and locates a woman who he's been pursuing for many years. When he visits her house, she's not at home and he gets a call that his trio has arrived on world. He is forced to abandon his personal mission and checks in to learn about a crime-wave the trio are on.

TABLE OF CONTENTS

CHAPTER ONE

Pitch

HAWKE licked his lips, tasting pungent, salty air. He wondered if the name Howard Ellis was supposed to mean something to him. Sounds of bells and people shouting were far away, smothered by the heavy silence that had fallen between him and the man who'd arranged for him to be here. Dust tickled his nose and Hawke rubbed it to prevent a sneeze. He then traced the embroidered stitching on the arm of his chair with a fingernail, the low scratching noise plucking out a slow rhythm punctuated by occasional pops, like strings breaking from a guitar. The weight of the gaze upon him was palpable.

"Discuss what?" he finally asked, realising that he was going to have to push the conversation forward.

The setting was so unusual that he wasn't surprised to feel a sense of intrigue dominating his natural suspicion. He had no idea who this man was, nor what the 'many things' they had to discuss might be but instead of feeling the need to flee, he wanted to listen. The Unit Commander was somewhere waiting outside, his classmates were by now moving through Oceangate—the jewel of the Authorities' operations in Gredann—and Hawke was here, in a strange lounge setting in the middle of an empty warehouse with a man he didn't know.

The ignorance didn't travel both ways. Howard Ellis knew of him and though the man seemed content to sit and stare at him through dancing dust motes, there had to be an agenda at play.

"How I can help you."

Hawke was used to demands being placed on him, on being politely forced to give in with the knowledge that consent wasn't necessary. He'd been certain that this was going to be more of the same. The idea of having help offered was unexpected and disconcerting.

"I don't need your help," he sneered, bristling at the notion that he was vulnerable.

Howard Ellis' green eyes glinted as he lifted a hand in a calming gesture. "You misunderstand. I don't mean how I can help you now, I'm talking about your future." The hand lowered, fingers dancing elegantly along the crease of his pants to smooth it. Afterward, they played restlessly against his other hand, linking and unlinking fingers as he watched Hawke intently. It seemed an excited gesture rather than a nervous one.

"My future?"

"Yes. In a couple of years you're going to be forced to decide what you want to be. I have no doubt that the Authorities would have you believe that there is only one path before you. One choice; to join their ranks and claw your way through their faceless machine, eking out an anonymous existence at the end of their leashes."

Hawke's eyebrows lifted and he was slightly awed. He'd only heard his kidnappers speak so viciously about the Authorities before and they'd never been so eloquent. Until that moment, he'd been entertaining the notion that this man had to be connected to the Authorities because he'd had a respected Unit Commander deliver him here. The mischievous glint in Ellis' eyes and the relish with which the derogatory words were spoken told Hawke that Ellis had no love for the institution. Or at least he wanted Hawke to believe he hated them.

"I brought you here to show you that you have another, better choice. A future far brighter and a position far more important available to you. Working for me."

There was ceremony evident in the delivery of Ellis' final words, an importance relayed by a slight vibration of emotion in the man's voice, in the way he looked into Hawke's eyes, the stillness that overcame him when he finished speaking. Hawke felt it and allowed the silence to settle around them once more, giving the importance of the declaration its due respect by thinking before he spoke. There was an element of ritual about this meeting he didn't dare overstep—just as a guest would wait for a host to offer refreshments in Boronia, even if he was dying of thirst. He knew he was supposed to consider every word this man said with appropriate solemnity.

"Doing what?" he eventually asked.

A broad grin split the older man's face and even though he looked genuinely happy, it seemed a harsh expression on his thin countenance.

"Business."

"What sort of business?"

"I have many, varied business interests that I'd invite you to be part of."

"Part of? Like a partner?"

"In many ways you would be my equal. Together, we could accomplish unlimited feats."

"Unlimited feats?"

"We'd accomplish many amazing things. As a team."

"Like a superhero team?"

Howard Ellis chuckled, uncrossed his leg and shifted so that he was leaning his elbow on one arm of the decorative armchair. He was angled towards Hawke, his hands folded in front of his stomach and his eyes dancing with delight. His gaze was nothing short of admiring and Hawke had been looked at like that enough times in his life that he could appreciate it for what it was. This man wanted something from him. What Hawke wasn't used to was the fact that Ellis wasn't trying to hide it and didn't seem to care if he knew.

"Of sorts."

"Pfft," Hawke had made the superhero comment as a joke, half expecting he might offend Ellis by not taking his words seriously and Ellis had answered him. He understood when someone was playing him for a fool. "In that case, working for you sounds riskier than signing up."

"Earnest endeavours yield the sweetest fruit."

Hawke wasn't sure what that meant and he shifted with agitation, feeling like he was being toyed with. He wanted to stop the games and he had an idea about how to do that.

"Why me?"

"You're unique."

"Because of my blood," Hawke spat.

Ellis tilted his head, regarding him curiously. "You say it like it's a bad thing."

Hawke glared at him, unsure how he could see it any other way.

"You've been amongst Authorities too long," Ellis stated and his words were acidic, his mouth a disapproving slash. He sat up, straightening his perfectly arranged suit jacket, as if flicking imaginary lint off the cuffs would as easily dispel whatever was annoying him.

"I wasn't left with much of a choice, considering Wanderers abandoned me," Hawke argued, knowing he was probably provoking the man's ire but also wanting to know what that looked like.

Ellis' mouth pursed and his hands fisted tightly on his knees but his deep voice was steady as he responded. "True. But we should focus on the future, not the past."

"You know my history," Hawke stated, feeling a mixture of horror and flattery. This man had gone to great lengths to bring him here and even though he wasn't part of the Authorities, he'd somehow gained access to classified information on him. Through the Unit Commander? Why?

"I do," Ellis agreed quietly and his hands slowly unfurled.

"You either know somebody important or you have a lot of money."

"You're very perceptive," Ellis complimented with a small smile. Hawke was surprised by how much he enjoyed hearing approval in this man's voice.

"Which is it?" he pressed.

"I'd have to say both."

"How come some of my questions get answered easily but others don't? You don't seem shy."

The smile broadened again and now Ellis' hands were flat on his legs. His upright posture was still perfect but the air about the man was more relaxed. "No, I'm not shy, but I don't want to overwhelm you."

Again, Hawke snorted derisively. "Maybe you shouldn't have brought me to a creepy warehouse in the middle of nowhere, then."

"I apologise for the location. It was the best I could do at short notice. It's the only place I could guarantee we wouldn't be bothered."

"You've gone to a lot of trouble."

"You're worth it."

Hawke's chest burned with pleasure and he had to stop himself from smiling. "So are you a Wanderer or something?"

"I'm an admirer of the bloodline," Ellis admitted, smiling coyly.

"And you don't like the Authorities?"

"I have a healthy respect for them. What I don't like are their restrictions and I believe that you and I working together would achieve what they want to withhold from everyone—but especially from Wanderers."

Hawke gave him an enquiring look.

"Freedom," Howard Ellis responded.

It was a simple word but it had a profound effect as it fluttered through Hawke. The skin on his arms prickled inexplicably.

"Sounds like a Wanderer thing to say," Hawke replied and a new thought quelled his soaring feelings. Howard Ellis thought he was looking at a full blood. His next words were spoken dully, resentment spiking his tone. "You should know that I can't travel through the natural Portal."

Ellis looked only momentarily perturbed before he was smiling reassuringly once more. "I've read that. It doesn't matter. You'll be more powerful than a Wanderer anyway."

"How?"

"You're registered already. When you reach fourteen, you will only have to notify your guardians of your intentions to live here as my charge and you'll be free. I will induct you, guide you and you shall be free to travel anywhere, to all the known worlds, on behalf of our business interests."

"You can't do that already?"

"I admit...I enjoy the anonymity I've worked hard to maintain. I don't risk mainstream travel."

"I see," Hawke said, a sour taste lodging on his tongue.

Howard Ellis was the head of his business, willing to risk everyone beneath him in order to protect his empire. As much as he was shining light on Hawke with all his compliments, ultimately he was looking for someone willing to play harder than him and to take the risks he wasn't willing to take. It was smart but cold and not exactly what he'd expected when he'd been told he was going to be helped.

He was simply watched and left alone with his thoughts for a time, allowed to wriggle on his fancy chair. It was too tall for him to sit back in it and have his feet touch the ground, which made him feel like a small child. It felt too eager to sit forward on the edge just so the tingling sensation of restricted blood flow in his legs didn't bother him. He wondered if the furniture was deliberately chosen to keep him uncomfortable and decided that it had to have been. This was a test, like they all were.

When Howard Ellis broke the silence at last, his words were hesitant and his voice had a hopeful quality to it.

"Would you do me the honour of telling me... what is it like, being a Wanderer in Authority custody?"

The gentle reverence in the words had Hawke frowning as he finally found an acceptable sitting position—settled back on the chair with his legs arched before him. He hugged them as he answered sternly.

"I'm not in custody. I'm not a criminal."

"My apologies," Ellis demurred, inclining his head. "I had thought the Authorities would put conditions on their care for you."

"Conditions?"

"Yes. I didn't realise they would give without expectation."

At last Hawke saw the point Howard Ellis was making and he bit the inside of his lip gently, disappointed he hadn't seen this coming. Although he respected the subtlety of the comments, it made him wary. The man before him was obviously manipulative and he knew how to get his way. Hawke resolved to think more carefully before he spoke but that didn't make his decision any easier. Should he betray his guardians to this relative stranger? Hadn't his sponsor Cayden earned his loyalty? But there was part of him that knew if he didn't tell Mister Ellis everything, he could expect the same in return. If he wanted to know more about what he was being offered, he needed to lay bare the entirety of his circumstances so that he could compare and make a fully informed decision about his future.

Before he'd consciously decided it was worth the risk, Hawke started talking. He told his companion about what life at Willets was like for him. He enjoyed the sympathy he gained, the outrage voiced by Howard Ellis when he described the prejudiced actions of the other boys, simply because of his blood. The fury burning in vibrant green eyes when Hawke described the teachers as being equally as biased was exhilarating.

There were numerous questions and captivated silences as he described his visits to the DOME. There was a pang of guilt when he talked about Dr Kelly Turner and the preferential treatment he received from Cayden, but he was reassured when Howard Ellis declared surprise and pleasure that he had such vigilant protectors to guide him.

Hawke was just getting into a discussion about the portals when the Unit Commander strode in, staring at Howard Ellis from the other side of the coffee table.

"It's time. I need to get him back," he declared gruffly.

Ellis' expression matched the way Hawke felt and the distinguished gentleman consulted his watch disbelievingly as he responded. "No, it can't be! Surely it hasn't been—almost two hours? Oh dear. We were... please," he implored Hawke, "will you come and visit me again?"

Hawke blinked, also disappointed that they hadn't discussed in more detail what this man could offer him.

"I don't think I can."

"I can make it happen," Ellis assured him, turning to look at the Unit Commander. There was a tense moment of staring before the wrestler-type soldier gave a curt nod. Ellis turned to smile at Hawke once more. "There. I shall send for you when it is convenient. I very much look forward to continuing our conversation," he said grandly, standing and offering an elegant hand to be shaken.

Hawke scrambled to his feet and was surprised when he shook it by how rough and calloused that hand was. "Until next time," he agreed, giving his best Boronian head bow before he was ushered away by the Unit Commander.

When they got to the exit, he turned and wasn't surprised to still see Howard Ellis watching them from his little patch of furniture in the distant middle of the warehouse. He gave the man a wave despite believing he wouldn't see it. Exiting the warehouse had him blinking against the bright sunlight as he got into the Unit Commander's vehicle.

He wasn't entirely certain what had just happened but he felt like he'd made an important connection, perhaps even a friend. It was about time his blood started working in his favour.

CHAPTER TWO

Prized Possession

DAESON was roused from sleep by a phone's warbling ring. He felt the bed shift as Omerri reached across and fumbled for the handset. When he looked over, he saw she hadn't bothered to lift her eye mask.

"Hello?" she mumbled, her voice croaky. "Okay, I'll send him."

The resentment that fell over him was a heavy blanket weighing him down. Daeson wanted to complain about the demand he was meeting lately but held his tongue. Any protest would sound like he didn't want to help or that he was being immature and selfish. They were accusations he'd already heard. What bothered him most was that he hadn't had a full night's sleep in over a month. He wasn't waking up tired but it was what he was waking up to that was his biggest grievance.

Daeson sat up and Omerri rolled over while tugging on the sheet. He got out of bed so she could take as much of the covers as she liked.

"Which room?" he asked.

"Wha—?" By the slur of her question he knew she was almost asleep.

"Interrogation or healing?" he barked, wanting an answer before she drifted off.

She mumbled a noise that sounded like 'heal' and his resentment grew more pronounced. He toyed with the idea of not heading downstairs, to let Nick suffer his injuries...except the chances were higher that the heal was needed for someone else. It was usually the men Nick took along with him on his after-curfew missions who got hurt.

Daeson dressed quickly into long-pants and a shirt, both of them a light material because the season was growing hotter. Summer was fast approaching, bringing his eighteenth birthday along with it. It had made sense to swap his winter birth to a summer one since arriving in the city of Gredann, on the world of Trent. Once he'd become involved with Omerri, he hadn't openly celebrated his birthday—she was emotionally fragile about the process of ageing and he'd discovered it was better to avoid the topic altogether.

Daeson went into the master bathroom—ignoring the spa-bath and extra large shower stall—and headed for the narrow floor-to-ceiling storage cupboard instead. It wasn't a storage cupboard but it looked like one. In reality, it was a private elevator.

When Daeson stood inside it, it was only just big enough for his shoulders not to brush the walls. When he'd questioned why it had been made so narrow, Omerri explained that it used to have a different purpose. Before the Authorities had retroactively installed plumbing, every house with upper floors had a waste-channel beneath their toilets. Once more modern conveniences had been installed, there was no need for the channels and they were either filled in or the space cleaned up and used for other things. Daeson realised this meant Omerri's secret elevator was gliding up and down a column designed specifically for shit.

It didn't smell but he still found himself trying not to touch the walls every time he used it.

Daeson stepped into the small space, pulled the gate across and latched it into place. There were only two buttons in the lift—neither of them labelled. The top button was for Omerri's bedroom at her house (which neighboured the Queen) and the bottom button took him into the depths of Nick's underworld.

He suspected there were more secrets within the Queen of Hearts than just an elevator that led into Omerri's personal space; there had been a few times when Nick would disappear into a room and then appear somewhere else without coming back out. Omerri had mentioned many times that she'd designed the Queen herself, to reflect as mysterious a personality as her own. At first Daeson had been impressed, then he'd become thoughtful. Now he just smiled politely, bored by a boast that was repeated word for word each time he heard it.

The elevator arrived with a small bump and Daeson unlatched the gate, peering out into the empty corridor before he entered. It took him only a few steps to arrive at the place he called the Healing Room.

Smoke coiled from incense sticks around the room, carrying the odour of sandalwood and jasmine. Tasselled cushions and silk pillows were tossed in corners. Peculiar statues and other-worldly figurines that represented unknown Gods littered every surface. The room was a mixture of dark reds, greens and purples, highlighted with gold. The music that played softly within was percussive and without melody.

Daeson felt at odds with this room. He liked it; the exotic decorations were fascinating and he wanted to know more about where they had come from and what they meant. He also didn't like it; it was a room that represented a lie and was often filled with screams of pain. It was strange how his emotions wouldn't mix. He would either experience one or the other depending on his mood. At the moment he loathed it.

In the middle of the room stood two men—Nick and a man with a black bag covering his head and shoulders. Daeson recognised him by his clothing and build. His name was Marcus and he was one of the live-in security guards at the Queen. He was smart and reliable, often guarding the door to the gambling den, sometimes going out on Nick's missions. He had kind words and a quick smile for everyone that came his way. Daeson was surprised that he was the kind of man that could stomach the illegal tasks Nick set for him.

The black bag moved from side to side when Daeson shut the door, Marcus reacting to the sound. Daeson knew that Marcus wouldn't be able to see him. Beneath the bag, Nick would have tied a black scarf around his head, over a black sleeper's eye mask.

It had been Nick's idea to protect Daeson's identity as a Healer from everyone at the Queen. Other than Daeson, Omerri and Nick, nobody else knew. It didn't stop Nick from taking advantage of that knowledge, however.

"Hold out your arm," Nick prompted. Nick was holding onto one arm but Marcus' other arm was pressed against his chest, the wrist bent at a peculiar angle. It looked broken. Marcus at first grunted then growled his pain through clenched teeth when Nick helped him to get his arm away from his body. Daeson shook his head; separating the limb was unnecessary but he knew better than to speak. Marcus would certainly recognise his voice.

Daeson approached, listening to Marcus' laboured breathing. He checked for the water cooler tucked away in one corner of the room, disguised by a draping of purple material.

In case anyone snoops, Nick had said. Daeson knew that if anybody snooped and Nick caught them, it was unlikely they would be able to tell anybody what they'd seen anyway. He'd never asked Nick if he'd killed anyone... because he didn't want to know for sure.

He reached out with both hands and gently pressed

his palms to Marcus' broken wrist; one atop and one beneath. He heard Marcus pull in breath to scream but it never came. The heal had begun and Daeson could feel familiar warmth radiating from his hands, soaking into Marcus' wound and correcting it.

When Daeson healed, he didn't hear sounds. It was like the thrumming and warmth of his hands blocked some of his other senses. His mouth and throat would go dry but he also felt an indescribable emotional connection to whomever he was healing. The connection was possibly the hardest and most overwhelming thing of all; especially now that Nick would sometimes bring strangers to him. At least he knew Marcus and already considered him a friend. It was unsettling to feel affection towards people he had no idea about.

"O Mighty Shea," Marcus said as Daeson completed the heal. His words were muffled but Daeson recognised the hail to the Goddess of Mercy. It was these overlaps between his world and theirs that intrigued him the most. The deities were the same—not only the same names but also what they stood for. The language the Docksiders spoke was a dialect of the one Daeson spoke. He could barely understand it, just like he'd barely understood Authoritan when he'd arrived in Gredann, but it explained how Omerri had managed to speak to him because she had both parts of the language. The implications between shared Gods and shared language between one world and the next spoke volumes but he still felt like he was missing a vital key.

"All good?" Nick prompted, staring intently at Daeson before his gaze dropped to Marcus' arm. It was no longer bent at a strange angle but Marcus was still holding it out.

Daeson nodded and stepped away while Nick

guided Marcus out of the room using the opposite door. It led into the main corridor and would be locked using a key that Nick had the only copy of. Daeson poured himself three cups of water and drank them all before he left the room, returning to the elevator.

He was exhausted. Healing others extracted a great deal of energy from him, though he would never feel it seeping away at the time. Not understanding his boundaries was dangerous; if he tried to heal someone beyond his ability, would it kill him? It didn't seem possible, that healing another person would deteriorate his own health... but was that what was happening? Was that how he healed others? Why did he always need to drink so much water afterward? He had no idea how his powers worked. He had nobody to teach him.

He wondered if his mother knew more. He was angry with her, denied access to her and the knowledge that she possessed. He thought she might be punishing him because he'd used the criminal portal three more times after her warning for him not to. He'd been awake each time but knew to feign sleep in order not to alarm the people who were sending him. He would travel through the portal-tunnel to his mother's mind-sanctuary but she wouldn't be there to meet him. The first time he'd been there alone he'd called constantly for her, searching through the rippling room before he'd been whisked away back to Gredann. The second time he'd been there he'd called out again, pleading for her to come to him, to answer some burning questions. The third time he'd kept his silence and looked around instead, trying to solve the riddle of the rippling room himself. He'd found no answers. He wondered if she was punishing him for holidaying with Omerri. It wasn't necessary that he travelled to Mwavey with her every year but he felt he had no other option. It was at a time when she was most vulnerable and needed him and he wanted to be there for her.

Daeson wasn't sure that Omerri would want him to come this time.

The elevator delivered him back upstairs and he stepped out into the darkened master bedroom. He undressed and waited for his eyes to adjust before making his way back to bed. When he climbed in, Omerri made a soft noise of greeting and turned to face him, throwing her arm atop him and curling against him. She was soft and warm and as he stroked her hair, he felt guilty for his critical thoughts.

He loved her, truly. It wasn't easy but she was worth it.

Daeson enjoyed working in the kitchens. It was the one place in the Queen that wasn't tainted with ulterior motives. He didn't have to spot liars, he didn't have to heal injuries, he didn't have to think about what the girls did to make their money upstairs. He was also out of the way of the Authorities who visited the nightclub downstairs. He felt useful and he'd discovered a joy for cooking that he hadn't expected. It was fun to create delicious food and make it look pretty on a plate. The head chef, Herme, had even called him 'talented'. The praise had buoyed Daeson for weeks.

He usually worked the day shift but one of the kitchen-hands hadn't shown up for work and Daeson had offered to fill in. Omerri was at an important Authority General's party tonight. For someone who ran an illegal enterprise, Daeson was surprised that she was invited to a lot of Authority parties. This world didn't make much sense to him.

Someone charged through the kitchen door, slamming it against the wall and not stopping it from swinging back with the same gusto. Daeson looked over to see who would risk Nellan's wrath—the night-time chef was a tall, skinny woman who could deliver a barrage of insults at incredible volume if someone dared upset her. Daeson had felt her fury only once when he hadn't wiped down properly for the night-shift workers and she'd sought him out to scream in his face. He double-checked that everything was spotless for the changeover nowadays.

It was Nick who'd entered the kitchen aggressively and Nellan said nothing. Daeson returned his attention to the risotto in the giant pot before him, knowing that he was Nick's target.

Nick stood very close, his chest against Daeson's arm. Daeson clenched his teeth, promising himself that he wouldn't respond.

"You told her," Nick hissed in his ear. Obviously he didn't want the secret to be shared further. "You fucking squealer."

Nick waited for Daeson to say something but when he didn't, Nick continued.

"I do all this shit for you; set you up in the kitchens to make you comfortable, keep you away from the Authorities, keep you *safe*, just so you can squeal on me."

Daeson couldn't let that go. He turned and glared at Nick.

"You don't do all that for me, you do it for *you*. You want to keep your prized possession working for *you*."

"You're a *prize*, now?" Nick spat. "You're no goddamn prize, running to Omerri like a little brat, tattling on me for having fun."

"She was passed out!" Daeson yelled.

"Keep it down," Nellan ordered and Daeson looked at her, angry that she wouldn't stand up to Nick and would berate Daeson for doing it. He lowered his voice.

"She was unconscious and you had sex with her anyway."

"I didn't put her on my bed, she went there herself."

"So? She can't change her mind when she's out cold."

"She wasn't going to change her mind," Nick snorted.

"Then why wouldn't you let me..." Daeson dropped his voice even lower. "Heal her?"

"You'd trust your secret with a drunk bitch?"

Daeson and Nick glared at one another.

"You knew sex with her was wrong if you wanted me to keep it to myself."

"I don't care if you tell the guys. I asked you not to tell *Omerri*." Nick's smile soured and he pretended to inspect his nails. "She's the jealous type." Nick stepped away from Daeson to lean against the counter nearby. Daeson didn't want to be drawn into what was obviously bait for him to respond to. He'd already learned that arguing with Nick was a waste of time. When Daeson said nothing and continued stirring, Nick peered into the pot.

"What's that you're cooking?"

"Chicken risotto," Daeson said, feeling like the worst had passed and wanting to move the conversation on. He was aching to know why Omerri would be jealous about Nick having sex with a passed out girl. Nick had obviously got into trouble for it. When Daeson had told her what he'd learned, Omerri said she was disgusted... but why would Nick use the word jealous?

"Give me a plate. I'm starving."

Daeson left the pot and found a shallow plate to

spoon some risotto in. He handed it and a fork over to Nick, who promptly began eating. Daeson thought that would be the end of the conversation but Nick spoke around mouthfuls of food instead.

"I'll be needing you for a questioning. I'm bringing someone in later."

"How much later? I've just done two shifts here," Daeson complained. "I need to sleep at some stage."

"Pull your weight. I never asked you to work in the *kitchen*."

Daeson stirred the risotto furiously, angry and helpless. There was no point talking to Nick, he would always have the final word. He was very good at making his argument and even though Daeson knew that Nick was overstepping, Daeson didn't know how to express it.

Salvation came in the form of another person entering the kitchen. Daeson didn't turn to look but he could feel Nick's attention had shifted away. He was relieved but also concerned that the other person might receive some of the residue of Nick's bad mood. He didn't have to worry.

The person who'd entered was a woman. Daeson didn't recognise her voice but heard the enjoyment in her tone at speaking with Nick. They flirted openly with one another but her tone grew serious when she told Nick that she had news. Daeson snuck a glance in their direction, just as Nick looked his way with a panicked stare. The blonde woman speaking with him seemed confused and Daeson wondered why. He turned back to his risotto and paid more attention to their conversation.

"About what, then?" Nick asked.

"About Kate."

Daeson didn't know a Kate. Perhaps that was the real name of one of the girls at the Queen of Hearts. He knew it wasn't Jade or Ruby.

"I... well, you know she hasn't been coping at the Bunker," the woman said.

Daeson had heard the term *Bunker* a few times. He knew it was somewhere Nick had used to live before coming to work at the Queen. Other than that, nobody would talk to Daeson about it and Omerri had grown furious when he'd mentioned it to her. She'd made him promise not to talk about it again, with anyone. The word had stuck in his head.

"She's a useless junkie," Nick said.

"Well, she's dead."

"And?"

Daeson wasn't surprised by Nick's callousness but the woman he was talking to obviously was, by the way she cursed him. Daeson jumped when Nick tossed his plate and fork into the sink beside him, thinking he was about to yell at Daeson for listening in, but Nick was still focussed on the woman.

Daeson felt bad for the unknown blonde. She obviously cared about her friend and he could hear pain in her voice as she appealed to Nick. He didn't know this woman but he felt partially to blame for Nick's ruthlessness towards her. Perhaps if Nick hadn't already been antagonised by Daeson's betrayal of his secret, he might've been nicer to the woman.

"I gotta' go," Nick said, announcing his exit with a sigh. "You coming downstairs?"

"Soon, I just need a drink of water." The woman's refusal at joining Nick won Daeson's respect. He could show her that someone cared, even if with a small gesture. Daeson grabbed a glass and poured cold water into it from the fridge. Nick was already gone by the time he handed it to the woman. She looked up at him first in surprise, then in gratitude.

"Thanks," she said quietly.

Questions itched to be asked. As he watched her drink, he wondered what it was that she did for Nick. She obviously did some kind of work for him, but the death of Kate had rocked her. She didn't seem to be comfortable with violence and death and Daeson felt a kinship with her.

He opened his mouth to ask her name... when Nick shoved himself in between them.

"Why don't you get back to work?" Nick growled. Daeson returned to the risotto, frustrated. He felt like everybody was keeping secrets from him and he was sick of it.

It was a week later when Daeson saw the blonde woman again.

The kitchen was open for staff breakfasts from six until eight. After the general populace was fed, the kitchen hands would eat, wipe down and then prep for lunch. There were very few special meals made on the fly—Omerri and Nick often ate at different times to everyone else. Daeson breakfasted with the kitchen staff and ate again with Omerri because she rose very late. Once she arrived and they'd eaten together, she would sometimes pull him from kitchen duty (the cleanup before lunch) to spend time with her. Whenever she did this, it would cause tension during Daeson's next shift. He'd discovered that if he wiped down and cleaned up as much as he could before Omerri's arrival, the other kitchen hands wouldn't make inappropriate comments. The head cook— Hermes—never did. Daeson assumed the older man knew Daeson didn't have to work in the kitchen, but that he wanted to. Still, Daeson wanted to earn his keep and not feel like he was getting special treatment. The best way to show this was to take the garbage bags out to the large dumpsters in the alley. It was a job everyone hated because of the smell and the very real risk of ripping a bag open.

Daeson gathered the two large black bags together, knotting them firmly at the neck and then bustling them out.

Hammond was guarding the door and kindly opened it for him.

"Thanks," Daeson said, shifting the bags awkwardly so he could move through the door and past Hammond without rubbing against anything.

Hammond didn't say anything but nodded his acknowledgement. Daeson had been told that the security guard held his breath whenever someone did a garbage run from the kitchen. Since hearing the rumour, Daeson saw Hammond press his lips firmly together every time he approached holding the large black bags. He'd never noticed such a thing before and this knowledge somehow humanised the steely guard. Hammond was polite but never friendly.

The air felt cool on Daeson's face and arms as soon as he stepped outside. Even on a hot day, the alley would be chilly. It only saw the sun at its highest point. A strip of light would travel down one wall to the ground and then up the other before disappearing in the space of a couple of hours. Daeson had watched it once, when he'd had nothing better to do than to think about his place in this city. It had been a struggle at the start but he'd found a way to be happy.

Now he was struggling to hold onto that happiness.

Omerri was losing patience with him. No, that wasn't fair. They were losing patience with each other. When he was away from her, his opinion of her would radically change. When he was in her presence, he would feel a rush of affection. Was such a thing normal? He'd tried to talk to her about it, to find out if she felt the same way and if they could work it out together. His questions were met with accusations that he was testing her love so he immediately dropped the issue, begging for her mercy with kisses, touches and compliments.

It remained unresolved between them; a constant shadow that etched a dark path in his thoughts until the light of her smile would cast it away.

He huffed and dropped the garbage bags onto the ground before opening the skip with some difficulty. The lid wasn't heavy but it was awkward. He heaved each garbage bag into the bin and closed it with a loud clang. The noise made him wince and he wiped his hands on his white apron, before turning and seeing her - the blonde woman who'd been disturbed by her friend's death.

Her hair was pulled tightly back. She was wearing a green parka over blue pants that hid her shape and her hands were wrapped around the straps of her backpack. It was vastly different from the outfit he'd first seen her in. She was staring at him with unfiltered interest, a smile toying about her lips like she was pleased to see him. He was flustered by her expression; it was like she knew all of his secrets.

"Hey, I didn't get to thank you last week for the water. Nick was being an ass, so thanks."

That's because Nick is an ass, he wanted to say. He held back because he didn't know how she'd react. She seemed to like Nick. The silence got a little too long so he filled it with something easy.

"You're welcome."

There was a pause but the woman didn't let it become awkward.

"So you've been here for—what...two years or something?—and we've never been formally introduced. I'm Synjan. Have you been avoiding me?"

Her smile grew, changing from the enigmatic, knowing one to something cheekier. Daeson wondered how she knew he'd been at the Queen for two years. Her question was direct and strangely accurate. Perhaps she already knew of the warning Nick had given him about her. He could simply say 'yes' and return to his kitchen duties, effectively cutting her off—that was what Nick would want - but Daeson didn't want to comply. He wanted to know more about Synjan. He wanted to know more about the Bunker. He wanted her to explain herself to him and the best way to get it from her was to make a provocative statement.

"I've been told to stay away from you."

CHAPTER THREE

Business As Usual

YNJAN blinked, the answer unexpected.

"By... Omerri?" she guessed, a disbelieving little laugh accompanying the words. The woman had never liked her but this seemed extreme.

"No, by Nick," the kitchen hand corrected.

Synjan frowned. "Why does he want you to stay away from me?"

"I'm not sure."

She watched him, trying to decide if he was telling the truth or not. He shifted beneath her gaze but it didn't appear to be because he was lying. He looked like he had more to say but he was waiting for her to go first. Was he being polite or did he have no more information to share with her?

"What's your name?" she asked, leading with the most pressing question.

"Daeson."

His name was unfamiliar and a ripple of amazement ran through her. There were occasions when it took a while to connect a name with a new face at the Queen but it eventually came together. She didn't recall the exact date she'd noticed Daeson's pattern close to Omerri's but she felt she was pretty close with her guess of two years. Considering the frequency with which she visited the Queen, Nick certainly *had* worked hard to keep her and Daeson apart. His odd behaviour when he dragged her away from the handsome kitchen hand last week made even more sense now. She needed to know why.

"Pleased to meet you, Daeson," she smiled at him.

"You too... Synjan." His smile looked sincere.

"What is it you do around here?" Nick had never barred her from mingling with any of the other staff so there had to be more to him than just being a kitchen hand. It had to be something to do with Omerri. Maybe the insecure old witch thought Synjan would take a shine to her blue-eyed toy and she didn't want to risk her pretty prize being tainted by the likes of her.

Daeson's eyes widened slightly. His mouth opened but no explanation came out. He didn't seem to know how to answer her and Synjan felt vindicated by his awkwardness.

"Let me guess; you've been told not to tell me that?" She smirked and took a step closer to him. He was a head and a half taller than her and she had to crane her neck to look up at him. Someone her size shouldn't be able to intimidate anyone as big as him but he tried to step back anyway. He looked mildly panicked when he smacked into the dumpster, glancing around like he wished someone would come and rescue him.

"Aren't you curious?" she demanded. She narrowed her eyes and tilted her head, silently inviting him to entertain theories about the conspiracy as well. The urge to touch him was strong so she let go of her backpack and shoved her hands in her coat pockets; he was spooked enough. "Not even a little?"

"A-about... ?"

"Why they want to keep us apart?"

"Um, well, I suppose Nick has his reasons—"

"Yes! That's what I mean! What are they? What do you *know*?" she asked, leaning forward eagerly.

Whether he might have found the inclination to hypothesise with her, she wasn't to learn because the air above them split apart with a thunderous, resonating boom. Synjan's gaze snapped upward but there was nothing to see beyond the usual dull sky of Gredann. Though it had sounded like a storm breaking overhead, there was no venom in those clouds. As bizarre as her theory was, she guessed what the noise came from; an explosion. Something in the city had exploded.

She closed her eyes in order to concentrate better and mapped. Her mind lifted, hovering above Dockside before moving north to Portside. Although she couldn't see any actual damage, she could determine the location of the blast by the effects it had on the people nearby. It took her less than a minute to determine that whatever had just echoed doom across Gredann had happened at Oceangate. Soldiers were swarming to the southern side of the campus like ants defending their nest.

Nick rushed out of the Queen, the bang of the door a sharp retort in the stillness that had erupted in the wake of the explosion. Not even the birds were confident about breaking it.

Synjan opened her eyes and wasn't surprised by the question she read on his face.

"It's at the base," she confirmed.

"Fuck!" he cursed vehemently, his gaze straying to where Daeson stood pressed against the dumpster. Nick did a double take as he glanced first at Synjan and then at Daeson. "Get back inside and stay where I can find you. I might need you," he growled.

With an obedient nod, Daeson scuttled away. Synjan watched Nick curiously, filing his instruction away to ask about later.

"Are we aborting?" Synjan asked.

"We can't afford to. This is our window."

"You don't sound confident."

"You heard that! What the fuck was it?"

"A bomb, by the sounds. On the south side of the compound."

Nick's lips pursed and she could see him

calculating. "Shouldn't interfere with our plans."

Synjan scoffed. "The whole place will be in chaos!"

"That could be an advantage." He sounded like he'd made up his mind.

"It *could* be," she argued, her disbelief clear.

"We're not going to figure it out standing here talking. Let's go and see what we're dealing with."

It only took him two steps to realise she wasn't walking with him. Impatiently, he leaned back and grabbed her by the upper arm, marching her towards where his vehicle was kept.

"Hey!" she protested, but his grip didn't waver nor his steps slow.

"Don't be ridiculous," he snapped. "I know I'm not hurting you."

"It's just... the situation's completely changed. This seems like a really bad idea!"

"You don't know that for sure."

"I can *see* how much scrambling there is—and most of it is around the kitchens!" Her words appeared to have some effect as he turned to squint at her but his feet didn't slow. Soon enough, his argument was restored.

"No. I'm not giving up yet. Not when we've gone to so much trouble to set it up."

"It doesn't feel right," Synjan argued obstinately.

"It's not about how it *feels*," he sneered, looking her over. "It's about how prepared you are. You've got everything, haven't you?"

"Not the ID."

"I've got it." He didn't hand it over—probably because he was too busy fishing in his pocket for the vehicle keys with his free hand.

"And the memory stick?"

"Of course."

She sighed, resigning herself to at least going to the

base to be sure of the situation. Nick was right. It *was* possible that the explosion could work in their favour... even if the uncertainty tightening her chest right now didn't agree.

CHAPTER FOUR

Bad Reputation

THE smell of frying onions assaulted Hawke's nose and the room was drenched white with steam. Clanging pans and shouts filled the air as the staff verbalised their cooking times to one another. Ill-fitting lids vibrated atop pots boiling over. Being in the kitchen during dinner service was like being on a planet rife with volcanic activity.

His skin felt greasier with every second that passed. No matter how often he scrubbed in the shower, he would get out of bed in the morning with last night's dinner smells clinging to him. There was a comic book he'd read once where one of the characters lived in a swamp and the artist had drawn wavy lines coming off their head to represent odour. Hawke felt like that swamp-character, only *his* wavy lines were the smell of day old bacon and spices.

He stood in the middle of a queue formed by twenty boys of various ages, all waiting for their bread baskets. Most of them were thirteen years old like him, he recognised them from the classes they shared.

They had the same task; to deliver a roll to every person seated at their sections within the dinner hall. Twenty long tables meant twenty boys serving. Hospitality duties were supposed to be rotational but Hawke was constantly rostered on. He was also called upon to clean toilets and mop floors with the other delinquents. He discovered that he would see the same faces on chores with him; the same kids getting into the same kind of trouble. They were losers who couldn't do any better. He was only here because he wouldn't let others make a victim of him.

"Move up, cheesehead." The order came with a shove in the centre of his back. Hawke stumbled forward and then whirled around to glare at the boy, who lifted his hands in a gesture of surrender. "Sorry."

Hawke turned back around and caught up to the rest of the line. The quick apology had placated him—in truth he wasn't angry about the insult; it was a generic one doing the rounds. If he'd been called something derogatory and personal, the outcome would be different. Still, he was pleased that his glare had commanded respect.

They shuffled forward again and Hawke got to the front of the line. He was handed a broad, shallow rectangular basket with a pyramid of bread rolls balanced atop it. They were still steaming from being freshly pulled out of the oven and the smell of them was mouthwatering.

Hawke wouldn't be able to eat his roll until after delivering everybody else's. Then he would have to take his leftovers back to the kitchen where they would be gathered together and then handed out for sharing among the boys after they performed full dinner service. By that time they would be cold and their surface hardened. Even though they would still be fresh and delicious, Hawke resented missing out on eating them hot.

The kitchen was always loud but the noise was nothing compared to the cacophony upon entering the dinner hall. As soon as Hawke shouldered his way through the heavy swinging door, he heard hundreds of conversations spoken with raised voices. He wasn't impressed by the Academy's indulgence of the students' behaviour at dinner time. Until the main meals were served, the students could chat as they liked.

Hawke worked his way along the table, keeping a

firm grip on the basket as bread rolls were snatched out of it. He'd not yet reached halfway down the table when his foot caught on something and he fell forward, landing with a smack on the floor. Bread rolls were launched out of his basket and made some tremendous distance across the tiles. His chest and elbows got the worst of the fall, and as he caught his breath, he could hear the laughter around him.

Hawke rolled onto his side and looked at what he'd tripped over. It was a big, clumpy black shoe with an extended leg that belonged to Polsen. The other boy was laughing along with the others but his stare remained fixed on Hawke. Fury welled in Hawke's aching chest, distorting the expression on his face. He could feel the sneer as it pulled his lips away from his teeth. He lunged to his feet, fists curled while staring Polsen down—Hawke wanted to punch that stupid smirk off his face. The laughter faded and the boys nearest to Hawke went quiet, interested to see what was going to happen next.

Hawke took a step forward, weighing up his chances of getting in at least one good strike. None of Polsen's bigger friends were on this side of the table... but Polsen didn't look worried. He looked excited. He even tipped his chin upward in a gesture for Hawke to continue coming at him. The challenge had been made. Hawke's muscles tensed, ready to leap when—

"Donovan!"

Mr Blatch's voice pierced his thoughts. Hawke looked up to see his maths teacher standing at the head of the next table. The only reason why Hawke could even hear him was because the entire dinner hall had gone quiet. Silence had spread from this section and infected every conversation as boys realised that something was happening.

Mr Blatch's shoes were the kind that clicked as he

walked and Hawke listened to each echoey step as he rounded the table to be in Hawke's direct line of sight. The teacher pointed at the floor beyond.

"Don't just stand there, pick those up!" he yelled. Mr Blatch's volume was unnecessary but he kept everyone's attention. Most of the boys were looking at their teacher rather than at him. Hawke spared a glance over his shoulder at the rolls scattered across the floor and by the time he looked back, Polsen had pulled in his foot and was facing his friends.

Had Mr Blatch seen what was happening? Had he taken note of Hawke's threatening movements and Polsen as his target? Was he saving Hawke from a possible expulsion? Perhaps he'd noticed nothing beyond the fall and just wanted Hawke to retrieve the rolls. Hawke didn't think Mr Blatch was that clueless. Other students thought little of their teachers, thinking them blind and deaf to the goings-on between the boys. Hawke respected Mr Blatch enough not to dismiss him. Blatch had to have known. As much as he liked his maths teacher, he wasn't happy that Mr Blatch had only called him out instead of yelling at Polsen for tripping Hawke in the first place.

Hawke went to the bread basket and crouched down, throwing rolls into it with heated cheeks and impotent rage. His elbows continued to sting but his breath was back now. The palms of Hawke's hands were hurting in an unexpected way; not like the sting of a slap but like he'd been cut. He inspected them before he picked up the bread basket.

Four red crescent marks were indented into the skin of his palms. He recognised them immediately as marks left by his fingernails. He really should trim them down, they'd cut into his skin when he'd made fists.

Nobody was laughing or staring at him anymore.

He was barely looked at when he returned with his bread rolls to the kitchen. The noise of conversations in the dinner hall had grown by the time he made his way back. He didn't think it was as loud as before and when dinner began, the boys were on their best behaviour.

"I heard there was an incident during dinner service."

Hawke raised his eyebrows as though he didn't know what the guidance counsellor was talking about. Naomi stared back at him over gold-rimmed spectacles, her mouth set in a grim line. Her hair was pulled back into a ponytail today, so tight that he thought she was trying for a pseudo face-lift, but it only made her look harsh and older than usual. He chose to interpret her expression as disappointment with his silence, rather than dismay at his behaviour. Over the years he'd learned to give her the benefit of the doubt.

Naomi loved to make excuses for him. He wondered how much she knew about teenage boys. He'd asked her once if she was a mother and she'd smiled and replied that she tended to mother everybody. He'd initially thought the answer was supposed to make him feel good about her. It wasn't until later that he considered it might've been a distraction; a way to rebuff him. She hadn't answered the question directly.

He thought she could be old enough to be a mother of teenagers. In the five years he'd been at Willets Academy, he'd seen her display a range of emotions. He wouldn't say they ruled her but there was never any question as to how she felt about something. He admired the way she could do that; feeling every emotion and displaying them without shame or letting them overwhelm her.

"Would you like to tell me about it?"

He considered her words. Here was the difference between Naomi from Willets Academy and Dr Kelly Turner from the DOME. Naomi would ask if he wanted to talk. Dr Turner would tell him to. His relationship with both women was vastly different as a result, even though he liked them both. He'd gone so far as to tell Naomi he was thankful for her help (even though he didn't think he needed it). Kelly didn't deserve his appreciation, though she had his respect.

"Sure. I tripped."

"Over what?"

He shrugged, not wanting to name names.

"Just clumsy?" she offered. The words were a device to taunt him and he knew better than to rise to the bait but he was still irritated by the implication. "Being clumsy bothers you?"

He must've let his feelings show somehow, either in his face or in his body language. He shrugged, hoping she'd drop the line of questioning.

"Is that why you get bullied? Because you're clumsy?"

"Naomi… " he complained. He didn't know how to phrase his complaint without giving anything away so stopped his protest with her name. She smiled at him over the rim of her glasses and he puffed laughter. "I'm not like them. They fear me."

"Are you someone to be afraid of, Hawke?" she asked gently.

"It wouldn't matter if I was or wasn't. I'm different and that's enough."

"Kellan Polsen says that."

Hawke gave her a sharp look, not liking what she was implying.

"I'm nothing like him," he snapped. "Polsen's a small-minded unintelligent thug who's reached his peak at this Academy. Maybe he knows it, maybe that's why he takes it out on everybody around him."

"Maybe," Naomi agreed. Hawke felt placated until she continued. "And why do you do it?"

"Do what?" he asked testily.

"Take it out on everyone around you?"

"I don't bully anybody," he argued, offended.

"You intimidate a great many of your peers," Naomi said. "Your name comes up almost as many times as Mr Polsen."

Mr Polsen sat strangely in her sentence, but he supposed *Mr Donovan* for himself would sound just as awkward. He wondered how his name 'came up'. He knew that he was likely a topic of disdain from other students but he suspected from Naomi's words that they didn't like him not because of his blood or because he went away on research tests all the time... but because he scared them. The same way Polsen scared them.

He remembered the way he'd been shoved and then instantly apologised to. Nobody would dare shove Polsen.

"Not the same way," he protested, but he was suddenly unsure.

"No," Naomi agreed. Hawke was relieved and also surprised by how great his relief was. Had he truly considered himself a bully? He didn't pick on the weaker kids. He picked on the strong ones.

"I challenge them. I challenge the bullies, that's why they complain."

"You don't know who's complaining, Hawke."

"You can tell me," he said before giving her his best smile. Naomi wasn't encouraged and he dropped it. "Seriously, the others should be thanking me. I'm standing up for them."

"For them or for yourself?"

"Okay, for myself. But they're getting the benefits of that."

"How so?"

"They get to see that it's okay to stand up for yourself."

Naomi frowned at him and leaned forward, her elbows resting on her desk and her fingertips alighting on her cheeks.

"How is it okay, Hawke? You've been suspended twice for fighting, you've been consistently cycling through detentions. How long has it been since you've sat down to eat dinner at the same time as your friends?"

Naomi adjusted her glasses so she could stare at him properly and Hawke felt betrayed. She was supposed to make excuses for him. Wasn't that what she always did? What kind of books was she reading that she now wanted to try a different angle with him?

What friends? he wanted to ask but it would make him sound like a loser. He didn't care that he had nobody here that would talk to him. He had acquaintances—the odd boys who would chat with him during their free time or needed his help with their academic work. He always helped them, always tried to involve himself by asking questions to keep the conversation flowing. Short of inviting himself into their circle of friends, he did it all. They would spare him a bit of their time but he was never good enough to be invited to join them.

There were only two people he cared about. Perhaps that was all he had room for, in his life. Even at home, in his own family, there were only two members he deeply cared for.

"I'm sorry to be so harsh," Naomi said, interrupting

his reverie.

"I know," he said. He forgave her for it because she didn't know any better. She read her books on child psychology, using whatever tactics they suggested. She might even have the experience of sons to draw from and this was why she was easier to talk to than anyone else at the school. She didn't understand him, though she tried. He thought she even comprehended how overwhelming it was for someone like him, who'd been thrust into this place from another world.

"You don't often show me your anger," she said, grabbing his attention. Naomi leaned back in her chair and picked up a nearby pencil so she could tap it on the closed file in front of her. It was labelled 'Budget'. "I hear about it from all manner of sources. So it's a thing. You've made being angry your thing."

"I have a lot to be angry about," Hawke reminded. It was an excuse Naomi had made a few times on his behalf.

"Yes, however, it's well-past time to control it. A young boy who went through what you did has to go through a stage of anger but a young man needs to come out the other side."

"My anger helps me fend them off," Hawke said. He failed to elaborate who 'they' were but Naomi didn't ask for clarification.

"I'm sure it does... but wouldn't you like to be at peace, Hawke? Wouldn't you like to feel something other than rage? I don't imagine you enjoy feeling that way."

Hawke shrugged. He didn't know if she wanted answers to her questions. They sounded more like she was wanting to make points than to find out what he was thinking. Normally, her questions weren't rhetorical but were phrased for discovery. He missed those.

"I have an idea how you can work through it. There's a martial arts class that teaches discipline and meditation—"

"I'm not allowed in that class."

Naomi gave him a warning look and continued, speaking slowly at first, speeding up when she warmed to her topic. "As I was saying, the class has done very well for those students who need a little extra help maintaining their self-control and I think that kind of class would benefit you. You're right when you say you're ineligible—too many fights have seen to that— but I've argued your case and received permission for you to have lessons during your study period after lunchtime. There's no room in the budget for a teacher but since your sponsor is a high ranking officer in the Authorities, I contacted Major Cayden to see if he could help and he told me yes."

She gave him a bright smile, full of excitement and hope. It suited her face and he answered it with a smile of his own, even though he wasn't sure he liked her arranging things behind his back. Her intentions were pure and the outcome was fantastic but he didn't like being reminded that no facet of his life was under his control.

"Okay," he said because she looked like she was wanting a reply.

Naomi's expression changed, becoming quizzical. Before she could ask him if anything was wrong or if he didn't like what she'd done or some other question that was easy on the outside but difficult to respond to, he offered more.

"Thank you. I'm overwhelmed."

He didn't say it with any emotion but the words were right because Naomi's broad smile returned and she grinned at him. With her pulled-back hairdo, the effect was ghastly. He figured out that her smile looked wrong because it wasn't in her eyes. She grew serious and dropped her voice.

"Don't let me down, Hawke. I've told Administration that you need this training to control your anger. If you keep getting into fights, you'll lose your opportunity and I'll lose face."

She was taking a chance on him. Hawke was responsible not only for himself but now for her. Naomi had proven herself a genuine ally to him and he truly was overwhelmed. He looked down at his lap because it was hard to look at her sincere and hopeful expression without feeling emotional.

"I'll do my best. I promise."

CHAPTER FIVE

Tables Turning

*S*TAY *where I can find you*, Nick had said. *I might need you.*

The ominous words sent Daeson retreating to the Queen. There were times when he argued with Nick but he chose his moments. As much as he wanted to demand what was going on, the explosion coupled with that phrase was enough to suppress his curiosity.

Once out of Nick's sphere, he began wishing he'd spoken. Daeson was annoyed that he always found his courage after the fact, or that the best words came to him after the moment was lost. If he'd been less of a coward, he would've demanded Nick take him along. The truth was, he didn't want to go. What he wanted was to talk to *her*.

Synjan. Now he had a name. How much could a name give him?

Daeson didn't return to the kitchen, knowing that Herme would bluster about an unfinished shift. Daeson liked the head cook's gregarious nature but right now he didn't want to be guilted into scrubbing pots. He had been given a glimpse of a puzzle piece and he wanted to find out more.

Ahead of him, in the corridor, he could see Amethyst leaning against the wall in her light purple lingerie. She'd started working at the Queen six months ago. He thought that she wouldn't know about Synjan but she was the most convenient person to ask. He could hear a lot of spirited conversations taking place in the lobby and the front door was wide open. Daeson thought people had likely gone outside to look up the street towards the Authority Base.

"Hi, Amethyst. Got a minute?"

She glanced at him, the fringe of her white-blonde hair falling almost into her eyes. "Okay?" she replied, sounding unsure. She struck him as a nervous kind of person but Jade painted a very different picture of the girl who'd been hired because of her specialties.

"Have you met Synjan?"

"Synjan? Oh, sure. She's nice."

Daeson didn't know what to say. The answer was unexpected. Amethyst filled the pause with a question of her own.

"Do you know what's going on?"

"No," he said. It was only a moment later when he realised she must've been asking about the explosion. He'd thought she was talking about the Synjan secret... which was only a secret to him.

Amethyst moved away, leaving him in the corridor to contemplate.

There had been a very strange moment in the alley, after Synjan had blocked him between herself and the dumpster. She'd closed her eyes and he'd felt oddly *peaceful*. It had been a familiar sensation and one he'd never forgotten. The Portal had given him the same sensation of calm.

Is she like me? Is she a Wanderer?

It didn't make sense that this was the reason Nick wanted to keep them apart. How often did Synjan visit the Queen? Amethyst knew of her and thought she was nice; how often had they spoken? He couldn't ask her because she'd joined the others in the lobby. He needed to find someone else, someone who wouldn't keep the truth from him.

Jade.

When he arrived at her room, the door was shut and he could hear movement inside. She had a client with her and he wasn't so eager for information that he was going to interrupt them. A door opened farther up the corridor and Daeson watched as an Authority soldier exited Ruby's room, hastily tucking his shirt into his pants. He didn't look Daeson's way as he passed him in long strides, heading for the stairs and clumping down them with a rhythm that sounded like he was taking more than one step at a time.

"That was lucky." Ruby's voice caught his attention and Daeson looked back to see her standing just outside her doorway. "Not that he was horrible or anything but it's nice to be paid for nothing." She laughed. "Somebody should set off more bombs."

"How do you know it was a bomb?" he asked, drawing closer. Ruby looked gleeful to have his attention. There weren't many things she said that he paid mind to and for whatever reason he couldn't fathom, she seemed to want his interest.

"Because he had one of those little black boxes with him," she shrugged and Daeson got the impression that she wasn't going to explain further. Perhaps she didn't know more.

"Can you tell me about Synjan?" he asked.

Ruby's reaction was immediate and inelegant as she pulled a face. "Why the fuck do you want to talk about *her*?"

"I only just met her," Daeson explained.

"Well..." Ruby hesitated, looking at him as though he'd done something wrong. "Nick said not to talk to you about her."

Daeson ignored the hint.

"What is it that Synjan and Nick do together?"

"Lots of nasty things, I bet. Want me to show you? I got a free session."

She might've been offering but Daeson knew she didn't really want him to take her up on her offer. He'd discussed Ruby's advances with Jade and they'd both decided she was after favours of a different kind. Even now, with her words hanging between them, Daeson could sense that her offer was insincere.

"How often does Synjan come by?"

Ruby huffed and returned to her room, ending the conversation by slamming the door. Daeson suspected that Nick's order not to talk about Synjan carried more weight than he'd initially thought. Ruby wasn't as defiant as she liked to think.

He thought he'd have more success downstairs. The club wasn't operating but he might be lucky and find someone who was cleaning up or restocking. The door panel wasn't open like it usually was later in the day, allowing access to the sitting room. Daeson went to the back of the small room behind the stairs where Dyna and Chad worked, and knocked. The large bodyguard was the one to answer the door with a scowl. It became a broad smile upon seeing Daeson.

"Hey, it's your favourite son," Chad greeted, looking at Daeson but talking to Dyna. She was often called 'mums' by the men who worked at the Queen. Daeson didn't know why and he'd never done so, but Dyna always had kind words for him. He liked her.

"What's the occasion, cubby?" Dyna asked as she twisted in her chair. The greeting was a pet name that she used with all the men at the Queen.

"I'm..." Daeson hesitated between asking her to unlock the door to the club below or asking her about Synjan directly. Dyna and Nick were often conversing together and he knew that, apart from himself, Nick was one of her favourites. "I would like to go downstairs."

"What for, now?" Dyna asked, friendly but curious. He knew she liked to know everything that was going on. Out of all the people to ask about Synjan, she was probably the best, but he knew her loyalty to Nick was greater.

"I..." It was no use, he couldn't lie. The words stuck in his throat and he gave a small cough. Chad came to the unlikely rescue.

"Do you have a thing for Topaz? Don't let Xenik find out, he's the jealous type."

Daeson stared at Chad while he tried to figure out what to say and how to say it without lying.

"Oh, don't scare the poor boy, Xenik's harmless," Dyna cut in.

Daeson didn't think 'harmless' was the best way to describe the large man who was often called on by Nick when a questioning didn't produce results.

"Flirt with Topaz at your own risk," Chad said and stepped away so he could reach past Dyna and flick the switch that opened the panel door.

"Thank you," Daeson said, pleased that the conversation had turned on its own—finally something was working in his favour—and headed for the club.

The neon lights were on but the light ball wasn't spinning. Daeson was glad because the turning lights made him feel dizzy. He wasn't here often enough to get used to it. Misu was working behind the bar, replacing almost empty bottles with full ones. He nodded at Daeson as a greeting but focussed on his task.

Topaz was gyrating suggestively against one of the narrow floor to ceiling posts near the DJ booth. She reached up and performed an acrobatic twirl that ended with her curled around the pole. Daeson advanced until he was sure that she saw him and waited.

It didn't take long before she stopped and stared at him, waiting for him to speak first. Topaz wasn't a big talker but in all of Daeson's interactions with her, she'd only spoken truth—much like Jade. She was more likely to say nothing at all if she didn't want to answer.

"I want to ask you about Synjan," he began. "Do you know her?"

Topaz nodded, her gaze flicking to Misu behind the bar. She left the pole to stand in front of Daeson.

"Nick says no Synjan for you."

"Why? Who is she?"

"She does special stuff, like other guys he pays. Only she's better," Topaz shrugged. "Girls here like her because she talks to us like people instead of gutter-trolls."

It took Daeson a moment to decipher her accented speech. "But why can't *I* talk to her?" he persisted.

"Don't know. Lady Omerri don't like independent women. Too good competition for you, maybe. They both got hooks in—" Topaz stopped talking suddenly, her eyes widening for a moment. Daeson felt like an opportunity to learn more had been lost. "Anyway, Synjan works for Ellis, not my business."

Ellis wasn't a new name to Daeson but just as difficult to find information about. He'd managed to catch Ellis' name a few times, the first time from Omerri herself when they'd holidayed on Mwavey. Mentioning the name had been a slip, he knew, and perhaps she was the reason why information about Ellis and Synjan was so difficult to come by. Nick worked for Omerri, though Daeson knew enough about their working relationship to understand Nick often operated under his own initiative.

"Ellis is Omerri's friend," Daeson pointed out, attempting to bluff knowledge from Topaz with what little he already knew.

"You say that like you don't know more," Topaz challenged, but her tone was light and her smile was easy. "Lady Omerri don't brag to you about turning this business around? Make it more special?"

Turning this business around? Omerri often boasted that she'd created the Queen of Hearts herself. Omerri hadn't been lying but neither was Topaz. How could they both be speaking the truth?

"She said the Queen was her idea."

"Long time ago she got this place, made it more special. I think just brothel, now has extra stuff with high-risk, but also..." Topaz made a gesture that meant money.

"So Ellis...?" Daeson had no idea what to ask. The conversation had led him down a track he hadn't envisaged.

"Ellis plays the property game. He has fingers in much property. You figure out yourself who owns this place. Maybe he sell it at good price, maybe nothing. I think like all men he want favours from Lady Omerri."

Daeson stared at Topaz, feeling every response melting out of his brain at her words. He didn't know why Topaz was telling him everything. She was the one and only dancer here who didn't sell favours so he didn't see much of her because she didn't maintain a room upstairs. They'd spoken many times since he'd come to the Queen two years ago but never about anything important.

"I see more question in your eyes," Topaz said. "The Queen is a riddle nobody solves."

She left him with those strange words, walking around him. Daeson turned and watched as she and Misu waved goodbye to one another.

The barman stopped wiping the counter to meet Daeson's stare.

"You going through?" Misu asked cryptically before gesturing with his head to the staff only door. Daeson shook his head and returned the way he came, taking his time in the stairwell to figure out his next move.

He was a part of the Queen's riddle, he knew. With

his secret Healing Room and while watching interrogations, he helped Nick become a force in the criminal world. It was easy for him to do as he was told and pretend nothing bad was happening—especially since Nick kept him separate from it. He could keep pretending nothing was wrong, he could continue being part of the Queen or he could control what he was involved in. It was hard to separate his relationship with Omerri from his position at the Queen—the two of them were entwined, but he couldn't just keep on going with his eyes half closed. Ignorance didn't absolve him.

He needed to talk things over with Omerri. He couldn't let her change the subject or distract him or do what she always did when he wanted to talk about things she didn't. This time he'd get answers.

CHAPTER SIX

Diverted

ICK thrust the ID card towards Synjan without taking his gaze off the road. "Here."

She sighed pointedly and jammed the card between her teeth before wriggling the rest of the way out of her parka. His driving through the winding streets of Dockside was difficult enough to endure without the added task of a costume change. They'd left in such a rush she didn't have much choice.

She'd only worn the large garment to conceal the Authority uniform on her walk to the Queen—apart from the fact that Ellis would've questioned her (thankfully he hadn't seen her), she didn't enjoy the looks she got when she walked through Dockside dressed like a soldier. The spitting and muttered curses were even less welcome.

Finally free of it, Synjan tossed her parka into the back. She straightened the short sleeves of her dark blue shirt as she settled back into her seat, checking that it was still tucked neatly into her trousers. The only identifying marks on the uniform were the Authority logo and her rank on each sleeve. The insignia was a simple design, denoting that she carried the rank of Authority Officer. It was only one step up from a plain Authority but it was something.

Rolling her hips, she pulled her ID wallet out of her pants pocket while her other hand rescued the card from her mouth. The wallet was designed to hold identification, with a plastic window on each side so that two sets of credentials could be displayed. Oddly, they'd gone on sale to the public a few months beforehand and Synjan had been surprised by the opportunity to buy an official Authority wallet to complete her rarely-used uniform. With the instigation of the Gredann resident identification card system, it all made sense. The Authorities were excellent forward planners.

As she wiped saliva off on her pants and tucked the ID Nick had given her behind one of the clear windows, Synjan impressed Officer Mikala Atkins' name into her working memory. Hopefully nobody tried to get her attention with that first name, because she wasn't sure how to pronounce it. Atkins was more easily deciphered.

"We're going to get caught," Synjan warned, putting the wallet back in her pocket and paying attention to where they were going.

"It'll be fine," Nick insisted, driving towards where most of the action she'd mapped was occurring.

"It's a bad idea," she countered, leaning down to the backpack on the floor between her feet in order to take a drink from her water bottle. If this plan did go ahead, she would need to be as hydrated as possible.

She straightened up to find a memory stick being held in front of her face. It went into her back pocket.

"Authority Teve Scanlan?" she queried, checking the name of the contact.

Nick gave her a dirty look for her trouble. He knew she had an excellent memory and had committed all the details of this plan to it. She had no need to check information.

"Assuming Scanlan didn't get blown up," Synjan added spitefully.

"Will you settle down? It's going to be fine."

She pressed her lips together instead of responding, unable to find the words to clearly express the nervousness eating at her insides. Nick didn't want to hear it.

Their arrival at Hibiscus Court revealed exactly what Synjan had expected; utter chaos. Nick pulled the car up well short of the temporary barrier the Authorities had erected and they stared in silence at the hive of activity ahead of them.

A large section of the fence was down but it looked like it had been rammed, rather than bombed. Most of the damage seemed to have occurred beyond the buildings standing by the perimeter fence (the recreational hall and the cafeteria Synjan occasionally visited). She could tell without mapping that the bomb site wasn't too far away though, probably the next building over.

This side of Oceangate wasn't a very logical target, unless disabling Authority personnel was the aim. It could have been some sort of gas explosion and not an attack at all. Nothing they could see was definitive. The scene was swarming with blue-uniformed workers running between buildings, ferrying bleeding victims on stretchers or loading them into vehicles that roared past them, heading for Gredann Hospital. Other workers were attending to the drooping fence line or delivering supplies to mend the unseen damage, while yet another very official-looking group seemed intent on documenting everything. They were standing back in a huddled cluster taking notes and photographs.

"Maybe it was an accident," Synjan breathed, feeling like her voice was very loud in the silent car.

"Maybe. It doesn't seem like anything important was hit."

"Nothing important. Just people,"she chastised.

"It wouldn't have been a robbery."

"No. The commissary and rec buildings don't hold much of value."

"The Administration Hub should still be fine," he

told her and she could feel his stare aimed at the side of her face like a physical touch.

The Administration Hub was the collection of buildings that housed the department she needed to get the memory stick to. It was centrally located on the base, well away from the action they were observing. Nick's assessment—although a guess—was likely accurate.

"Probably, but how can I get there?" she demanded.

"Through the front gate."

Her jaw fell as she gaped at him. A clicking sound at the back of her throat was audible as she struggled to find the words to tell him how stupid that idea was.

"Synjan," he said earnestly, turning to face her as best he could behind the steering wheel, "you have an ID card. You look a lot like Atkins and with all this—" he gestured towards the action at the end of the street they'd parked on, "I bet they won't be looking too hard at people coming onto the base right now."

"Or maybe they'll be looking extra hard because they're trying to find whoever did this!" she cried.

Nick shook his head firmly. "Look at them. They're investigating. If they were still chasing people down, they'd be tearing around like madmen. Either they've already got the people who did it or it was, like you said, an accident. They're focussed on first aid and checking whatever matters most to them is still intact. You'll pass inspection."

She stared at him, his arguments whirling around her head and no logical rebuttals coming to her. Foremost was a sense of utter terror that he was expecting she'd be able to walk up to the main gates of this massive base and gain entry like she belonged there. She'd never done anything so brazen. If she was right and they were fully scrutinising everyone trying to enter, she'd be spotted. Blood tests and the Gods-knew-what came very soon after that and she'd never be free again. Was he seriously expecting her to risk signing her life over to the Authorities just to complete his stupid mission?

Apparently he took her silence as assent because he started the car and drove around to the front of the base. He pulled into one of the angled parking spaces and switched the car off so that they could once again admire the Authorities' handiwork through the windscreen.

Access Point Alpha was clearly signed and was approximately a hundred metres ahead of them. It stood on the other side of an urban square meant to make the approach to Oceangate more appealing. The cement and pebble expanse boasted a sporadic assortment of trees shading bench seats, some grass sections, a couple of small fountains, some rubbish receptacles and an enormous, ugly statue right in the centre. The coppery artwork depicted a group of life-sized Authority soldiers and scientists holding various poses of shock, awe and victory as they gathered around a large, bullet-like object poking out of the bottom of the statue—it was the scene of an Authority probe landing in some distant soil on a new world. It was a depiction of heroism and dominance that only served to make her feel worse.

Since it was a main thoroughfare, Alpha entry had a wide path to the right, for emergency or large vehicle access and for those exiting the base. An armed soldier stood guard either side of the wider throughway.

The entry pavilion was to the left and consisted of four pedestrian lanes defined by sleek metal and stone electronic turnstiles, backed up by two baggage scanners and walk-through x-ray machines. The extra equipment was slightly to the side so as not to disrupt the view of a circular garden holding another statue and flourishing greenery beyond, framed by a circle of stone pillars. This dramatic scene constituted the entry courtyard. All of it sat beneath a feature roof set at an extreme angle, probably designed to make visitors feel like they were being drawn into something spectacular.

Synjan wasn't feeling it. She didn't even know how the turnstiles worked, though she felt she could rely on following the lead of others entering before her. There was a surprising amount of soldiers heading onto the base at that moment and she realised with a sinking sensation that Nick was right. Extra personnel seemed to have been called in to deal with the emergency and the four guards milling between the turnstiles and the more serious inspection equipment seemed intent on maintaining the flow, rather than holding people up to check their IDs.

As she sat there mapping the scene to get a better idea of what to expect, only three people were detained and that was because they were armed or were carrying bags. They were run through the x-ray equipment with a minimum of fuss and sent on their way quickly.

"Go now. You'll be fine," Nick said.

His sudden comment caused her to jump because she'd been concentrating so hard. Her eyes flew open in surprise and he laughed at her, which didn't improve her mood.

"If you say so," she snapped, leaning down to have one last long drink from her water bottle. She'd have preferred taking it with her but didn't want to risk the delay of extended scrutiny while she waited for it to get scanned. She wasn't wearing any weapons for the same reason—a smooth entry was what she wanted. She'd have to rely on her own skills and the capricious whims of Elvara, the Goddess of Fate, beyond that. "Hopefully this won't take long," she stated, opening the car door and sparing Nick one last glance.

"It'll be easy," he told her, brandishing the smile that usually got her pulse racing. It had no such effect on her today. "I'll be right here. Waiting," he assured. It made her feel slightly better that he'd wait and she mustered a weak smile.

"You better be right about this."

"Trust me. You'll be fine," he scoffed, waving her out of the car.

She closed the door and took a moment to right her clothing, press a fluttery hand to her pinned-up hair and inhale a steadying breath before she set off. She was Authority Officer Mikala Atkins, reporting for duty. She lifted her chin and squared her shoulders, walking with purpose and an exterior confidence she certainly didn't feel on the inside.

CHAPTER SEVEN

Fighting Chance

AWKE had dressed in his gym clothes and shown up early at the weights room, betraying his eagerness to be trained in fighting. Naomi had spoken of discipline and meditation and he'd promised not to get involved in any fights.

In hindsight, the request was unreasonable. He couldn't guarantee that he wouldn't be attacked. Willets losers like Polsen would keep coming at him, usually bringing two or more thugs. If Hawke could defend himself against multiple opponents, then any fights started would be over quickly, leaving less chance for discovery. If he could learn some off-world moves, he'd be able to surprise them. Hawke would only need to give them a solid pounding one time—or maybe a few because they were slow learners—and then word would get around that he was too good for anyone to fight.

That was the gist of the conversation he'd had with Cayden and the reason he was here waiting. His sponsor had found someone to train him and their arrival was imminent.

The idea of learning to best others elevated his mood. He was pumped enough to start shadow boxing while fantasising about all the faces that he would pummel. He'd worked up a sweat by the time he was joined.

"You're not holding your fists high enough," Cayden said from the doorway. Hawke turned and smiled even though he was embarrassed by the criticism. He opened his mouth to respond but when he saw who stood beside his sponsor, he froze.

Hawke recognised the blonde man and shock tingled at his nape. He knew that stony expression, that impossibly tall and rigid posture, the chiselled physique and business-like demeanour. This was the man that took him to see Ellis when he went to Trent. Hawke had never learned his name and it seemed strange that here was where that would happen.

He tried to blink away his surprise as Cayden and his companion approached, focussing on the more familiar face even while his mind stuttered over the other man's presence. Obviously he'd known that Hawke would be here but it was difficult to know if he'd volunteered for this task or if Cayden had assigned him to it. If it was the latter, that was an exceptional coincidence. Hawke was more willing to believe that the soldier had positioned himself to be selected.

He was taking a risk that Hawke wouldn't identify him.

"Major," Hawke greeted while performing a lazy salute. The rank was new and Hawke could see the glee in his sponsor's eyes when he commented on it.

Cayden chuckled and pulled him into a sideways embrace—just enough intimacy for them to be comfortable with. "Hawke, this is Unit Commander Kegan Frederickson. He's the best instructor I know," Cayden said, clapping the Unit Commander on the back. "Hell, he's the best soldier I know."

"Shouldn't he be busy fighting bad guys then?" Hawke asked, looking at the mountainous Unit Commander, who now had a name. Cayden's brows drew together but Kegan Frederickson's expression remained impassive. Hawke pulled in his lips to stop himself from making another comment.

"I have a team for that," the Unit Commander said, and offered his hand for the shaking. "Pleased to meet you, Hawke."

Hawke shook his hand, feeling surreal.

"I hear you've been having some trouble?"

Hawke merely nodded. He'd heard more of this man's voice in these past few minutes than he had over the past year. Suddenly he didn't know what to say.

"I'm here to help you with that. Looks like you're ready to work."

The Unit Commander looked around the gym. Hawke glanced at Cayden and back again, wondering how this odd triangle had sprung up. Hawke knew Frederickson was obliged to Ellis in some way, but what was he to Cayden? Where did the blonde man's loyalties lie? Was Cayden a willing accomplice or ignorant to his companion's criminal ties? Hawke wouldn't believe Cayden capable of treason.

"That's a suspicious look," Cayden accused with a chuckle.

Hawke felt the weight of the Unit Commander's stare as he maintained eye contact with Cayden. He gave a deliberately casual shrug. The Unit Commander would be able to isolate telltale signs of Hawke's guilt but how easy would they be for Cayden to spot?

"Not at all, sir. If you trust him, I trust him," he remarked placidly. From the corner of his eye, he noted the commander's posture stiffen.

"Good, because Kegsy's good people," Cayden confirmed emphatically, dropping a concerned hand on Hawke's shoulder. "How've you been doing?"

"Alright."

"Really?" Hawke's shoulder was given a little squeeze with the question.

"Yeah. Avoiding trouble."

Cayden nodded and checked his watch. "Unfortunately I can't stay but I wanted to introduce you to Kegsy myself, so you know that you're in good hands."

Hawke shot 'Kegsy' a dark look that was met in kind. Cayden appeared oblivious.

"I'll leave you both to it. Stay out of trouble, Hawke."

"Sure."

Cayden shook Hawke's hand and slapped Kegsy on the shoulder before leaving. The gesture looked familiar.

They stared at each other until Cayden was completely out of the room.

"What do I call you?" Hawke asked.

"Commander will do. Or U.C. if you like. I'll call you Donovan."

"How did you even pull this off? Did you make friends with Cayden to get closer to me?"

"Yes, because the worlds revolve around you."

"Hell of a fucking coincidence."

The Unit Commander glanced at the doorway before closing in on Hawke, who took a couple of steps backward. He was grabbed by the shirt front and pulled close. "Say what you've got to say," the large man growled.

"You're a double agent," Hawke accused. He was surprised his voice didn't wobble like the rest of him was.

"I'm not a traitor," Frederickson said, releasing Hawke with a look of disgust.

"But Ellis isn't—"

"Don't."

The order was low and menacing and stopped Hawke momentarily. "Don't?"

"Say his name. Not here. It's all I ask."

They both knew where the power lay as soon as the plea was spoken. Although Hawke was pissed off that he was caught in the middle of a secret he couldn't fathom, he relished having the upper hand. "I want to know how you came to be here."

"Bad luck," Frederickson said grimly.

Hawke glared at him. "I think there's more to it. Tell me."

"Or what? You'll tell Cayden?"

"I know how to keep my mouth shut."

Frederickson regarded him. His light blue eyes were intelligent and bored into him for a long time before he nodded. He took off his watch and then his jacket, revealing a black t-shirt. Hawke got a good look at the way the muscles in his thick arms moved when the Unit Commander tossed his jacket over an equipment rack.

When the giant moved over to the long blue mats propped up against the wall and pulled one out, Hawke got the impression he'd been dismissed—along with a conversation that was aggravatingly unfinished. Hawke helped him get out another and as they faced off, he realised his frustration must be easy to read because he was given a goal.

"I'm here to train you. You can ask your questions later. If you're good enough, I might answer some of them."

It doubled Hawke's determination.

He was shown how to warm up, his body pushed into stretched positions he'd never considered. When he queried the necessity of them, he was answered succinctly yet eloquently. The commander had a consummate knowledge of the body and how it worked. As they progressed into the session, Hawke was given details he hadn't expected, curious about the corrections he was given and amazed at how much more efficiently he moved when he followed the advice.

The focus was predominantly on his balance,

though it began to feel like he had none when he was repeatedly dropped on his back. His frustration grew and he suspected he was being taunted. Part of him respected that he wasn't treated leniently; the rest of him resented being constantly proven inept.

"This is ridiculous!" Hawke complained, getting to his feet after being knocked onto one knee. Frederickson took advantage and shoved him while sweeping a foot behind Hawke's ankle, causing him to fall heavily onto the mat. It hurt and Hawke was winded. The commander stood over him, a giant dressed in black with his hands on his hips.

"Had enough?" he goaded.

Hawke scowled as he got up, watching the other for telltale signs of attack. It made his trainer smile.

"Better. Keep your eyes on your opponent."

"For all the good it does me," Hawke sniped.

"You haven't hit the floor as much as I expected you to."

Hawke wanted to argue but he saved his breath instead.

"You're a fast learner," Frederickson continued. "You just need to stay on your feet. Fighting from the ground is an entirely different set of skills."

"Right," Hawke answered sarcastically.

Surprisingly, the commander laughed and despite Hawke's annoyance, it was a nice sound. He realised he respected his trainer, even if he didn't trust him.

At the end of their session, Hawke was breathless and sweaty. Kegan looked the same as when he'd first walked in. Hawke's arms ached from keeping his fists up, his legs ached from moving around in a weird position (that he'd named a ten-percent squat) and his whole body ached from every time he'd hit the floor.

The commander shifted the mats back to their original location against the wall. Hawke watched

Frederickson collect his jacket, lay it over his forearm and approach. Kegan focused on putting his watch on as he spoke.

"Think you deserve to ask questions?"

"Fuck, yes," Hawke declared emphatically.

The man mountain grunted his amusement. "That kind of profanity carries a detention here, doesn't it?"

"What are you going to do? Report me?"

"Thought you were smart, not smart-mouthed."

"I'm smart, too," Hawke grinned.

"Being intelligent doesn't make you *smart*, Donovan."

Hawke frowned but he thought he knew what Frederickson meant.

"Is that one of his sayings?"

When the commander looked at him blankly, he clarified. "He has a lot of sayings, I noticed. My favourite one is 'In the end, everyone answers to somebody.' Do you know it?"

The square jaw set and he could see emotions flaring in Frederickson's blue eyes but Hawke continued.

"I thought it was about death. At the end of your life, you get judged. But now I think it has more everyday use. You're here and it's the end of your secret, understand? And now you have to answer to somebody. Me."

"Screw you, Donovan."

Hawke blinked, now realising how much he'd angered the Unit Commander.

"No, I'm not being shitty," Hawke countered. "I'm just... making conversation."

"I've said enough."

"I want to know more about Ellis, you with me?"

The blonde man's expression became murderous as he glared at Hawke and then looked at the door.

"Nobody's here," Hawke reassured, following his trainer's gaze. He was paranoid about Ellis' name. Hawke didn't want to piss off the Authority any more. "Sorry. I didn't mean to... mention it. Why does it matter anyway? Is he a bigger deal than I thought?" Hawke's eyes sparkled.

"No."

"He says he needs me."

"I think he's overstating."

"How?"

"There's a difference between need and want."

Hawke breathed a puff of annoyance at the literal interpretation of Ellis' words. There was a prickling of awareness that Frederickson would only stand a certain amount of questioning before he walked out. It made more sense to Hawke to clarify his position than to ask why he was in it.

"What do you think I should do?"

For a moment, it looked to Hawke like he wouldn't get an answer and he watched a muscle tick in the commander's jaw while he chewed on whatever he wanted to say. What eventually came out wasn't very helpful.

"I think you should decide what *you* want."

"If I work for Ellis, would it be *outside* the Authorities?"

"Yes."

So Ellis *was* a criminal. All the things he'd talked about accomplishing with Hawke at his side had seemed less than legal but he'd never been sure. Until now.

"He makes it all sound very appealing."

"He's good at that."

"Yet you won't tell me not to work for him?"

Frederickson shrugged. "I made my choice."

He made his choice? Enlightenment washed over

Hawke and he looked at the commander with newfound interest. "You chose just the Authorities?"

Frederickson nodded.

Hawke remembered how angry Frederickson got when accused of being a double agent. He decided to accept the Unit Commander's words as truth.

"So why did you—?"

The Unit Commander cleared his throat. "I should get going."

Hawke glared, angry to be cut off from asking what he thought was a pivotal question.

"Remember to stay on your feet and keep out of trouble."

Memories of the taunting made him feel more vulnerable than he cared to admit. He embraced the anger that was already rising instead. "Hey, I don't start trouble. I can't help my blood."

Frederickson frowned curiously at him. "They pick on you 'cause you're a Wanderer?"

"Yeah."

"Have you Wandered?"

It seemed a strange question and Hawke blinked. "Yeah?" he drawled, wondering what his trainer was alluding to.

All he got in return was a thoughtful nod. "I'll be back next week, same time," Frederickson announced as he headed towards the exit. He paused when he got to the doorway and turned to look back at Hawke. "We'll make them regret it," he said emphatically before he disappeared down the hallway.

CHAPTER EIGHT

The Hunter And The Prisoner

EXPEDIENT as his flight was, the Hunter was unable to reach Yulanigh Bay in time to affect the outcome of the Wanderer pursuit. When he exited his aircraft, he was met by an Authority that hustled him into a waiting vehicle, delivering updates as they went.

Of the trio, only one male had been secured while the female and second male eluded police capture. All leads on their whereabouts seemed to have vanished in the last half hour and the locals were baffled by their flawless disappearance. The Hunter sneered, unsurprised that the local police were too incompetent to catch experienced Wanderers; the interlopers probably hadn't even used their powers to assist their escape.

Knowing he needed to clean the mess up, the Hunter instructed his driver to take him to the local station where the Wanderer was being kept. As they drove, he ignored the worshipful conversation coming at him, contemplating what Narelle Lawson might be up to at this moment. Would he manage to deal with his business in time to visit her again that night? He hoped so.

At the police station, the Hunter strode up to the reception desk and showed his badge. The guy behind the glass had an impossibly square jaw, complete with dimple. He raised his eyebrows at the Authority ID being flashed at him and then looked up warily.

"Can I help you?"

"I'm here to get the prisoner you arrested."

A frown told him he didn't need to elaborate on exactly which prisoner was being discussed but Mr Square Jaw picked up the phone and pressed a button that likely connected him to a supervisor.

"This is Kendricks on the front desk. I've got a Hunter here, says he's come to collect the prisoner." Silent nods and a grunt while Officer Kendricks was spoken to, and then he said, "Okay, that's what I thought," before he hung up. "We've got a unit inbound from Austra," he declared.

The Hunter knew the world and was aware that it boasted a Wanderer testing facility. It seemed they wanted to take the prisoner for study rather than deferring to his directive, which outranked theirs. He was incensed.

"That's against protocol," he seethed. "I'm on world first. I've complied explicitly with my pursue and dispatch orders. I authorised the resources used and my division will bear the costs, not theirs. I have jurisdiction!"

Kendrick sat back behind his glass window, raising his hands innocently. "Sorry, brother, don't shoot the messenger. What goes on between your people has nothing to do with us. I can't change it and I can't authorise you taking the prisoner but, hey, if it helps, they're not due for another hour so how about I let you interview him? I can buzz you into the cells?"

The law enforcer at least knew how to defuse an irate superior because his offer was a good one. The other two Wanderers were still at large. The Hunter could get some intel that would help him find them and eliminate their threat instead. Fuck the Austra team.

"Alright," he agreed. "A conversation will have to do."

Kendricks flicked a switch and directed his visitor through the bullpen to the stairs that would get him down to the cells.

The Hunter went where he was told, taking stock of the four cages lined up on his right as he entered the basement. The Wanderer was in the end one, on his own. Noting the surveillance camera placement in the fluorescent-lit space, the Hunter stuck to the wall opposite the cells, his shoulder brushing the painted bricks as he walked. He preferred the Austra team not to see his face and if he was against the wall, he would remain out of view.

The Wanderer seemed to be of a similar mindset because he was slouched against the back of his cell, forgoing the questionable pleasure of sitting on an unmade platform bed in order to face anyone that might come towards him. His shoulders were against the same kind of grey-painted bricks the Hunter's were, though the Wanderer had his fingers tucked into the pockets of his jeans.

His cell wasn't as bright as the others and the Hunter soon realised why; one of the lights was flickering on and mostly off. It was enough to see by but annoying when the intermittent flashes struck. The Wanderer was tall, over a hundred and ninety centimetres, with broad shoulders and a bulky frame. He probably got caught because he was the biggest and slowest. He had brown hair long enough to brush his shoulders, a full beard and a scowling expression. He was likely in his twenties but could've been older, it was hard to tell.

"That was sloppy," the Hunter told him mildly. "Getting caught."

The Wanderer watched him but said nothing.

"It's only taken me two days to catch up with you—you know who I am, don't you?"

More silence.

"I'm a Hunter. You know what I do?"

Maybe there was a flicker of recognition, it was hard to tell.

"I hunt down illegal bastards like you and punish them for Wandering."

Eyes were rolled but no comments came.

"Right. So you know what you're up against here. Luckily for you, I won't be escorting you out. That honour goes to the DOME team. Do you know what that stands for? Domiciliary Observation and Medical Examination. How does that sound? They're on their way to get you, to take you back to their testing facility. You'll live... but you might wish you hadn't."

The Hunter smiled coldly but found himself growing increasingly agitated by the Wanderer's silence; his disdainful demeanour was infuriating. For some reason, he didn't seem to care that he'd been arrested, locked up and was about to be sentenced to life as a lab animal.

His cockiness probably sprang from whatever power he had. It was likely one that could affect his surroundings—but how? It was doubtful the guy was an Elementalist. He'd have used the elements to free himself at the scene, as a Controller would have used the power of suggestion to his advantage. They weren't the only options, just the most obvious.

"I'm going to find your friends, you know. Wherever they are. I'm going to put a bullet through each of them."

Was that a muscle twitch in the jaw?

"Maybe you don't care because they've left you behind. They obviously don't give a shit that you're going to be tested. They're probably off fucking or laughing at how stupid you were to get caught."

A snort of derision came and the Hunter was pleased that he'd finally got a reaction. At least he knew he was being understood.

"What's that? You weren't stupid? Is that because they set you up? Sacrificed you to save themselves? Selfish assholes, leaving you to be the bait while they run off to get romantic. You should probably tell me where they were headed. They don't give a fuck about you and your path is set; you may as well guarantee they get what they deserve. From me."

"You have no idea what you are talking about." The words were uttered softly, accompanied by some head shaking. An accent proved that Authoritan wasn't the Wanderer's first language.

"Oh don't I? Do I strike you as new at this?"

The Wanderer had fallen quiet again but he was frowning now. A little more goading should have him breaking his silence.

"Every. Time," he ground out, almost stepping forward towards the cell door before remembering that he was purposely staying back to maintain anonymity. "*Every time* I've come across a group of more than two, you fuckers turn on each other to save your own skins. Usually, I don't even need to get you apart before you're flipping, negotiating a better deal for yourselves."

There was venom in the look he was getting from the back of the cell now and the Hunter basked in it, beginning to enjoy himself because he knew he was having an effect.

"So where are they? Waiting for you?" he scoffed.

His mockery was met with predictable silent disapproval but the Wanderer folded his arms across his chest and shifted his feet.

"Not if one of them's a Navigator. They're already planning to leave. Might've even done it, if the Portal was close. Typical vermin, infecting the worlds as they travel and never in one place long enough to contribute. Always on the move, breaking laws and creating havoc for innocent world inhabitants. Making guys like me chase them."

It almost looked like the Wanderer would break. He opened his mouth but then closed it, clenching his jaw and turning his head so that he didn't have to look at the Hunter. It was a telling action, giving away how the dam of silence could be unstoppered.

"It's their own fault. Yours too. If you didn't Wander, I wouldn't have to shoot you."

At last, he hit the mark and the Wanderer exploded with anger, taking a step towards the cell door as he began shouting out his objections.

"You seriously have no fucking idea what you are talking about! The Authorities can *never* know what it is like to be a Wanderer. All they are interested in is trying to control what they do not understand. You do not know who we are and what we are, so you can never understand us!"

"Is that so?" the Hunter jeered.

"Exactly so! The Authorities are like children who get upset when we do not play their game and when you cannot force us, you kill us to make yourselves feel better. You are more powerless than we are, tying yourself in knots with your rules and regulations."

The Wanderer's superior attitude was grating on all of the Hunter's nerves. He wasn't having such a good time now and the urge to teach this righteous asshole a lesson was strong. "You call me powerless when you're the one behind bars," he scoffed.

"From where I am standing, *you* are the one behind bars," the Wanderer replied, grinning. There was something wrong about his confidence. "You cannot do anything to me while I am in here because of your own laws. See? Powerless."

The smug quality of his reply was enough for the Hunter to lose his temper.

"Let me *show* you how much power I have," he snarled, drawing his sidearm. He cocked it, the metallic click echoing loudly off the brick and mortar walls. It was the only noise in the place. As soon as his finger moved to the trigger, the Wanderer's eyes widened with genuine fear and then the very large, very solid Wanderer seemed to... *waver*. As the Hunter stared down his gun at him, the prisoner disappeared.

He was a fucking Ghost. Even as the thought registered, the faint shimmer that was the Wanderer's ethereal form moved towards the bricks and through them. The Hunter blinked, scanning the cell for any detectable movement but after a minute he realised it was no use. The Wanderer had escaped; it had likely been what he was planning to do all along (the Authorities had never managed to keep hold of a Ghost, for obvious reasons). The Wanderer had been giving his buddies as much time as possible to get away. He'd probably ensured he got caught in the first place, to distract from the pursuit.

The Hunter slowly re-holstered his gun. No doubt his extended arm and weapon had been detected by the camera, but he hadn't been thinking about that at the time. Now, he was finding it very difficult to think at all. He turned and walked out of the detention area, ignoring the calls of disbelief and fear coming from the occupants of the other cells.

As he passed in full view of the camera, he looked directly at it and spared it a shrug.

CHAPTER NINE

Obstructed

HE walk to Access Point Alpha went far more quickly than Synjan expected. She fell naturally into line behind another uniformed soldier, peering casually around him as they shuffled forward. Like animals into a slaughterhouse.

She cringed at her own comparison, pushing it out of her mind. Her nerves were frayed enough without imagining something even worse. Sure, one wrong move here could end her life as she knew it—and Ellis had no idea what she was up to—but she didn't need to overdramatise the situation. She took a deep breath, comforted by the subtle smell of the ocean on the air, and focussed on what she had to do.

On top of the turnstiles was an infrared scanning plate. As they approached, everyone withdrew their ID cards and waved it across the panel. This caused the plexiglass barriers set discreetly in the turnstiles to retract, allowing access. The glass was hard to see until she got closer; obviously the aesthetic aspect of the base's grand entrance was important.

Her heart was hammering as she got closer to taking her turn. She tried to look impervious to the process, as if she'd been through it daily for many years, but she wasn't sure she was pulling it off. Her gaze kept being drawn to the armed soldiers standing beyond the turnstiles, inspecting the pistols they had holstered at their waists. The two near the exit also had high-powered rifles, butts cradled comfortably against their shoulders. She could imagine all too easily having them trained on her if the card Nick had given her didn't work.

What if Authority Atkins had discovered it was missing and reported it already? Would there be loud alarms or would it just be some kind of irritating beep that declared the card she'd just tried to use was on an alert list? There were four people lined up behind her now, what if they pressed in too close for her to turn and run back to Nick? Was there additional facial-recognition technology at play that she couldn't see? She'd inspected the roof of the entry pavilion as she'd shuffled forward and hadn't seen any cameras but it was new technology on Gredann and who knew what kind of advances had been made in concealing things like that?

It was her turn.

She swallowed but her throat constricted painfully. Licking her lips, she watched the soldier ahead of her walk away fluidly. She had to move. Staring at the screen beside her, she stepped forward, flicked open the wallet and waved it across the scanner. Just as she'd seen everyone else do. Her body was rigid, every muscle coiled as she waited the minor eternity it took for her card to register. She was ready to run, ready to fight, hundreds of scenarios flashing through her mind in preparation—

There was a beep, but it was just a noise of acknowledgement. The glass barriers slid back silently.

Synjan hoped that it didn't appear to take her too long to get going; she moved as soon as her brain processed that nothing had happened. Nothing bad had happened.

One of the guards watched as she moved past him but his attention soon moved beyond her. The base was filling quickly and Synjan used the distraction of moving through the crowd to regain her focus. It wasn't easy to dismiss the tumbling oblivion she'd been contemplating. It took some long breaths and determined strides to get her emotions under control. She wasn't paying attention to where she was going during that time so there was a moment where she had to stop and get her bearings.

She wasn't heading for the Administration Hub—not as directly as she could have been, anyway. With a turn and a quick walk down a narrow space between two buildings, she could see her sprawling four-storey target looming ahead of her, just beyond her immediate surroundings. Her course corrected, she continued on at a swift pace. Her gut was still churning and she wanted to be on the base as short a time as possible.

The Oceangate Administration Hub was a set of buildings that branched off a central spine, like legs from a spider. It housed a vast network of various administration offices within it. Nick had advised Synjan that her best entry point would be through the General Services section, at the front and centre, as it served as the main point of access for the hub. Everyone from visiting elites down to Gredann city couriers walked in through the large plate glass doors because every other administrative department could be reached through it. She also wasn't exactly sure how to reach the department her contact worked in, so she'd also be able to get instructions at the reception desk.

It was oddly quiet as she approached the doors set beneath the 'General Services' label. There'd been no other foot traffic in the area and there was an eerie silence hovering around the whole precinct. She had a sinking feeling as she approached the doors. When they refused to slide open once she got close enough to press her nose against the darkened glass, she knew something was wrong. Cupping her hands around her eyes, she did her best to see into the lobby beyond the glass but it was too heavily tinted to make out much of anything.

Mapping didn't make her feel any less anxious, as she could see no people inside this part of the building. She stepped back from the doors and looked around, absently gnawing on the inside of her bottom lip. Since she wasn't sure how to get to her contact if not through General Services (though who knew if Teve Scanlan was still in place?), Synjan couldn't give up. She spied a card reader set onto the wall to the right. Her ID card! Fishing it out of her wallet, she hurried over to the reader and swiped it.

An angry, honking beep sounded from the machine. It was obnoxiously loud in the preternaturally quiet air. The LCD panel set alongside the swiping channel flashed BAD READ at her, so she turned the card around and swiped it again. This time, there was a happier chirping noise of recognition before a piercing trio of ascending notes blared out of wherever the fuck this thing had a speaker concealed. She flinched and looked around, feeling paranoid about all the noise.

UNAUTHORISED ACCESS was flashing at her from the message panel when she looked back.

She swiped it again and exactly the same result occurred. She swore at the machine and that was the moment she became aware she wasn't alone. Two soldiers were approaching, shoulder to shoulder and watching her. She looked over, feeling thoroughly exposed in front of the locked building, and thought she made eye contact with one of them. She turned back to face the glass doors desperately. It was stupid but she swiped the card again, hoping for a different outcome. The noise of the shrieking rejection notes was almost loud enough to drown out the beat of their heavy boots on the road. They mumbled something to one another and she heard the rhythm of their footfalls change.

"Hey!" one of them called out as they started

jogging towards her.

Synjan turned and squared up to them, her heart in her mouth. With a glance she confirmed that there was no one else around, no witnesses. She had no idea what the three whistling beeps meant but it seemed these men did and they wanted a word with her about it—the panel had said she was unauthorised to attempt access. The soldiers seemed convinced.

She slid her card back into the wallet and put it away as they ran intently towards her. Her hands fisted against her thighs and she shifted stance so that her feet were offset and her weight was on the front one. She turned slightly, presenting a smaller target with one shoulder towards them. This was her only chance to prepare, so she assessed them as they moved, deciding which one she'd hit first and how she'd avoid the other's grasp.

If only running away was an option.

Schooling her expression into one of polite confusion, she chose to address them as they closed the last few metres. "What's up, gentlemen?" she asked as casually as she was able.

CHAPTER TEN

Homecoming

THE taste of the portal coated the back of Hawke's throat. From experience, he knew that nothing would get rid of it, he had to wait it out. He was lucky he hadn't acquired the intense nausea he saw in others, who emptied their guts into tall, narrow paper bags accompanied by sounds that he preferred not to hear. Not long ago in his Fundamentals of Psychology class, they'd covered a topic on 'compassionate illness'. The teacher had touted how highly evolved a person's empathy was if they threw up when someone else did. Hawke had considered it and decided the theory was unsound. He thought it had more to do with when people were primitive and ate something poisonous... it made sense that the instinct to throw up alongside another was etched by survivalism, not compassion. If it was a reaction that a person could suppress, could it be called evolution? He hadn't bothered to share his opinion, figuring the teacher would just side with the textbook.

"You look deep in thought," Cayden commented beside him. Hawke looked over and nodded, not wanting to explain what had been on his mind. The Major looked sweaty and pale. Hawke had noticed in spite of the many times Cayden had travelled by portal, he never seemed to improve. Hawke was different; he no longer felt queasy on waking and instead of Cayden waiting for him to recover, it was now the other way around.

"You've portalled a lot, haven't you?" Hawke asked.

"You could say that."

"How many times a day?"

"You can't portal more than once a day, or even every day."

"Can't?"

"It's not recommended. Studies have shown that the body is impacted by constant portalling. To keep the tourists safe, we don't allow them to portal sooner than two weeks apart.

"I've portalled in and out of the DOME within a week!" Hawke cried.

"Yes, but you have six week breaks to recover afterward."

Hawke stewed for a while before another realisation came to him.

"The Junior Oceangate project," he said. He didn't usually mention it to Cayden because those were the times he'd gone to see Ellis. "We only stay on Trent for one week. All of us."

"Yes, and you *all* have six week breaks to recover," Cayden repeated.

Hawke didn't think Cayden had understood his earlier indignation. He'd thought that he'd been risked just because he had Wanderer blood and the DOME was keen to get at it.

"I'm surprised you're thinking about this," Cayden said gently, capturing Hawke's attention. "I thought you'd be excited about where we are."

Hawke looked around the waiting room. It was dressed in the usual couches and armchairs, plush rugs under coffee tables atop clinically white tiled floors. Unlike most other waiting rooms, the paintings weren't abstract, but depicted mountain vistas.

He'd never portalled to this world before, never sat in this room. He didn't feel like he was anywhere different or special, it was just another waiting room on just another Authority Base.

It didn't feel like home, even though that was where

he was.

Boronia.

The Authority base on Boronia was nestled deep in the Tortured Isles. When Hawke learned this, it made a horrible kind of sense why there were so many legends of unforgiving seas and ruthless pirates. He wondered aloud what happened to those who dared to explore in spite of the risks and when his questions were met with silence, he understood enough not to bother asking again.

The ship he boarded with Cayden was a strange breed of modern technology wearing old skin but he didn't notice until it was pointed out to him. Authorities dressed as Boronian seafarers swarmed the ship with efficient precision. Orders were fast and clear, the work seemingly effortless. The sailors' muscles bulged with the work and at first Hawke admired their strength, respectful of their arduous tasks. Then he was told that the sails were of a special material that weighed less than half the normal weight but was as strong. They also didn't need the wind to billow them out to maintain their speed, as the ship had been fitted with modern propellors that moved them at a pace unequalled by any ship upon this world. Hawke's respect for the sailors lessened, even though their false tasks were still gruelling and continued to make them sweat. He was invited onto the bridge where computer screens showed the ship's progress on a map and relegated the captain to nothing more than a babysitter for the auto-pilot.

Cayden spoke in a tone that belied his admiration

while Hawke remained silent, eyeing all of the instruments and feeling disappointment swell in his chest like a poisonous balloon. His mind understood the benefits of convenience while his heart felt like he was being cheated. He recognised the sensation of helplessness within him—he was well acquainted with it by now, in his thirteenth year of life—but this time he thought it was driven by protectiveness for a world that didn't have a chance against the Authority machine.

Willets Academy, being not just a school but also a vehicle of propaganda and a recruiting pool for the Authorities, had taught him more about the workings of the organisation than he'd cared to know. He now understood that there were many worlds that achieved the 'opportunity' to become an Authority shaped world and enjoy the technologies that every Authority world had to offer.

Worlds like Varrell and Austra, who'd become almost identical to one another—including some inter-world corporate brands—were Charlie worlds, shaped and fully embracing their governance by Authorities. Worlds like Cazul and Earth, however, were Delta worlds—also shaped and just as identical but they still didn't know that portals existed. Once they did, they would become carbon copies as the Authorities streamed in and took over, forming a worldwide governing body. More Delta worlds became Charlie worlds every day.

Then there were low-tech, Bravo worlds like Trent, whose resources were too rich for the Authorities to ignore. They took control, plundered what they could and used the rest to show off, often blocking technological development to suit their own purposes. And the likes of Boronia, a world classified as Limbo because it had managed to capture Authority attention and was being guided toward yet another formulaic pattern that would lead them directly into Authority hands—under the banner of equality—but a development strategy hadn't been formalised for it yet. Limbo was less of a call-sign and more a state of existence for such worlds.

It was knowledge like this that made him resent the power the Authorities wielded. He stared at the instrument panels without seeing them until Cayden led him away. They stood side by side at the railing, looking out over the ocean and the calm metre swells, smelling air that Hawke thought was supposed to be salty but smelled like nothing at all. Cayden spoke about a variety of things that seemed to dance around the true subject but Hawke didn't really listen. He didn't care to know.

"Hawke," a hand on his shoulder alerted him to Cayden's intensity. Hawke stared at him uncomprehendingly, not knowing what had last been said, noticing for the first time that his sponsor had wrinkles around his eyes and grey in his three day beard. When had Cayden started to look old? "Are you worried about meeting them?"

"I haven't really thought about it," Hawke said honestly. He'd been thinking about everything else except the family they were travelling to. Was that normal? He could imagine both Naomi and Dr Turner telling him it was, that this was a coping mechanism. He didn't think other thirteen year old boys thought as much about their own motivations and internalisations as he did.

Cayden looked dubious, his gaze assessing.

"Does it not yet seem real?"

Nothing seemed real, especially not on this ship.

"Not yet. Maybe it will later," he said, injecting hope into his voice and relieved when Cayden gave him a reassuring smile. There was no sense sharing his bitterness. Cayden had pulled many strings for him to come home and he was grateful.

Four days later, the ship docked at a citadel called Rummager's Perch. High stone walls prevented Hawke from seeing more of the fortress beyond. As Hawke disembarked, the large iron gate set into the wall cranked halfway up, allowing them entry into the citadel. He and Cayden, dressed in the fashion of a region beyond the Tortured Isles, stood in a dirt courtyard as guards worked in pairs carting goods to and from the newly docked ship. Cayden looked peculiar in his high collar and ornamental green jacket. He also wore wide-legged pants that were tied tight halfway down the calf, and black socks that turned into pointed-toe shoes. Hawke was dressed in the same manner with different colours, except for the black sock-shoes.

"Are the guards Authorities too?" Hawke asked quietly, in case they weren't.

"A few of them," Cayden replied. He gestured at the narrow two-storey building nearby, sitting at the bottom of a steep hill. A wooden plaque screwed into the exterior wall informed Hawke it was a cartographer's place of business.

"Do you not know where we're going?" Hawke asked, alarmed. Cayden explained that they were supposed to meet their guide within and Hawke felt foolish for asking. Of course Cayden would know where they were going and of course they were going to have a guide come with them... because they were posing as newcomers.

Inside was a short, stocky man with wispy white hair. He was dressed more casually with a leather vest over a loose tunic and pants. Hawke envied his comfortable clothes. The man squinted at them and spoke in Authoritan, like he knew who they both were.

"Take a seat, Foygle will take you through the mountains. He'll be here shortly."

'Shortly' turned out to be a two hour wait. Hawke spent the time looking out the thick glass windows, watching as the courtyard became a dance of inventory placement. He was bored until some crates fell off a wagon, then he enjoyed the spectacle as too many people tried to take charge. The crates were loaded up and Hawke turned to face Cayden, who was tapping a report on his tablet. Hawke watched, reading as much as he could until he was sensed and Cayden quickly flicked it off.

"I thought you were still looking out the window."

"Aren't I allowed to see your work?"

Cayden shook his head, surprising Hawke. "Not really, it's classified."

"Is it about me?"

Cayden gave a short, unfamiliar chuckle. Upon hearing it, Hawke was positive that the classified information *was* about him.

"Why would you write your classified report beside me?" Hawke prompted.

Cayden pressed his lips together for a moment, thinking before he replied. "Because there's very little to do here. It was rude of me to do something that excludes you. I apologise."

"Why don't you want to tell me which division you're a part of?"

Cayden blinked.

"That came out of nowhere."

"No, it didn't. It's all part of the same secret," Hawke gestured at the tablet.

"It's not a secret, Hawke. It's *classified*. There's a difference."

"The division you work in is classified?"

Cayden puffed frustration and shook his head. "No, but—"

"Then why won't you tell me? What is it that you do? Is it something you think I'll be upset about?"

"No, I..." Cayden was pensive. "I don't know what you'd think."

Shock travelled down Hawke's spine and nestled in his stomach, churning.

"You told me you didn't work for the DOME," Hawke said, having managed to extract this information out of Cayden many years ago. Had the denial been a lie? Was this the reason he'd become a sponsor to Hawke in the first place?

"I don't. I'm stationed on the same world as you," Cayden said. "What's going on with you today? Are you concerned about meeting your family? There's still some days' travel."

"This is not about my fucking family."

"Hey!" Cayden's brows wrinkled and drew down.

"Give me slack," Hawke requested. "Deep thoughts, that's all. You with me?"

Cayden looked like he was debating his reaction and settled on a brief lecture. "I'm with you but you have to accept that in full. Don't strike out at me."

"Alright. Okay," Hawke agreed, glad to have defused what might have led to tension between them. He looked out the window again, noticing out of the corner of his eye that Cayden had made the tablet disappear.

Hawke saw a boy run through the courtyard, maybe two or three years younger than him. The boy was headed directly for the cartographer and Hawke thought there might be a message that came with him saying that Foygle wouldn't be showing up today.

The boy spoke rapidly with the cartographer in a Boronian dialect that Hawke didn't understand, gesticulating grandly as he spoke. He looked over at

Cayden and Hawke before disappearing into a back room and then emerging with a bow in his hand and a quiver of arrows slung over his back. There was also a utility belt cinched at his waist. It held at least one knife that Hawke could see. A few more words were exchanged and then the cartographer addressed them.

"Foygle will take you through Red River Pass and leave you at the gates of Marvapan."

Hawke realised then that the boy was Foygle, not a messenger. More importantly, the city of Marvapan was mentioned. Hawke recognised the name as a destination he'd always wanted to visit. It had sounded so interesting during his geography lessons. He'd heard tales of locals wearing brightly coloured material swathed around their bodies and binding their feet. He remembered Denis telling him stories; about girls who would dance naked on stage, animals jumping through rings of fire and fighters duelling until one of them died. He wanted to see the full body tattoos of the Wise Ones whose entire life story was imprinted upon their skin.

"We're still a long way from Galantyne," Hawke told Cayden, even though he suspected his sponsor already knew.

"About a week by coach plus however long it takes us to get through the Pass."

"You'll get through before nightfall," the cartographer promised, then gestured for Foygle to take the lead.

Cayden and Hawke followed him out the door.

They exited the citadel by the west gate, which was more like an iron door than a gate. When it swung outward, Hawke was surprised to exit directly onto a narrow mountain path, where only two people could walk side by side without fear of pitching over the edge. Hawke peered down at the river that ran beneath the citadel and was likely their only fresh water source. Even though he knew the name 'Red River Pass' likely didn't mean anything, he was disappointed not to see the colour red anywhere. The water was silver; the mountainside that it had eroded was a duller grey. It was like the world had dropped all of its colour. Even the sky was bleak and overcast. Short gusts of wind made standing at the path's edge uncomfortable.

Two pack mules travelled with Foygle, Cayden and Hawke. One of the mules carried their luggage. Hawke didn't ask what the other mule carried; he had an idea that Rummager's Perch was a location that smuggled many goods into and out of Marvapan. Exotic goods likely travelled down this path by mule and were shipped out to sea. How much had the pirates organised before the Authorities took control? Did that mean the Authorities had taken on the role of pirates?

"Where's Filip?"

"Filip?" Cayden asked, puzzled. Hawke was astounded that his sponsor didn't remember.

"Filip Don Something-Or-Other, the man you brought with you when you first took me to the DOME."

At first Cayden stared blankly before Hawke saw realisation light up in his eyes. "Oh! Him! I don't have a lot to do with him."

"But wouldn't he be the captain of one of your special ships here?" Hawke asked.

"I honestly don't know," Cayden said.

The path widened as they rounded a bend and Foygle picked up the pace. Conversation was reserved to essential comments and Hawke thought they were making good time until Foygle started gesturing that they were too slow.

"Do you understand him?" Cayden asked hopefully when Foygle yelled over his shoulder at them and then smacked the rumps of the pack-mules. There wasn't a lot of options for the beasts to go so they quickened their pace.

"Kind of. He keeps talking about the moon imps chasing us."

"Is that a real thing or a folk tale?"

It hadn't occurred to Hawke that it would be anything other than a folk tale so he shrugged. He considered that a moon-imp might be some kind of nocturnal predator. It motivated him to walk faster, though the soles in the sock-shoes were too thin to cushion his feet properly and he could feel blisters forming. Hawke swallowed his complaints until they arrived at a monumental staircase cut into the mountainside. Its many steps rose so far up that Hawke couldn't see the end, though he could see plenty of switchbacks. He allowed himself a groan but saved the rest of his breath for the climb. Sweat beaded on his upper lip, which he licked away. He couldn't do much about the annoying trickle down his back. They were supposed to be incognito but every step had him wishing for his regular clothing over this costume.

The pack mules navigated the stairs with ease but Foygle left them behind in order to scout ahead. Hawke and Cayden heard him cry out gleefully from somewhere above before he returned with a large, dead snake coiled around his shoulders, skewered into place with an arrow. Hawke thought of Foygle as the kind of boy he'd like to befriend, though he was sure that the other boy thought little of him and his ridiculous shoes.

Red River Pass ended as abruptly as it began. At the top of the stairs was a cave where two men stood guard. Both were dressed in the same uniform as those in Rummager's Perch but these men also held shields. Hawke recognised the cat-eye etched into the metal as Marvapan's city insignia.

Foygle entered the cave first, leading them to where a tattooed woman stood beneath the warm glow of a fire-lamp set into the rough cave wall. She stepped forward and unlaced one of the packs from the mule brought to her. She checked inside the pack before lacing it closed and handed Foygle a small pouch as payment. It didn't look very full but when the boy peeked inside, he seemed very happy.

They moved deeper into the cave, more fire-lamps lighting their way, until there was a split. Foygle gestured for them to take the left fork, speaking rapidly. He handed over the reins of the mule that carried their belongings and then disappeared along the right hand tunnel, slapping the rump of his mule as he ran. Hawke supposed he was off to deliver the second pack and wondered how they were supposed to navigate a large, unfamiliar city without a guide.

Their tunnel sloped upward at a sharp angle. The pack-mule was well trained and kept their pace without prompt, its lead slack in Cayden's hand. When they surfaced, Hawke squinted at the difference in brightness. As washed out and grey as Red River Pass had been, the city of Marvapan was its opposite.

The sun beat down on them with unrelenting harshness as they walked to the middle of a paved courtyard. The fountain at the centre blasted cool water into the air, its off-spray sprinkling over Hawke and Cayden as they drew closer. When they reached the fountain, a dozen people dressed in colourful, sheer clothing swarmed them from all sides, all talking over one another, vying for their attention. They were boisterous and excessive, shoving and elbowing one another. Hawke drank in the experience, fascinated by their tattooed faces and golden skin. Cayden pointed at one of them who eagerly took the reins of the mule from him while the others groaned and headed back to their places, leaving the fountain and courtyard as empty as it had been when Cayden and Hawke had first stepped in.

"That was amazing," Hawke said, needing to acknowledge what had just happened.

Cayden grinned at him. "I was told how to pick a guide in this city, but even a warning doesn't prepare you for it."

They followed their new guide through an aisle of market stalls, banners and pennants flapping in the constant warm breeze. An array of spicy smells assaulted Hawke's nose as he passed a stall with coloured powders in barrels, the next stall filled with the pungent aroma of marbled cheeses. He was surprised to see somebody getting a tattoo from a stallholder, neither of them concerned about the dust swirling around them from the street or the heat of the sun from above. Sweat continuously trickled down Hawke's back and he found himself wishing one of these stalls would sell sunglasses to counteract the glare.

"How high up are we?" Hawke asked, thinking that they must've broken through the clouds to see skies so clear.

"Not that high. It looked like we climbed a mountain but it was more like the sheer face of a large hill."

"But it was overcast."

"The wind here pushes clouds along pretty quick. I saw patches of blue before we'd reached the cave."

Hawke had been too busy staring at his feet during the stair climb to notice the weather change.

"It's really warm," Hawke commented. He'd been distracted from his blisters by the madness of the city around them. As the qrowds thinned and there was less to look at, he became aware again. He did his best to keep up with the scurrying pace of their guide ahead, wondering why everyone here seemed in a rush.

"It's the exercise making you hot."

"Walking around isn't much exercise," Hawke scoffed.

"We did just climb a mountain," Cayden reminded Hawke. "Did you want a drink? There's a flask of water not packed too deeply."

"I can wait."

Their small group arrived at a stable with a line of carriages parked along the wide dirt road, ready for hitching. Their luggage was taken off the pack-mule by their hasty guide and squirrelled away in one of the carriages' carry areas but not before Cayden rescued the flask. The pack-mule was then led into the stable, where Hawke supposed it would be fed and watered before making the trip back to Rummager's Perch. Cayden and Hawke waited until they were directed into the small building nearby. For the first time, Hawke understood the Boronian that was used, for the young woman who managed the business spoke it as Hawke had grown up speaking it.

"What destination have you?"

"Donovan Court."

"The Court is the noble land overlooking the township of Donovan?" the woman clarified, pulling a rod out of the wall where maps hung.

"Yes, thank you," Cayden said stiffly.

The woman unclipped one of the hanging maps and pushed the rod back into place where it settled with a clunk. Hawke could hear the maps brushing against each other as they swung about from the motion.

The woman laid the map flat on the table and pointed out where Marvapan was in relation to Donovan Court, then she took out a thick measuring wheel that looked like a dough-cutter to Hawke. There was a painted dot at one edge. She rolled it from Marvapan to Donovan Court along a twisting red line, counting out a number every time the dot circled around to the bottom. Hawke mentally counted with her and they both ended up at five and a half.

"Do you have messengers?" Cayden asked as he paid for the use of the carriage. Hawke noticed that Cayden paid with small gems instead of coins.

"I have birds. Do you wish to send one ahead of you?"

"Please do." Cayden pulled a cream coloured note out from the pocket of his jacket and handed it over. Hawke had already been shown what was inside, he'd helped compose it. News of his imminent return would reach his family so they could prepare for his arrival. He stomach lurched, alerting him to his nervousness.

The woman took the note and she and Cayden negotiated the new cost. Ten minutes later, Hawke and Cayden were sitting inside the carriage that held their luggage beneath, on their way to Hawke's home.

Donovan Court.

The countryside was familiar to him in the same way as dreams. Hawke was jostled rhythmically on his seat as he watched the scenery roll past the window. He listened to the rumble of carriage wheels and the muted clop of hooves on the dusty road as the horses pulled them closer to their destination. He and Cayden were in their final day of travel.

He felt grimy and tired even though they'd stopped and rested at various townships along the way, bathing in private tubs or in opulent bath-houses. He missed the convenience of running hot water and flushing toilets. As each day brought Hawke closer to reuniting with his family, his stomach knotted more tightly. Hawke's mouth overflowed with spit that he continually swallowed. Opposite him was Cayden's gentle, sympathetic smile. He hadn't expected to feel this strange, cloying tension with each passing hour.

"You'll be fine," Cayden said.

"I'm a bad liar," Hawke said.

"Stay as close to the truth as possible," Cayden advised.

The carriage turned onto a smoother path, where the dirt had been properly compacted and the vibrations settled down. Hawke pressed the side of his face to the wall of the carriage in order to better see out the front.

Standing proud at the end of the long drive was the manor of Donovan Court. The building looked smaller than Hawke remembered, though it was certainly still grand. Living in the large and lengthy four storey academy had tainted his appreciation of the manor's size and facade. The manor was an ill-decorated block of a building with no sills on the narrow windows and a ridiculously sized front door.

"How does it look?" Cayden asked, and Hawke could hear the hopefulness in his tone.

"Not quite as I remembered."

"You've grown in the meantime."

Hawke diverted his gaze from the window to meet Cayden's encouraging stare.

The carriage came to a stop and Hawke hesitated. Arriving at Donovan Court in this manner made him feel like a visitor not only to his family home, but to his own world.

When they got out of the carriage, the driver hopped down and took their bags in each hand, waiting for them to lead.

"I thought they would be out here to greet you," Cayden said.

"They'll be in the foyer so we can make an entrance," Hawke explained.

"I'm familiar with the custom."

Hawke stared at Cayden, realising that the Major had expected his family to break the usual convention in favour of their emotions. Hawke was surprised that Cayden would feel this way since he was of the Authorities, who were full of regimental traditions.

"Should we start speaking Boronian again now?"

"Yes, we should."

Hawke was amused that Cayden had answered him in Authoritan. He appreciated that the Major had learned a great deal of Boronian so he could accompany him on this trip but languages weren't a strong skill of his. His accent was awful enough that it was difficult to understand him at times. It suited the story that he was from overseas and spoke a dialect of Boronian that had transformed too greatly to be recognisable from the original language. Their story would be that Hawke had taught him formal Boronian.

They approached the huge double doors and stood before them. The driver moved to the side and pulled on the cord that clanged the bell. The doors opened immediately afterward, revealing that the servants on the other side were ready for the ceremonial entrance. It was possible they'd been waiting even before the carriage had turned down the drive.

As the doors opened farther, Hawke's family were revealed, standing in arrowhead formation. There were a few differences.

He should've seen his parents first, except Umber was standing in the position were their father should be. This meant their father was away on some kind of business, leaving Umber to manage the affairs of the estate. It was likely that he hadn't heard of Hawke's impending return in time to make it back.

While Hawke had been away, his eldest brother Umber had already made his choice in marriage and wed a young woman Hawke vaguely recognised. There was a small boy perhaps two years of age standing beside his mother. He had her dark hair and eyes. Umber's wife also had a belly that promised another child soon. As the doors widened farther, Hawke saw Giselle with her hand high upon her chest and Denis standing restlessly beside her. Both of them looked like taller versions of themselves and it made Hawke feel younger and smaller.

His gaze found his mother next, who stood at Umber's other side, her eyes glistening and her hair greyer than he remembered. If it wasn't for tradition and ceremony, he had no doubt she, Denis and Giselle would have run to him and hugged him. Standing in a line opposite Hawke's siblings, there were two unknown men and two teenage boys. Beside him, Cayden made his announcement once the doors were fully opened. His voice boomed and echoed around the tiled hall.

"Greetings from Irian Cayden of Ulsa Maya, Region of Dondellian."

Dondellian truly was a Boronian location but the Major had used his home world in place of his estate name.

"I have brought home your son, Lord Hawke Don... *Aron* of Donovan Court."

Hawke was sure the mistake was overlooked due to high-running emotion. Denis broke the ceremonial greeting and approached Hawke at a sprint. Hawke only had time to catch his brother before they were both sprawled on the floor. He laughed off the impact, though Denis apologised and tried to help him up, attempting to embrace him at the same time. Cayden got them both on their feet and soon Hawke's family gathered around, welcoming him home.

"Your father would have..." Hawke's mother began but was unable to finish her sentence before her face crumpled and she pulled Hawke into a tight hug. He looked over her shoulder at Umber, whose lips were pressed tightly together, holding back news.

He knew. Looking at Umber's face, he knew. His father wasn't away on business, he'd died. Hawke was disappointed that his father wasn't alive to see his return. After realising that this was the only emotion he felt at his father's passing, guilt came next. He wanted to care more but couldn't. His father had been a man of stately matters and observed rules. He'd been emotionally absent and the rigid post against Hawke's rebellion. Hawke felt a sense of loss but he didn't know what he was mourning. Cayden had replaced his father a long time ago. He didn't have much time to think about it when he was being manhandled between his family members so he let the grief remain with his confusion and swallowed them both in favour of celebrating his return to his family. He shed no tears until he saw them in his mother's eyes and at that moment he felt like he'd truly come home.

After he composed himself, Hawke was introduced to the two unfamiliar men. They were fathers escorting their sons. The young men sought Giselle's hand in marriage. Hawke had missed the formal event introducing her as an eligible young woman. These two contenders had possibly also missed the evening and wanted to make their intentions known.

They entered the sitting room as one large group and Hawke flopped onto a low chair with winged arms. He noticed Umber and Giselle shoot bothered frowns in his direction and he straightened before the questions came.

The play on truths began.

Hawke did most of the talking due to Cayden's stilted grasp of the language. He spoke about the horse thieves who'd stolen him to stop him from raising an alarm. Hawke embellished that they were intending to ransom him back to Donovan Court. They'd travelled far north with him and beaten him for attempting to run away. He deviated from the truth when he described how they'd knocked him unconscious and it had led to a loss of memory beyond his own name.

"They sold him to a skipper," Cayden interjected.

Hawke didn't like the rest of the planned story about running off once the ship docked and then ending up on Cayden's estate, for it lacked adventure and excitement.

"We were boarded by pirates!" Hawke blurted. To his delight, he received many and varied reactions. When he glanced at Cayden, he knew that he would be forced to account for himself later.

But that was later.

When he saw his mother's devastated expression, he relented.

"They didn't hurt me. I sailed with them for a bit and was dropped off on the coast of Dondellion."

"I heard pirates show no mercy," Umber challenged.

"Thankfully this lot did," their mother replied, shooting Umber a glare.

Hawke was enjoying himself and opened his mouth to tell of more excitement but Cayden interrupted.

"They docked at a smuggler's town. Hawke ran off. He found my estate. Our house was familiar. He insisted he lived there. I was intrigued. I took him in, for he had no-one. In time his memory returned. I immediately prepared to travel here."

The staccato style telling of Hawke's past was more due to Cayden's struggle with the language than his desire to leave out details. Hawke was aware that Cayden's comprehension of Boronian was a great deal better than his ability to fluently speak it.

"You've brought him home and for this you must be rewarded," Hawke's mother announced.

"You are very generous," Cayden said with a small nod. Hawke didn't like this idea. It might be the custom to reward a person who'd helped out a noble family but the Authorities didn't need it. Hawke felt like the reward should've been given in the other direction; after all, the Donovan family had lost a son and the Authorities had gained a test subject.

Cayden saw Hawke's face and must've seen the resentment on it. Cayden gave him an almost imperceptible shake of the head. What did it mean? Was it a warning not to make a protest or not to tell any more lies? Hawke squashed his indignation down, even though he could still feel the weight of his hatred on his chest. He told himself that Cayden shouldn't be the target of it.

The conversation progressed rigidly. Hawke was surprised at how difficult it was to talk to his family, how challenging it was to relate to them or care about the events that were circulating in their lives. The warm greeting had been promising but now that they were trying to catch him up, he found himself disinterested. He hid his disappointment when hearing about new inventions that sounded backwards and found himself at a loss for words when asked about his opinion of the neighbouring estate converting their lacklustre cornfield into a pig farm. He imagined, if he'd stayed at the estate, that he would be just as outraged that their neighbour would start such a low-brow business as a piggery. Now, he couldn't care less. He also didn't express his opinion about the relationship between piggeries and the abattoir in the conversation that came next. Why couldn't their neighbour stable horses, or continue with falconry? They were *hunters*, not farmers. Hawke yawned behind his hand.

"Join me for a walk, brother," Denis said, standing. The invitation didn't seem optional but Hawke was glad, for he'd been wanting to reconnect with Denis most of all.

Cayden remained in the sitting room and Hawke and Denis were warned by their mother that the dinner bell would ring in less than an hour, so they shouldn't venture too far.

While they were upstairs visiting rooms that Hawke recognised but felt detached from—rooms in a house from a previous life—Denis asked a revealing question.

"Do you not feel you belong here anymore?" His tone was sorrowful.

Hawke realised he'd managed to hide none of his true feelings, at least from his brother. He still knew him well.

"I don't know if I belong anywhere," Hawke said honestly.

"That's grave news," he said. "You speak with a strange inflection now. Like a foreigner."

They entered the armoury, though the room was decorative rather than practical. The shined wooden floor was where Hawke and Denis had their favourite lessons, and other than a few new pendants and ribbons won at events held whilst Hawke had been away, the room hadn't changed.

Denis plucked a light sword from the wall and unsheathed it.

"Am I at risk?" Hawke said wryly.

"Have you been keeping up with your lessons or do they bore you as well?" Denis asked.

"You sound bitter."

"No." Denis sighed and swung the sword in an arc that Hawke made sure he was well away from. "Sorry. I have an array of emotions that battle within. I expected you to be the same, which was foolish."

"Then we are both fools," Hawke said.

His brother talked strangely yet in a familiar rhythm that Hawke was beginning to match. It wasn't just the language that was different but even in the way that it had been used. Coming here was like slipping into a pair of shoes that had been well-worn, that were comfortable and a favourite of his... but were now too small for his feet.

Denis gave him a smile and then tipped his head towards the wall of weapons. There was a rack that was supposed to be used for practice but Hawke bypassed it just as Denis had and took a sword off the wall that he'd always admired; one that was named many things by other worlds, but in Boronia it was called a *tayeta*.

"You still like that," Denis said, grinning.

"I was supposed to get a *tayeta* of my own."

"Just take that one," Denis gestured with the sword in his hands.

Hawke didn't know whether to be pleased or saddened by the suggestion. The assumption made was clear and he avoided replying by staring down at the ornamental sheath as he moved a little farther away from Denis, showing his brother his profile before he unsheathed the sword and began to go through motions that were still ingrained in him.

Denis joined the routine and side by side they swung and thrust their swords at invisible foes in fluid motion. Both of them stopped when they heard the chime of a bell echoing up the corridor.

Hawke faced Denis, who looked as sweaty as he felt, and the pair of them laughed at the state of one another. Hawke sheathed his sword and placed it back up on the wall while his brother did the same. Hawke had hoped to speak more with Denis, for they'd always been frank. He felt like his brother could be close again... but there was time. Together they headed for the dining hall.

During dinner, Hawke decided he liked one of Giselle's suitors better than the other. The father and son from Yarrow Hill had been invited to stay at Donovan Court, for Giselle had spent a great deal of time with that suitor during the festivities. The other pair from Koralee Circle had turned up unannounced. The father declared his son hadn't yet spent enough time with Giselle. In spite of this socially unforgivable act, Hawke preferred their more genuine natures.

He hadn't expected his opinion to have any standing but after dessert, when returning from the bathroom, Giselle stopped him in the corridor a fair distance from the sitting room. The family had gathered in there to talk again and she seemed keen to keep this conversation between herself and her youngest brother.

"You've chosen a good time to return, Hawke," Giselle said, her cheeks pink and her eyes bright. "You can offer me your preference of brother-in-law."

"What? Why does it matter who *I* like?" he asked, flummoxed.

She looked sympathetic to his confusion.

"Hawke, I wouldn't dare leave you out of your right to have a say, simply because you've only just returned home. I know it must overwhelm you." Her eyes widened before she reached for Hawke's hand, holding it in hers. "Do you—do you *remember* the tradition?"

she asked apologetically.

The tradition was that their father was supposed to state a preference, but since he'd passed away, the onus fell upon the brother to dictate. If there were multiple brothers, then they all received a vote as to which estate they would allow their sister to marry into.

"I remember," he said.

"Please tell me who you like best. Umber and Denis are in disagreement and I've been at an absolute loss which of their opinions I should adhere to."

"Isn't it better to have a stalemate so you can select your own husband?" Hawke suggested, not liking how Giselle was speaking. When he'd left Donovan Court, she'd been wilful and strong-minded. Was she having a joke at his expense? Why did it bother her about two male opinions beyond those of her suitors?

"Your opinion removes the issue of brotherly favouritism. Neither Umber nor Denis would be cross at me if you tipped the scale."

Hawke finally realised what she wanted to achieve and he felt pleased to help her out.

"I understand now. Let me know which of the two you'd like me to announce my preference for and I can make my declaration when the time comes." He smiled encouragingly but she dropped his hand and took a step back, glaring at him without comment. It dawned on Hawke that she truly wanted to know which of her suitors he wanted her to marry.

"Don't *you* prefer one over the other?"

"I'm asking that of you!" she challenged.

"It's not *my* decision. You'll be required to live at your husband's estate, be the mother of his children. Surely you—" he stopped when a servant scuttled by and continued in a quieter tone. "Surely you have a favourite among those two? I barely spoke to them."

"They did enough talking that you should know what they're both like," Giselle said, sounding defensive. "You're my brother, your opinion is more important than mine."

Hawke swore in Authoritan.

"Since when have you blindly followed tradition or devalued yourself in such a way?" he accused. "You constantly challenged our parents and the value of the old ways when we were young."

"No, Hawke. That was you and Denis. Mostly *you*, and look what happened to you because of your wilfulness," she hissed. Giselle's hand flew to her mouth and she stared at him, horrified by what she'd said. Hawke waited for her to recover, perhaps even to apologise—though he preferred this hot-headed version of her. At least she had some spine and his memory of her wasn't completely wrong.

After she lowered her hand, no apology came. "Don't make your settling in difficult, Hawke. It's a simple matter."

"I won't be settling in, Giselle, so the point is moot."

"You're not going *back*!" she said, though her words themselves were contrary, they sounded more like the kind spoken in shock.

He was angry with her, upset that she wasn't the sister he remembered, that none of this was what he remembered. He realised he would be breaking his mother's heart but at least she would know that he was alive and happy.

"You're best suited to Gregorson at Yarrow Hill since, like you, he would never break tradition. I'm sure the two of you will be happy making mindless children together."

He stormed back to the sitting room, leaving Giselle in the corridor behind him—her cheeks pinked for a different reason than when they'd first started speaking.

Hawke knocked softly on the guest room door, though the sound echoed along stone floors. At least the wall panels muted it somewhat.

"Come in," Cayden called without first asking who it was. As Hawke entered, he saw Cayden standing by the window where he looked like he'd been waiting for someone. He wondered if Cayden had been expecting him. "Are you alright?" Cayden asked in Authoritan. Hawke adopted the language also, finding it easy to slip into even though his native Boronian was more familiar.

"I don't want to stay here."

"Has something happened?"

"This isn't my home anymore. I can't fool myself that I can live here again."

Cayden stared at him until Hawke looked down at his shoes, feeling hot pricks of tears behind his eyes. The expression on his sponsor's face was unreadable, almost peculiar. Hawke believed he was letting Cayden down but the chasm he felt couldn't be put into words.

Hawke had lost everything. The Wanderers had taken him away from his home world forever because he no longer belonged. The Authorities had kept him away for reasons he still didn't understand.

The Authorities, in spite of their restrictions, had opened his eyes to life beyond the insular world of Boronia and its frustrating traditions. He'd always known that his home world didn't value the opinions of the working class or women, but he'd never considered the depth of its problems before. Giselle had hammered the truth home with her absurd request that he should choose her husband.

Hawke heard Cayden move away from the window and approach him but he didn't look up, even when he was embraced. The gesture brought a great deal of emotion to the surface, which spilled out of him as he cried into Cayden's chest. He wasn't shushed or his hair caressed; Cayden simply held him until the wave of despair passed and Hawke regained control of himself. Embarrassed, he pulled away and spoke to the wall.

"Sorry," he said, his voice hoarse.

"We can visit again, another time."

Hawke rubbed the remains of his tears away with the back of his hand.

"That would be great."

"For now, how long would you like to stay?"

"A week," Hawke said, even though he wanted to leave right away. He didn't want to be accused of making a hasty decision. Ultimately, he was running away because he no longer felt prepared to face his family. There was so much he'd forgotten; memories had blurred into favourable impressions and details had faded. Now the imperfections were overwhelming and he needed to deal with them. He didn't think he could process his thoughts and emotions while he was here but he would try. A week would be like a month, no doubt.

His lower lip began quivering but he didn't want to cry in front of Cayden anymore. Hawke turned and left the room, hoping that Cayden wouldn't say anything to his departing back. He was grateful when he was allowed to escape into the corridor and into the privacy of his bedroom, a room that was both familiar and claustrophobic, despite its grand size.

CHAPTER ELEVEN

Not Just A Number

WHEN Daeson entered the penthouse, he was surprised to see Omerri in disarray. It struck him, how dishevelled and flustered she looked. He'd only ever seen her lose her composure when he made love to her, and even then she was elegant and beautiful. Right now she looked wild; she was twisting her hair with one hand while the other held some sheets of white and yellow paper. He figured whatever was written on that paper was the reason she was acting this way. Now was not the time to ask her about Synjan.

"Omerri?" he questioned, closing the door behind him so nobody else could see. The gesture was unnecessary because nobody would be wandering around the top level but it was instinctual for him to protect her as much as he could. He knew Omerri wouldn't want anybody else seeing her like this. "What's wrong?"

She spun to face him, her eyes wide but not just in fear. She was angry too. Hers was the stare of a woman who knew something bad was going to happen. The emotion behind her expression migrated to his heart, causing him to feel alarmed as well.

"This!" she hissed, shaking the papers at him. "This!" she said again, either because he hadn't replied quickly enough or because it was all she could bring herself to say.

"What is that?" he asked, stepping towards her. He stopped when she snatched the papers back and held them against her chest like a treasured secret.

"That stupid man!" she exclaimed, shaking her head

and not making eye contact with Daeson. Tears rolled down her face. "Those stupid men. Those stupid, *stupid* men. Damn them for doing this in the first place. They're going to find you."

Her words turned a knot in his stomach and gooseflesh broke out on his arms. He wanted to ask her who was going to find him but he didn't want more nonsensical answers spouted his way. He pushed down the instinct to grab Omerri by the shoulders and shake her and used a soothing voice on her instead.

"Come sit with me," he said, holding out his hand as he approached. He felt like he was speaking to a small, frightened child rather than the sophisticated woman he knew her to be. "Tell me from the beginning."

As she watched him, he could almost see her thoughts turning behind her blue eyes. He had no doubt she knew that panicking wasn't helping but he didn't think she could stop herself. There was a moment when he thought she would reach out for him and do as he asked... but then she huffed and stormed a short distance away, shaking the papers at him again.

"Don't talk to me like that!" she snapped. "This is a serious problem and it's going to have serious consequences. Damn the Authorities."

When she mentioned that it was a problem concerning the Authorities—

They're going to find you

—fear coiled around his heart like a snake, squeezing lightly and lying in wait. He could feel his patience slipping.

"What have they done?" Daeson asked, straightening.

"They're setting up the entire city with identification cards. If you have a birth certificate, you fill out some paperwork and apply by mail, but if you don't, you get a different form and have to go through their processing stations."

Processing stations. Daeson had no idea what such a thing was but it didn't sound good. The only word for 'processing' that he knew of was the food processor in the kitchen, but he didn't think they would be putting him through anything like that.

"I'll be put through a process?" Daeson asked.

"And they'll use needles," Omerri clarified. It was easier to make the connection.

"They'll be taking a sample of my blood," Daeson guessed again, more sure this time.

"They were, yes, but we were going to bypass all of that to keep you safe..." Omerri smiled winningly at Daeson, the pride in her face and voice were clear. "But then that *idiot* filled out the forms wrong and now it's too late because they've already gone!" Omerri wailed, speaking in riddles again. Daeson frowned at her. He felt bad when her shoulders slumped and she began to sob, standing in the middle of the room. Daeson went to her and wrapped his arms around her, kissing the top of her head, making shushing sounds. His emotions were warring; he wanted to soothe and comfort her but he also wanted to force her to explain herself better. His patience was rewarded when she started speaking again between sniffs.

"I don't... want to... lose you," she said, hitching in breaths.

He felt like a cad. She was severely upset on his behalf and he was only concerned about knowing what was going on as fast as possible. Did it matter if he waited a few more minutes to calm her down? He held her more tightly before releasing her so he could walk her to the chaise. There was a box of tissues upon its arm and he sat her at that end. Daeson waited while she fought her emotions for control, his gaze stealing to the documents in spite of himself. He couldn't read anything because the writing was small and the papers were scrunched in her fist.

"Are you feeling better now?" he asked after she'd lightly blown her nose and dabbed her cheeks. Her eyes were rimmed red but other than that she looked her usual self. Omerri nodded, looking embarrassed by his concern.

"I'm sorry you had to see all that."

"I—"

Wasn't bothered, he was going to say, but his tongue refused to move and the words stuck in his throat. Her tears had bothered him. He felt like that was his failing, not hers.

"I'm glad I was here for you," he said instead.

Omerri nodded and placed the papers on her lap with the yellow page on top. She smoothed the creases out with her hands while frowning down at them. Daeson could see now that the yellow page was some kind of form. The words in the heading were too long for him to puzzle through but he didn't try to sound them out, expecting that Omerri would be able to tell him.

"This is the form Nick filled out for you. The Authorities keep the top part for their records and we keep the bottom sheet. They use the white copy to enter it into their computer systems. With—"

"A what system?"

"Computer. It's a... kind of machine brain that remembers everything you tell it."

Daeson was overwhelmed. Ruby had spoken of little black boxes that sent messages and now he was finding out about a machine brain? It was harder to concentrate on the rest of Omerri's words as he wondered how much knowledge of this world had been kept from him. Why hadn't Jade told him?

"They put the information into the computer and

another machine attached to it makes a card, your ID Card. Every time you have to shop or work or are chosen for spot-checks, you have to produce this card."

"They're going to put my blood on the card?"

"Supposedly they want everyone's blood type—some ridiculous scam for streamlining the hospitals, but it's just a fabrication to find the Wanderers among us. It's not like the hospital at Bardon City would bother calling us up in Gredann for some Type B to be sent over because the Authority soldiers are blood donors anyway. All of that's on record so it's not like—"

"Omerri," Daeson said gently, interrupting her tirade. He hadn't understood much of it but he could tell that she was getting sidetracked. At first she looked upset by the interruption but then she nodded.

"They want to take your blood to find out if you're a Wanderer. The only way to stop them is to either produce a birth certificate—which is access to forgery contacts I don't have and there isn't enough time for—or to have you in their system as processed, with your card pending and the form already filed."

Daeson was shocked.

"So how—?"

"Nick has someone who can do it from the inside. Your card will be made and sent out with the rest. If we make as few ripples as possible and give them as much of an internal paper trail as we can, they're less likely to notice."

Daeson made the connection for who their Authority contact was.

"Synjan," he breathed. If she was an Authority, no wonder Nick had wanted him to stay away from her. Couldn't he have just said that? Perhaps they hadn't trusted the fact he could only speak truth. But who would possibly question him about his knowledge of a spy?

Omerri didn't look happy at his declaration. "Well, Synjan's involved, yes," she conceded, her voice betraying her ill feelings. "You're not supposed to know her name."

"I won't tell anybody about your secret Authority contact," he promised.

Omerri laughed a merry tinkle. "She's not an authority in anything, darling. She just pretends."

Daeson was confused. If she *wasn't* an Authority after all, then why keep knowledge of Synjan from him? He wanted to know what the problem was, since Omerri was telling him that everything was handled.

"So why are you upset? What's gone wrong?"

"Because Nick, that idiot," she moaned to the ceiling before looking at Daeson with haunted eyes. "He got your age wrong. He's written down that you're eighteen and nobody would believe that as soon as they look at you and you can't lie."

He was confused. "But I don't have to lie. I *am* eighteen."

She stared at him, her expression blank. There was a long pause before she spoke.

"You're eighteen years old?" she asked. Her hands stilled and she appeared as a statue, though a blinking one.

"Ye-es." By the look on her face, he realised that she'd had no idea. "How old did you think I was?"

"You... you look to be in your *twenties*! Or perhaps even a well-preserved thirty!"

He knew the second declaration was a lie but he thought he knew why she wanted it to be true. He knew she was older, that she was extremely sensitive about her age, that she hated every birthday and ran from it to Mwavey, where she didn't have to think about it. He hadn't noticed that they'd never spoken about how old *he* was. His desire not to upset her had kept a greater secret between them and now she looked like she was in shock.

She went pale suddenly.

"Blessed Shea, you were *sixteen* when I met you? When we... ? Blessed Shea, you were just a child!" she screeched, leaping to her feet and whirling to face him.

"I wasn't a *child*, I was a man!" he replied. He stood up and she recoiled.

"You're barely a man *now*!" she argued.

"I was man enough for you at the time," he shot back, angry at her ridiculous accusation.

She stared at him as though he'd struck her. Her cheeks flared pink and her lips parted. He didn't think that his words had been particularly offensive but the look on her face made him wish he could take them back to phrase himself better. Unfortunately, they'd already tumbled out of his mouth.

"It's sick. It's wrong. It's sick and it's wrong!" she screamed. "Get out! Get out!"

"Omerri, I'm the same person—"

"GET OUT!"

He felt like his ears cringed into his head, so forceful was her command. He walked backwards from her, his resolve melting under her stare. She looked horrified and disgusted and it was the idea of being with him that was making her look that way.

Hurt, Daeson turned his back and retreated into the space beyond the penthouse door. He walked without purpose, moving down stairs and entering another corridor. He found himself at Jade's door. It was open but he didn't have the nerve to enter. He stood just outside of the doorway, looking into the room decorated in shades of green and wondering whether he should talk about what had just happened. Every time he went to Jade to unload his concerns, he felt like he was behaving improperly. Omerri's jealous comments about his friendship with Jade were enough to make him feel guilty, even though he didn't believe he was doing anything wrong.

"Why are you just standing there, buddy?" Jade's voice pierced his reverie and he realised she'd stepped into view. Daeson stared at her and she reacted by pulling him into the room and closing the door after him. His guilt rose a notch, knowing Omerri wouldn't like them being together in a closed room. "Sit down."

She led him to the foot of the bed where they both sat down and he took her hand, drawing comfort from her touch.

"Omerri... " he couldn't bring himself to say it but Jade said it for him.

"You two had another fight?" she guessed, her free hand touched the side of his face. "You need a shave."

It was typical of Jade to soften or trivialise confrontation with other commentary. He'd asked her once if speaking about arguments made her uncomfortable. She'd explained that it was her way of showing that life goes on or that an argument didn't mean that everything was over. He thought it a crude method but he also liked her perspective—he'd learned to appreciate it.

"She doesn't want me anymore."

"Oh Daeson, that's not true." She paused, then: "She didn't *say* that, did she?" Jade asked with alarm.

"No... but I don't need it said to know it's true."

"Last time I checked, you did."

"She found out how old I am."

Jade's fingers clenched in Daeson's hold and she said nothing. That twitch said more to him than the words she didn't use. He'd never known her to be struck speechless before. It was possible she wasn't saying anything because she agreed with him; Omerri didn't want him anymore. Something in his chest tightened and he drew in a strangely uneven breath.

"Let's do some reading!" Jade said, her suggestion exploding out of her and startling him as she leapt to her feet. He looked up at her in bewilderment. "It'll pass the time. Time needs to pass, right?"

She was right. Omerri had been blindsided. It didn't matter if Daeson hadn't knowingly led her astray, he'd lied to her through omission. The deception wasn't anything he felt guilty about and he thought this was an indication of how much he'd changed. When he'd first arrived on the world of Trent, he'd believed any deception, intentional or not, was wrong. Now he understood about miscommunication. Now he understood about individual perception.

"This is the last one I can help you with," Jade said, confusing him momentarily as he returned to the present. The book that she placed upon his knees reminded him.

"Why the last?" Daeson queried.

"Because some of the words in here are a struggle for *me*," she said, tapping the cover. "This is the last reader for non-Authority education."

"You went to school until the Authorities wanted you to sign up?" Daeson asked.

"Buddy, I left school before they got the chance to ask." Jade tapped the cover again and Daeson started reading. Apart from a couple of words that he had to ask about—and had Jade looking through a dictionary to explain—the reading was easy.

When Daeson closed the final page, his skin broke out in gooseflesh and he grinned at Jade.

"I did it."

"Yes, you did."

"I can read now."

"You've been reading for a while, but yes, you've finished."

"I can read now!" Daeson repeated. The promise to himself had felt so long ago, but it was the first success that he felt he'd achieved. After all of his failures, after everything that had gone wrong, after stumbling into Omerri's care and letting her look after him, he'd finally achieved something for himself. The elation he felt made him want to leap in the air and shout with glee. Daeson did stand up but he didn't know what to do with himself other than to spread his arms out. Jade took that as a cue to stand up and hug him and Daeson laughed and wrapped his arms around her—his best friend—and spun her around while they both whooped and laughed.

The door opened, surprising them both. Ruby stared at them from the doorway with a smirk. Daeson lowered Jade to her feet.

"The door was shut," Jade complained.

"You didn't have anything booked in," Ruby said with a shrug. "Clarin wants you. He's been waiting ages and refused the other girls."

"What other girls?" Jade snapped. Daeson knew that Jade was protective about her clients and that Ruby knew this too.

"She's lying," he sighed.

"How the fuck would you know?" Ruby snarled, annoyed that her taunt hadn't gone as expected.

Jade threw Daeson a warning look. After two years, he was surprised that news of his talent hadn't travelled the Queen along with the rest of the gossip. In this place, if someone found out something in the morning, everybody knew about it by the afternoon. When it came to Daeson's truth ability, Nick and two of his closest men knew, Omerri and Jade knew, and that was it. It hadn't travelled beyond them.

"Anyway, Clarin is downstairs waiting on you. That ain't no lie," Ruby said petulantly, throwing a contemptuous look at Daeson.

"Tell him I'll be a minute," Jade said, then looked at Daeson.

"You go ahead. I'll get out of here." He offered her a smile, still feeling buoyant about his achievement. It would be nice to celebrate further with Jade, but since she was busy, he could find another way to mark the occasion.

CHAPTER TWELVE

Deviation

HE soldiers came to a unified halt a couple of metres away from Synjan. They were smiling but they were likely smart enough to recognise her tense posture. A buffer was a good idea—either that, or they didn't want to intimidate a female colleague by running at her from up the road.

"That won't do you any good," the taller one told her helpfully, gesturing at the card reader where she'd had no success.

"Yeah, I figured," Synjan mumbled, switching gears quickly. Since neither of them had used the words 'arrest', 'unauthorised' or 'shoot' in their opening sentence, she decided she wasn't in as much trouble as she'd anticipated. They'd come over to be of assistance. If there was one thing she knew how to exploit, it was a man that was willing to help her. She relaxed her fists, shrugged her shoulders and pouted prettily. "I don't know what I'm going to do!"

The two soldiers exchanged glances and the shorter, younger one took a half step closer to her. "What is it you need?"

"To get in here!" she cried in exasperation, thumbing towards the glass doors that wouldn't open. It dispelled any lingering tension as all three of them shared a small laugh.

"Most of the admin staff have been re-deployed to cope with the bombing," the older soldier told her. He looked to be in his thirties and was carrying a little more weight than his companion. She'd assessed him as the weaker link and was glad now that she hadn't had to break his knee to subdue him first.

"It's the new goal protocol," the other chimed in sympathetically. "Did you not do the mandated training last month?"

Synjan was pleased to have confirmation that there had been a bombing but she didn't appreciate having to make up lies because she didn't understand what the rest of the conversation was about. She shook her head, sliding her fingers into her pockets and subtly squeezing her breasts forward as she rocked on her feet. The younger one's gaze shifted predictably.

"I'm not stationed at Oceangate," she confessed. "I'm just here for a week as an attaché to my Lieutenant, so I really didn't need this bombing to shut half the base down—not when I barely know where I'm going as it is!" Her exasperated declaration was punctuated by a cute look that her avid audience responded positively to.

"Aw, I know what you mean!" the younger one exclaimed. "Where is it you need to go?"

"I need to get this," she produced the memory stick from her pocket, "to the Human Resources Department, which is somewhere in this building I assume?"

"Affirmative," the same soldier said before he turned to look at the other male. "How d'you think she could get in there in a lockdown?"

"Gee, I'm not sure she can," the elder hummed, leaning to the side to look at Synjan's arm. "There's the main entrance up the back but I don't think she has the rank. Although, if that doesn't work, officers should be able to get in through the loading zone—"

"Oh! Yeah, they can!"

"And she'd be able to get to HR from there, I'm pretty sure."

The younger one gave it some thought, tilting his head a couple of times and looking up at the sky as he imagined making his way through invisible corridors to Synjan's destination. She was unsettled by the amount of time it took him to 'get' there and worried that she was unlikely to complete this mission without a guide.

"She can! You can," the shorter soldier finally confirmed with an encouraging smile.

"Uh, so where am I going, exactly?" she giggled.

The two of them explained that the HR Department she wanted to reach was in the south east wing of the Administration Hub. It had its own entry—that they described in adequate detail—but, as with General Services, it was probably locked down so they told her how to get into the building via the loading area where the base's truck deliveries came and went. They both agreed she had the rank for access there but were divided about her being able to wend her way through the myriad corridors internally afterward. The younger thought yes, the elder thought no.

After thanking them profusely, Synjan declared that she'd have to take her chances and find out for sure, as her lieutenant was more likely to be upset if she didn't return soon. They all shook hands and parted, Synjan hurrying away in the direction she'd been advised to go.

She realised as she went that the Administration Hub was aptly named—it was an enormous conglomerate of connected buildings. The main spine was four storeys high but the offshoots rarely were. Most were constructed from brick or white stone, though a few of the newer-looking parts featured a lot of glass and chrome. The modern sections were better planned, with access tunnels cutting through their ground levels and landscaping around them that highlighted the beauty of the cliff-top base.

Her route took her much closer to the bomb site than she'd anticipated. Oddly, even though there was a marked increase of people swarming around the crater—operating machinery to move collapsed brickwork or simply standing around watching—she felt safer. She was more anonymous in a crowd of dark blue ants occupied with their tasks.

Across the end of one of the buildings beside the carnage was a very large and messy painting of one word—G.O.A.L. She had no idea what it meant but it brought to mind the comments of the soldier she'd got directions from. He'd said something about goal protocol training. She'd assumed it was to do with aspirations but now she wondered if he'd meant something to do with this word. Was there some sort of Authority/G.O.A.L. connection she didn't know about? It didn't seem a friendly label, scrawled hastily beside a bomb site as it was.

Thoughts of conspiracies and enemies left her mind as she spied the doors she was looking for on the next building over. They were a little less grand and identified as 'Human Resources' by a modest sign in the grass beside the path. The result was exactly the same when she approached. HR was locked down, just like the rest of the admin building. Even worse was the flighty feeling in her chest when she briefly mapped. This section was equally as deserted within as General Services had been.

It didn't bear dwelling on. She'd come onto this base, risking far more than she'd ever gambled with for Ellis and she was going to finish the job—or at least keep trying until it was proven absolutely that she couldn't succeed. She'd been denied entry to two places but there was one more option. Without a backward glance, Synjan headed for the delivery area.

She located the two extra-wide driveways she'd been told was the entrance to the loading zone without complication. They sloped down another storey below ground to accommodate their large visitors, dissolving into shadows beneath the overhanging building. What surprised her was that the two sides had signs above them saying 'In' and 'Out' and she hadn't been advised which one to choose. She wasn't sure if there'd be a difference as far as internal access went.

After a momentary pause, she ran down the 'In' half and found that the divisions were cosmetic, defined by painted lines and arrows so that vehicles going in different directions didn't collide. Otherwise, it was a cement wasteland, with vast amounts of space allowed for trucks to back up to the extremely high loading platform attached to the building. Inbound deliveries came to the left, outbound were loaded on the right. The doors beyond the loading dock were huge rolling metal sheets—all of them were down, despite there being three trucks mid-load at the platform.

As she ran forward, Synjan could see that the vehicles and their pallets of goods had simply been abandoned once the bomb tore apart the base's daily routine. Unfortunately, the staff had locked down the building by securing the rolling doors but they weren't what she'd been looking for anyway. On each end of the platform was a person-sized entry door with a card reader and code pad beside it. That was her way in.

Mentally sending a hopeful appeal for mercy to every God she knew, she hastened up the stairs leading to the door at the 'In' end. Pulling Officer Atkins' ID card out, Synjan paused and took a deep breath. The buttons for typing a code in were holding her gaze but they only increased her nerves. Her two advisors had both agreed her rank would afford her entrance to this section of the hub but neither had said anything about a passcode. Surely it was extraneous?

She swiped her card. This time, a single short note

came from the machine and she heard the locking mechanism in the door shift. Finally, it worked! Her moment of triumph was quelled when she noticed some unusual options appear on the LCD. Whether it was because it was connected to the code pad or an upgrade due to its location, the screen here was larger and a different colour. 'Officer Mikala Atkins' appeared on the top line with a date and time displayed beneath it—obviously, her access to this building was being recorded on the overall system.

After five seconds, the words rolled away and four options—corresponding to buttons beside the screen—appeared for her to choose from. 'Account', 'Print', 'GPS Tracking' and 'Permissions' were displayed.

It was the third one that piqued her interest. Even though she wanted to finish this mission very badly, she pressed the 'GPS Tracking' button. It brought up another set of options. This time, they were all time frames beginning with '1 hour' and finishing with 'Older than one week'. She selected '24 hours' and gasped as a miniature map was displayed on the screen, alongside two more options—'GPS' and 'Street Address'.

The map showed the movements of the ID card, clearly identifying the Queen of Hearts as the place it had spent the majority of its last twenty-four hours (until it had moved to Oceangate, where it was represented by a dot sitting exactly where she now stood).

The Authorities had a locator chip in every one of their cards, so they knew exactly where they—and, by extension, their owners—were at every second of every day. Would it be the same for the resident cards? She shuddered to think so.

It was only as her hand reached towards the door

handle that the greater implications of what she'd just discovered hit her. She froze. A horrible sensation of angst, fury and despair began in her gut and radiated through her in an instant, overwhelming her with an instinctive reaction she could only define as *wrongness*. Nick had thought the bomb would work in their favour but everything inside Synjan was screaming that it wasn't.

The ID card she had was being overused. She'd been hacking at this building from three different sides and now, as she finally gained entry, her card had told someone on this base that she was in. Mikala Atkins might have permission to be at Oceangate but Synjan had no idea where she worked. The fact that she'd just logged in at the loading zone could be fine but Synjan highly doubted she could get that lucky.

The base had essentially shut down so that all possible assistance could be funnelled to the wound that marred it. She was not meant to be in this building at this time and sooner or later, someone was going to notice. Maybe the bomb was giving her some leeway by keeping those people busy but she'd just found out that she was carrying the thing that would help locate her immediately. She couldn't get rid of it yet but it was only a matter of time before the item lauded as her saviour became her undoing.

Only a matter of time. Fuck Nick and his stupid, crazy plans.

Still, she wasn't going to surrender without a fight. The cell-clenching feeling of inevitability was washed away by urgency as Synjan opened the door and shoved her way through it. She found herself in a utilitarian area that mirrored the cement emptiness of the outside. Her blood was up now and she ran across it, head whipping from side to side as she tried to decide where to go. One thing in her favour was that this area seemed to be a hub within the hub and she soon came upon signs with arrows pointing to the various departments.

Her mind switched to the comfortable groove of focus she normally had during a mission and she moved through the inner maze of buildings at a constant speed. She tried to avoid it but whenever she found locked doors, she swiped her card. Every use was a weight added but it was unavoidable. In between barriers, she ran. She was certain that she'd get to the HR section and find no-one there to help her but she was equally determined to be able to say to Nick that she went and she tried. He'd accept nothing less.

When Synjan finally did reach her destination, it was exactly as she'd expected. Deserted. A bitter note of satisfaction coated her tongue as she stood beside another empty reception desk, staring through an open doorway into a cavernous room of cubicle workstations. She mapped to confirm that she was completely alone in the space and was secretly relieved when she was. Opening her eyes, she recalled Nick's instructions for how to find his contact and circled around the reception counter. She walked down a hallway that went between small glass-walled offices.

The first doorway she looked in was filled with makeshift computer banks, the room seeming too small to hold the amount of strange-looking, sophisticated machines it did. Poster instructions were plastered on the walls above every monitor and though she didn't read them properly, as she turned to continue her search for Teve Scanlan's office, one word registered in her peripheral vision. She stopped mid step, blinking a couple of extra times as her mind caught up with what she'd just seen.

Spinning on her heel, Synjan went back into the room to investigate.

CHAPTER THIRTEEN

Test Subject

DOCTOR Kelly Turner sat opposite Hawke in a matching armchair, a coffee table between them. A grand mural covered the wall beside them. It created the impression of sitting on a balcony looking out over a beach and the ocean, with swimmers and sailboats sharing the water. Dr Turner flicked her finger around the screen of her electronic tablet before she spoke.

"I hear you've had some interactions with Cornelius Academy. Some dances?"

Cornelius and Willets were connected in many ways, though girls went to one and boys to the other. Hawke had missed out on a few of the earlier social events due to his detentions and punishments for ill-behaviour. He'd thought he wasn't missing out on much but since visiting the Cornelius Academy recently, he'd discovered he quite liked being surrounded by girls.

"Two dances and one sporting event."

He couldn't help but smile to himself at the memory. On each occasion he'd managed to secure the attention of a girl and steal some alone time. It was risky for him to enter the girls' dormitories under threat of suspension or even expulsion, but so far he'd been snuck in there twice. The first time had led to some heated kissing with a girl he couldn't remember the name of, but the second was indelibly etched in his memory. Sarah. She'd taken him to her room where they'd crawled under the covers of her bed and discovered sex. She'd seemed knowledgeable enough that he thought he was the only one doing the discovering, but he didn't care. He'd felt like he'd gone to the dance as a boy and returned a man.

"You met someone special?" Dr Turner asked, her lips curled in a light smile.

"Kind of. Not really." Sarah had left him messages that he hadn't replied to, wanting to leave his experience with her untainted. If he found out more about her and ended up not liking her, she would no longer be an amazing memory but a sour one.

"You've kissed?" Dr Turner asked.

"Yeah."

"Anything more?" she prompted.

Hawke shrugged, uncomfortable with talking about his sexual experiences. Dr Kelly Turner stared at him, her gaze intense. Hawke did his best not to shift or wilt beneath it.

"Hawke Donovan, have you lost your virginity?" she asked, setting the tablet down on her lap. Her tone was warm and playful. She looked like she might be impressed if he indicated he had. His grin was obviously enough to confirm because she chuckled. He thought her expression had become more respectful. "How long ago did this happen?"

"Three weeks ago."

"Did you enjoy it?"

"Yeah," he said, as though her question was ridiculous. Of course he enjoyed it. Who wouldn't?

"When's the next event at Cornelius?"

"Next month there's another dance."

"Your social calendar is filling up."

"I'm closer to turning fourteen now, I guess. The Academies have graduations every month for those who sign up. Soon it'll be in my honour, along with whoever else was born in July."

"Are the dances formal?"

"They're more like parties. Dressed up but not

stiff."

"Will you be meeting up with your girlfriend then?"

"No. I don't know. She's not my girlfriend." Hawke frowned.

"You didn't want her to be your girlfriend?" Dr Turner guessed.

"I... don't know." Stupidly, he hadn't considered the benefits of being involved with someone who would let him have sex. "I don't think she wants to be. Not now."

Dr Turner didn't say anything but she didn't look at him disapprovingly like he'd thought she might. He'd anticipated a lecture about respect.

"So what are you going to do at the next dance? Hook up with someone else?"

The question threw him off balance. It was weird to talk about this stuff to a woman, even if she *was* a doctor.

"Um, yeah. I guess."

"You're uncomfortable talking about it?"

Admitting it would make him feel like a child. At the same time he didn't want to discuss it. He wanted to talk to Tavi about it, but he wasn't due back for a holiday to Ulsa Maya for ages yet.

"It's personal."

"Okay. Now that you're sexually active, we're going to have to run a few different kinds of tests, alright?"

"Sure," Hawke agreed, knowing he didn't have much of a say regardless. It was easier just to go along with everything.

She left and he stayed up playing video games until the television in his room went black and the lights dimmed. Grunting his frustration, he dressed in pyjamas behind the privacy screen and climbed into bed. It wasn't long after that before the lights switched off, except for the strip of light beneath the door of his connecting bathroom.

When he awoke, he used the bathroom, dressed and played some more video games. Breakfast was delivered at a convenient time in the game and he wondered if they were watching him and planning every move accordingly. He switched the console off and ate dutifully before setting the tray aside. He wished he knew what time it was but there were no clocks anywhere.

He'd just started exploring the bookcase for interesting titles when a man dressed in an all pink uniform (indicating he was more senior than the yellow-uniformed nurses) entered Hawke's assigned room. He was carrying a large blue plastic wallet.

Hawke was handed a small plastic cup with a lid and given a number of instructions as to the technique of filling it. Blushing a furious red, he interrupted the nurse's spiel not long after it began.

"Stop. Wait. Why do you want my sperm?"

"For the usual tests." The answer gave Hawke nothing.

"I want to talk to Major Cayden."

"Your sponsor doesn't need to sign off on the—"

"I don't care! I want to talk to Cayden!" Hawke turned and pelted the cup against the far wall. It hit the mural in the middle of the ocean and fell to the ground with a clatter, bouncing and then rolling a short way away. It made small arcs on the floor as it settled. Hawke spun back to the pink-uniformed man, who was open-mouthed.

"That kind of behaviour—" he began.

"Go get him!"

The man turned and left the room, taking his blue plastic wallet with him.

Hawke watched him go, his heart hammering in his chest. It was the first time in a long time that he'd been scared of the tests. They didn't hurt anymore and technically this one wouldn't hurt either, but the implication of the DOME getting his sperm...

Hawke waited for Cayden while sitting on his bed, back against the headboard and hugging his knees. It seemed to take an eternity for his sponsor to come.

When Cayden entered the room, he had a puzzled expression on his face. Hawke guessed he hadn't been told about why he'd been summoned. Hawke got up off the bed as Cayden approached, intending to explain himself stoically and plainly. Instead his words came out in a jumbled rush.

"Wait, Hawke, I don't understand, slow down," Cayden said gently, leading Hawke back to the bed where they sat side by side.

Hawke took some breaths and calmed himself, knowing he wouldn't have Cayden on his side unless he presented all of his facts.

"They want my sperm," he began. Cayden looked surprised and concerned at this news, which inspired Hawke to explain further. "I don't want to give them that. I don't want them to make test tube babies to keep here like pets. I don't... I don't want them to make me a father."

"I... of course not," Cayden said, frowning deeply. "I usually get told about your schedule here, there was nothing about taking a sperm sample."

Hawke knew Cayden got told but he didn't know how much control his sponsor had over the tests themselves. He wasn't assigned to the DOME but Hawke being in his charge had to give him some leeway.

"I think it's only because they found out I've..." Hawke didn't know how to finish his sentence and he blushed.

"Aha, I see," Cayden said, looking away. "You do realise that you have to be fourteen before it's legal, don't you?" he said to the room. Then he looked back at Hawke who was wondering if that question needed a response. "I hope she was fourteen. If she was a… uh," Cayden looked away and Hawke wanted to put a stop to wherever his sponsor was going with that.

"She was one of the graduates, so yeah." Hawke was surprised Cayden was being a prude about it.

"Well, I agree that you can't have your sperm taken, especially not against your will. You're underage, regardless of whether you're sexually active or not, so I'm sure I'll be able to stop them."

Cayden's confidence was reassuring and Hawke felt his anxiety melting away. Absurdly, he felt tears close to the surface and he gulped deep breaths to keep them away. The technique worked and also earned him a comforting arm around the shoulders from Cayden as well.

"I'll handle it," Cayden promised softly.

After he left, lunch was delivered along with a ten page questionnaire that Hawke was supposed to fill out. He worked his way through it even though it was tedious and he thought the questions were stupid. He wanted to prove he could co-operate and it could only work in his favour.

Still, the thought of the DOME running this test when he was fourteen years old—because then he'd no longer be a minor—was daunting. If he signed up, who knew how many times he'd be ordered to wank into a cup or donate his blood or perform their many tests? He was more useful to them as a laboratory specimen but that had to change.

Nobody came to collect his sperm. The next interaction he had was receiving dinner. He ate and drank everything, thinking it strange that they'd supplied him with a much better meal than usual. He had a thick steak, cheesy chips and coleslaw. Instead of water to drink, he had an apple juice. He took it as an apology and ate it all. He'd intended to play video games after dinner but he was too tired to bother. The stress of the day had drained his energy and he headed for bed.

He didn't quite make it. The room seemed to be darkening and his limbs felt heavy. He caught the edge of the bed but couldn't stop himself landing hard on the floor. Before everything went dark, he was acutely aware that being drugged could only mean something bad was going to happen.

Hawke woke up the next morning in bed, dressed in pyjamas he didn't voluntarily change into. He recalled falling to the floor and his cheek still ached from where he'd landed on his face. After pressing it gingerly, he reached down and felt his testicles. They weren't hurting but—

They were tender. It was a strange sensation, like he'd been kicked there yesterday. It wasn't hard to guess what had really happened; they'd drugged him and he'd had his sperm surgically removed. He'd thought there would be more pain but their method was obviously not very intrusive. Feeling helpless and violated, Hawke curled into a ball on his side and sobbed.

The Authorities always got what they wanted and he hated them for it. They were the machine that munched the bones of whatever small creatures got in the way. They were deciding the quality of his life and were also taking from his body as though it belonged to them instead of to him. He might be their ward and he might be a Wanderer, but he was still a person. They were treating him like he was their property.

The door to his room (prison cell) opened and he turned, intending on shouting at whoever it was to get out. He said nothing when he saw Cayden hurrying over to him, determination and anger blazing on his face. He moved to the wardrobe where Hawke's few things were kept and started throwing Hawke's clothes into the overnight bag.

"We're going home," Cayden said, not looking Hawke's way. "They had no right. They had no right." He looked at Hawke next, his expression uncertain. Hawke wanted to absolve him of the blame—Cayden obviously had less influence than he'd believed—but he couldn't bring himself to speak. Cayden returned to packing.

Hawke and his incensed sponsor left the DOME soon after. The only delay had been Hawke changing out of his pyjamas. Cayden had packed all of his clothes before realising that Hawke hadn't dressed yet. Whatever had been packed last—jeans and a t-shirt— ended up being what Hawke wore.

They were heading out of the building together when Hawke found his voice.

"Who told you?"

"Turner. She admitted what they'd done, wanted me to do damage control."

"Damage control?" Hawke asked warily.

"Fuck her."

Hawke was shocked. He'd never heard Cayden swear before. He knew that his sponsor was really angry but this was proof. The pair of them headed for the carpark, a detour Hawke hadn't expected. He'd anticipated that they would go straight to the portal.

"Why aren't we going back to Varrell?"

"It's too soon. We have to wait a few days before we're able."

Hawke didn't ask more questions, not knowing what else to ask, what else to say. He felt better already because he had Cayden on his side, angry on his behalf, looking out for him and getting him out of the DOME after they'd gone too far. He hadn't realised Cayden could even do that. Or could he?

"Are you going to get in trouble?" Hawke asked as they arrived at an ordinary-looking black sedan. Cayden pressed a button on the car keys and the indicators lit up while the car bleeped.

"Nothing I can't handle. Get in."

Hawke usually sat in the back passenger seat but this time he went for the front. Cayden took a moment to toss Hawke's bag into the back and then they were leaving the carpark.

"What are we going to do for a couple of days?" Hawke asked after they approached the front gates of the base. His muscles tensed, thinking they would be stopped. Cayden showed his ID and identified Hawke, using his full name. One of the soldiers at the front gate radioed in and then gestured for them to continue on.

"I thought I'd take you to see Union City. You haven't had the chance to be a tourist and Union City is one of the most beautiful on the world of Austra."

The base—where the DOME was—ended up being in the middle of a desert. It was a large base, with green grass and tall trees and nothing to give away the fact it was intensely isolated. It was sprawling enough without the added knowledge of the DOME underground.

"How far away is it?"

"Not that far. A little over an hour's drive, maybe."

It took almost an hour before the desert transitioned to plains. Hawke could see the hazy blue outline of mountains in the distance. The countryside was incredibly flat and only now and then would they pass a homestead.

"Why do people live out here, on their own?" Hawke asked, wondering why someone would choose to cut themselves off.

"Maybe they enjoy their own company over others'," Cayden said, then looked at Hawke. "I've always thought you might like to live that way."

"Me? No. Why would you think that?"

"You're not terribly social, are you?" Cayden goaded with a smile. He returned to watching the road while Hawke considered his words.

"I guess I like my own company," he admitted, "but I'd probably still want a house somewhere that's got lots of people around, like in a city."

"Really?" Cayden sounded astonished.

There was silence for a while as Hawke watched the scenery change from plains to a great deal of greenery and a winding mountain road. The degree of ascension was quite steep and it wasn't long before Hawke could look out the window at a severe drop. Sheep peppered the hills, their constant trek up and down the mountains etching lines that looked painted on. Union City was revealed quite suddenly as Cayden rounded a lengthy curve. One moment it was hills and grass and sheep, the next there was an urban sprawl of red suburban rooftops in concentrated blocks and tallish buildings beyond them that constituted the city's centre. From their vantage point at the top of the mountain road, Hawke thought he could see a distant shimmer that was possibly an ocean.

"Is Union City on the water?" Hawke asked excitedly. The idea of water sports excited him; skiing, swimming, snorkelling, sailing... there were a great many activities that he thought would help him mentally recover.

"That's Union Lake, what the city's named after. Not the biggest lake in the world but certainly the prettiest," Cayden said with a smile. "It's a testament to Authority city planning. Do you still like museums?"

"Yeah," Hawke said. He wondered why Cayden

would ask him in a way that implied he might lose interest.

"Then I'll take you to the Museum of Light tonight. It doesn't open until eighteen hundred—six at night."

"I know what eighteen hundred means," Hawke reminded him.

"Of course," Cayden replied.

Hawke wondered if Cayden corrected himself to Drue and Tavi, neither of which attended an Authority Academy. Both of them went to school on Ulsa Maya, coming home at the end of their lessons every day.

"Why didn't I go to school on Ulsa Maya?" he asked.

Cayden was quiet for a long moment, his expression blank as he steered the car around a number of turns.

"Because I didn't adopt you," he said finally. "You're a ward of the Authorities and I'm only your sponsor, a point of contact for you to make requests of. You were supposed to go to the Academy here, in Union City, but I wanted you on the same world as where I'm based instead."

It wasn't lost on Hawke that going to an Academy in Union City would mean potentially many more visits to the DOME. Cayden had been looking out for him even before he'd known Hawke, showing mercy for a child who couldn't help his blood and had been unlucky enough to shift worlds as a hostage.

"Thank you," Hawke said. The words didn't feel enough to express his gratitude but the smile he received from Cayden in response made him feel better.

CHAPTER FOURTEEN

The Hunter And The Barfly

KILLING wasn't the only thing that brought a hunt to an end; asshole Wanderers going to ground—because they knew their fucking lives were in immediate danger—had the same effect. Its technical term was 'Postponed Hunt' and the Hunter was forced to declare his trip to Baxter as such by twenty hundred that night.

After having his time wasted being interrogated by the Austra team (who were obsessive when it came to questioning perfectly clear video footage), the Hunter spent a fruitless afternoon searching for the Ghost and his partners. It was logical to conclude that the Wanderer Ghost had passed on the information he'd learned while incarcerated. If the trio had been planning to Wander soon, they would certainly have called it off. Movement with so much scrutiny upon them would be suicide. They'd no doubt decided to stay put.

Given the hour, the Hunter chose to stay in Yulanigh Bay. With customary efficiency, he organised a flight west the next day that would see him back in Narelle Lawson's neighbourhood mid-afternoon. He selected the highest-priced hotel, securing a room not quite at the top (no point giving the pinheads in accounts too much to squawk about, a modest room with a spectacular view was sufficient) and ordered a change of clothes while he showered. The jeans, underwear and shirt fit well and he headed down in the hotel's glass elevator to look for some entertainment.

With years of experience at this job, the Hunter had

picked up tricks completely unrelated to work that kept him a more well-rounded individual. He'd learned that he could find a woman to take to bed in any of the twenty-four hours he wanted, but where he looked dictated what sort of quality he would find. He never paid for it but otherwise there were no rules.

After business hours, the best options were found at the bars and eateries in the inner city. The fashionably-suited crowd were sharks by day but once they finally stepped away from their offices, they became much softer predators that craved no-strings-attached hookups. Women who'd prioritised their careers were still women, desiring the finer things in life (to feel human and vulnerable beneath his caress) without the guilt of wondering whether the sex should lead to a relationship. They shared a similar mindset with the Hunter, as did those that inhabited his second-choice hunting ground; medical staff.

If he couldn't get to a business-district watering hole before ten o'clock, he'd head for the nearest hospital. In his experience, there was generally a twenty-four hour bar that catered to the shift workers that left the local medical facility at odd hours.

Where the business crowd wanted guilt-free sex, the doctors and nurses he approached were generally looking for a life affirming carnal marathon. Having left the scene of whatever bloody, pernicious incident they'd just had to fend death away from, those that hung out at medical bars were usually looking for the first best reason to feel alive and know that the horror they'd endured was not everything in the world. It was generally a very athletic experience.

Beyond those general precincts, the game was anybody's and the Hunter had to be in a particularly needy mood to play. Tonight, he was early enough that he wouldn't have to worry.

He entered the bar on the ground floor of his hotel and was quite pleased with the offerings. Navy, grey and black suits were everywhere, milling about in small groups or pairs, some going solo. One woman sitting at the bar caught his eye when she heard the door open and turned to see who it was. She was obviously waiting for someone particular but when their gazes met, a twinge of approval made him feel her presence down to his toes. He respected a woman who could have that sort of affect on him. He looked away only to be sure there was no-one that appealed more and then headed towards her.

"Long day?" he asked as he slid onto the stool beside her.

"I'm waiting for someone," she told him, her voluptuous mouth lifting with the barest hint of a smile. Her eyes were heavy-lidded and her skin was the colour of silken cocoa. He could imagine exactly how she would feel wrapped around him.

"Can they do for you what I can?" he murmured, returning her smouldering look with one of his own. There was no point being coy about matters; his expression assured her that he certainly could make good on his silent promise.

She smirked, her tongue delicately wetting her lips as she tilted her head and appraised him. "Probably not, but that doesn't change the fact I'm waiting for them."

"Are they running late?"

"A little."

He tsked. "Disrespectful."

"I suppose you would never treat a woman like that?"

He laughed, enjoying the way she was mocking his pickup game. "I wouldn't say never. But what I would say is that I'm here... and they're not." His final few words were delivered close to her ear, his tone enquiring.

She turned her head towards his and there was a suspended moment where she could encourage him, push him away or lean over and kiss him but none of those things happened. The door to the bar swished open again and she looked towards it instead. "They're here," she grinned as the two women who'd just entered spotted her and started squealing their greetings from across the room.

The Hunter retreated. He hadn't eaten and the bar was attached to the hotel restaurant, so he found a table with a good view of everything. The woman who'd sparked his interest went with her friends to a more comfortable seat but remained in his line of view. She looked over at him occasionally and her friends giggled about him more than once but it didn't progress any farther than that for over an hour.

During that time, he finished his meal and made his way back into the bar area. He set up where he could see the trio of women as well as one of the televisions showing a sporting game of some sort. He wasn't interested in it but he pretended to be while he nursed his drink. Two other women approached him at different times and though he chatted with them, he wasn't interested in either one so he politely sent them away after a brief conversation.

When he'd been in the bar almost two hours, the last of his initial target's friends left and she walked over to his table, arranging herself with innate elegance on the seat beside him.

"Still here," she observed with a sultry smile.

"This is my hotel and I didn't want to go to bed alone."

"You had offers."

"I told them I was waiting for someone." His look

was direct and meaningful. She exhaled lightly, her lips parting as she allowed his words to wash over her.

"I'm not too late?" she asked huskily.

"Right on time," he grinned before he finished his drink and took her hand.

As they left the bar and headed for his room, he couldn't help but think about the fancy glass elevator they were about to ride up in and all the things he could do to her before they reached their destination.

CHAPTER FIFTEEN

Cry Wolf

THE small office that Synjan walked into had tables of computers against every wall and two long trestles pushed together in the middle. There were chairs huddled in the open spaces—as if their occupants had rolled back and got up in a hurry—and different types of boxy machinery interspersed amongst the computers. Synjan doubted the room always looked this way; the posters and tangled vines of power cords snaking along the carpet under the desks gave it a temporary air.

Walking up to the nearest poster confirmed her suspicions. It was the word 'resident' that had caught her eye as she was leaving. The walls were covered with explicit instructions on creating Gredann's Resident ID Cards. This room had obviously been set up to cope with the extra workload that cataloguing the city's citizens had placed upon the Authorities. Soldiers from other departments were probably rotating through the task so some genius had decided to stick the instructions detailing what to do on the walls, to minimise talk time and make the whole system more efficient.

Synjan whispered a sigh of thanks. She wouldn't fail after all. She read the instructions thoroughly and then sat down at a computer beside one of the other bits of machinery—it was a card printer. Boxes of blank cards, envelopes and ring binders of paperwork were stacked up beside it, making this a complete solution to her dilemma. As long as it was fast.

The computer was unlike the clunking artefact she

was accustomed to using at the Bunker and it was also more advanced than Ellis' personal system. Still, she could see where to insert the memory stick and one touch of the mouse revealed that it was on, she just needed to log in. After a brief inspection she found there was an ID card system connected to the computer so she tried that. Mikala Atkins was soon connected and she was away (trying not to think too hard about the fact that she'd made her location known yet again).

Following the wall instructions, she started up the card printing program. Nick had kept the information on it to a minimum, there were only two files—a picture and the written details to go with it. She hoped he'd made it look like the other photographs the Authorities were taking, otherwise she doubted the card she created would be worth anything. She clicked the photo file open as she glanced up at the example on the poster, ready to compare it, but shock took over when she looked back at the face on the screen.

It was Daeson. Nick *had* made sure to match the background to the Authority photograph on the wall but that was no longer her concern as she looked into the handsome face of the man she'd met just that morning. He'd been kept away from her for two years, had no Gredann birth certificate and was essential enough to the organisation that Nick had gone to extreme lengths to get this to happen, yet she knew nothing about him. Where was Daeson from, if not Gredann? Why was he the best kept secret this side of the Ryn Sayriss Alps? Was his life worth more than hers?

Anger bubbled inside her as she opened up the data file and read through his details; Daeson Farmer, blue eyes, brunette, one hundred and eighty-five centimetres tall, A positive blood type, no distinguishing marks, fair complexion. His primary residence was the address she knew to be Omerri's home—the princess, not the Queen—which she found astounding.

She copied it all into the card creator dutifully but every key stroke fuelled the resentment within her. Why was this Daeson person so fucking important? What was he to Nick? Was it all because Omerri was sleeping with him? Why the fuck didn't she know more about him?

While she fumed, she worked and it took her less than five minutes to create the card and seal it into an envelope that she addressed to the Queen. She slid it in amongst a completed stack near the door because she couldn't afford to carry it out with her. When she returned to the computer to log off, indecision stayed her hand. She stared at the information still on the screen, considering deleting all data from the memory stick permanently. She supposed Nick had another copy and it shouldn't prove necessary anyway, not with the card already created.

The feeling of negativity she'd had lingering over her throughout this misadventure finally decided her. She wiped the information, thinking about what might happen if she was caught with it. For added security, she snapped the device in half before she put it in her pocket and logged off. Feeling more in control, she stood up and mapped to be sure she was still alone.

Any sensation of positivity immediately seeped out of her and fear bloomed in its place. There were two soldiers heading towards her. She was on the third floor, they were on the second but there was, essentially, only a short hallway and a set of stairs between them. She'd mapped just in time to realise she was about to be hemmed in.

With her heart hammering, she ran out of the office

and sprinted in the opposite direction to where they would emerge. She had no idea where she was going but she couldn't afford to hesitate. For all she knew, they were coming after her because they'd noticed her unauthorised presence in the building. She wanted desperately to dump the ID card in case they had some way of tracking her as she ran, but she couldn't afford to do that until she was outside.

It had taken her an hour to get in; now all she wanted was out.

There was a stairwell in the back of the Human Resources Department and she was pleased that she could open the door without needing identification. Even better, the stairs went all the way to the ground floor. Her feet were a blur as she raced downwards, wanting to jump multiple risers at a time but not game to make too much noise.

At the bottom, Synjan erupted through the doorway and into a large, wide corridor that had many offshoots and office areas attached to it. After a quick glance around, she decided on a direction and went, looking to and fro as she ran. A side hallway with a glass door at the end caught her attention and she skidded to a halt for a better look; the door had shrubbery visible through it. It led directly to the outside!

When she got there, however, she found that it had no handle. Swallowing down the fluttery beat of panic constricting the top of her throat, she withdrew Officer Atkins' ID card and swiped it in the slot beside. A grating beep came but nothing clicked in the door. The promise of freedom made her desperate enough to swipe her card again. She was mortified when a much louder clanging filled the hallway with deafening enthusiasm. It sounded like a fire alarm and it seemed to be coming from everywhere at once.

If the soldiers hadn't been chasing her, they would be now. She mapped as they started running and knew she'd have to keep watching them because they were coming from the larger central stairs ahead of her. In the direction she'd been intending to go.

Determinedly, she set off again, rounding corners on a leaning curve in order to maintain her speed. This was something she was very good at; she ran regularly and she had a lot of stamina to draw on. She was certain she'd need it.

What she wasn't used to was the level of panic gripping her. Even in fights where the odds were stacked against her, she managed to maintain her focus. But here and now, this was very different. If she was caught, she was unlikely to die. She'd be imprisoned and tested, possibly tortured and forced to reveal Wanderer knowledge. The times she'd faced death seemed very simple in comparison to the potential shackling of her soul.

It was almost all she could think about. The terror was a constant weight, her despair increasing every time she couldn't open a door or find a way to the outside but she kept going. There was no other choice.

Although she vaguely knew the building's layout, in reality it was an incoherent maze. Navigating an endless arrangement of identical corridors while staying ahead of her pursuers felt an insurmountable task. She could map their whereabouts—twice that ability saved her as she hid and let them continue on so she could double back—but it was as if they had the same talent as her. With unerring accuracy they always managed to get back on her trail and she was convinced it was something to do with the ID card. She needed to dump it.

The longer the game of dodge and chase went on, the more she started seeing other people trickling back into the administration building. It gave her hope. Eventually, inevitably, she ran around a corner and found a woman walking towards her. She smiled as she trotted up and said she was turned around and confused about where she was. She asked for directions to the closest exit and although the soldier seemed wary, she told Synjan where to go.

With heartfelt thanks, Synjan set off at a run once more. When she rounded the final corner and found herself in the reception area, she was cautiously excited. The sliding doors were operational again and there was a crowd of people milling around. The air buzzed with words like 'cleanup', 'bomb, and 'goal'. Seeing an opportunity, she bumped into a man wearing a non-regulation jacket and slipped her card into an accessible pocket.

Getting rid of the ID was like being unshackled. Stepping outside was even better.

She didn't slow down to get her bearings but she also knew she had to look less like a fugitive fleeing the scene of a crime and more like an underling hurrying through the base to appease her superior. This time, she had a better idea of where she was going and wasn't afraid to cut between buildings or hasten between the swarms of people returning to their work areas. She noticed she got a few second looks but no one stopped her.

Her pursuers were delayed by her sleight-of-hand but she had a decision to make. Synjan was confident she could maintain her lead long enough to get to the front of the base but if she veered in an unexpected direction, she might get even more time or be off the grounds sooner. Should she head for Access Point Alpha or try another exit?

Doubt plagued her. She'd dumped the card but that wouldn't hold them off for long. Plus, she didn't trust that there weren't extra ways the Authorities could find people if they wanted to; cameras that were hidden, spying on her, watched by people behind computers able to communicate with the men looking for her. Synjan had seen the ear pieces Freddie used on his missions and knew about the technology the Authorities had. Everything they needed was at their disposal. She couldn't trust that using her talent would be enough to come out on top. Not with today's circumstances. Not the way she was feeling. Not today.

It was decided; the most direct route was best. She was closest to Alpha.

Synjan heard the cacophony before she reached the internal courtyard. It still didn't prepare her for the throng of people gathered there. She began wending her way through clusters of uniforms; some cradled clipboards, a few observers held annoying clicking devices but most were like those in the foyer—standing around talking about the bombing.

She couldn't see beyond the wall of dark blue so she had to map her way to the gate. It was the only place where a sea of patterns was moving steadily away from the base. A guard stood motionless on either side of that multihued tide, watching stoically. Everything in Synjan felt full to the brim, like if she didn't start running soon, she'd implode. No way would those guards let her through if she tried to race past them. Walking was a necessary torture.

A short distance ahead, she spied a sizeable group heading for the exit. They were perfect for her to join except their shirts were light blue. She didn't know what that meant but knew she'd have to risk leaving with them. Her stature could be used to her advantage; she could get in the middle and be partially shielded.

Inserting herself amongst them was easier than expected. She garnered a few sideways looks that turned into smiles. A brief exchange with another woman about the crazy day they'd had allowed her to manoeuvre herself into the centre. Their mood was more positive than hers and it was infectious.

The sensation faded as she passed the guards and heard a message broadcast on their radios.

"Alert. Be on the lookout for a female using the ID of Officer Mikala Atkins. Believed to be blonde, wearing officer's uni." Both guards acknowledged the call behind her but neither of them cried out.

Synjan kept walking. She looked for Nick's vehicle in between the people surrounding her. She felt insulated by the group and could envision her partner's reaction when she slid in beside him, able to tell him about her successful mission. It was tantalising.

She'd closed over half the distance of the square when one of the guards first called out.

"Hey!" he yelled. Some of the people walking with her turned but most ignored the call.

"Halt!"

It was bellowed across the urban courtyard and it got the desired reaction. Her comrades—conditioned to follow orders—stopped this time but Synjan didn't. She walked faster, able to see her freedom seemingly a few steps ahead. Nick frowned through the windshield.

"Halt or draw fire!"

Synjan bolted, sprinting towards Nick. The adrenaline became a wash of euphoria that she revelled in. Nobody was running after her and there were too many people in the area to risk shooting through, despite their warning.

Nick gunned the engine to life and flung the passenger door open.

For all her doubts, her bad feelings, her fear, she'd done it.

CHAPTER SIXTEEN

Fourteen

THE window to Mr Blatch's office was a single hung style and had been cracked open. Hawke figured it was kept that way to let airflow through without letting in a breeze that might shift the papers inside. Amid the shrubbery planted along the building's exterior, Hawke slid his fingers in the window's opening and forced it upward until there was a gap big enough for him to squeeze through. He tossed a small burlap sack in, hearing it *thunk* onto the floor, before he half jumped, half crawled in after it. There was a horrible moment when he thought he was stuck, visions of being discovered with his hips and legs dangling outside and evidence of his intended mischief in the sack below him... and then he felt gravity helping him along, tipping him over and landing him roughly on the floor despite his braced arms.

His face was near the sack and the smell of the thing inside it repulsed him enough to have him scrabbling to get away. The smell would get worse once he was done, he knew. He would have to work fast. Not only was this a bad place to be caught, he also had Kegsy waiting for him and he was already twenty minutes late.

Hawke grabbed the burlap sack by the neck and took it with him to Blatch's desk. Part of him wanted to clean the papers off to save the work his favourite teacher had already done but the rest of him knew that he had to be ruthless. His antics were supposed to be committed by a student that hated the maths teacher and sparing Mr Blatch in any way could be a clue that this was a setup.

Hawke dumped the sack onto the desk and untied the leather thong that held it closed. The smell of the dead ferret within assaulted him; the musky, coppery scent of the animal seemed to cling to his skin and attach to the follicles inside his nose so that he could smell nothing else. Grimly, he pulled the body out and laid it upon the desk, bloodying papers. Hawke spied the letter opener atop a stack of sliced envelopes and picked it up, wielding it like a knife. He intended on disembowelling the corpse, leaving behind a hot, sticky mess of blood and guts. Just thinking about it was enough to turn his stomach, though; he couldn't go through with it. If he did, he was likely to vomit all over it. Hawke wiped the letter opener's handle using the sleeve of his sweater and put it back.

Without the horror of a defiled animal, he would have to go the distance somewhere else. Hawke moved to the small, neatly organised bookshelf and pulled out handfuls of books, letting them fall in disarray. Above the shelves hung a painting of a decorated Authority— some General or other who'd probably helped found Willets. Hawke grabbed the letter opener again, pulling his sleeve over his hand as a makeshift glove and slashed at the painting. The oil was cut but the canvas it was painted on showed no signs of damage. Hawke contented himself with making stripes through the paint, annoyed that the canvas was too robust to rip.

Mr Blatch's leather chair wasn't made out of real leather but from some peculiar plastic leather-look stuff. It ripped satisfyingly when Hawke plunged the letter opener down the back of it, sawing his way through to the bottom. He punctured holes into the seat with malicious glee, somehow taking joy in all the destruction he was causing. He felt wild. He felt free.

It was hard to know how long Hawke would've

kept going if he hadn't been interrupted. It could've been the worst possible thing to happen but when he turned guiltily to see who it was, he cackled. Polsen stood in the doorway, frozen in shock. Hawke threw the letter opener at him but his aim was off and it landed a short distance from Polsen's feet. Amazingly, Polsen stepped inside the room to retrieve it, letting the door slowly shut behind him. It didn't quite close all the way but it was all that Hawke needed to make his escape. He ran for the window, hearing Polsen's, "What the fuck?" behind him.

Hawke aimed and dove headfirst with his arms straight out in front of him. His trouser legs scraped painfully on the window frame on the exit and he hissed in breath. Hopefully he hadn't left any evidence of himself behind. His landing was a little hard but not terrible, for Kegsy had trained him in the art of rolling.

He peeked through the garden's shrubbery before he sprang out onto the path, sprinting around the back of the buildings towards the gymnasium. He imagined Polsen might be looking out the window at his fleeing form but he didn't risk a look back. The backs of his legs were burning and he was ignoring the pain as he ran.

Hawke burst into the small gymnasium side-room where he trained with Kegsy. No longer relegated to the weights training area, they had more floor space to interact in. As Naomi had predicted, Hawke got into less fights since he'd started his training. Polsen was still the ignorant brute he always was but Hawke now managed to handle him better. Hawke and Naomi had discussed how and why, with Naomi reasoning that he was more at peace with himself and wasn't exacerbating an already hostile issue. Hawke himself put forward the theory that word had got out about his highly tuned fighting skills and less boys were coming at him.

Kegsy had been doing some kind of exercise on the square mat that was their sparring area but he got up when Hawke ran in. The Unit Commander watched quizzically as Hawke shucked his sweater and tracksuit pants, revealing the singlet and shorts he wore for training.

"I've been here the whole time," Hawke said, hoping Kegsy would go along with his request.

"What?" the large man asked, clearly unimpressed.

"I've been here the whole time," Hawke repeated, this time meeting Kegsy's stare. Hawke's heart pounded more from the adrenaline of what he'd just done rather than the mad sprint to the gym.

"If you say so."

It was impossible to miss the disappointment in Kegsy's tone as he agreed to Hawke's declaration. His clothes were tossed in one crumpled heap in the corner of the room and Hawke performed some unnecessary warm up exercises before adopting his usual sparring position. Kegsy took one lingering moment to stare at Hawke before they began their lesson.

Less than ten minutes later, Principal Fielder-Wiley knocked on the door and entered. Polsen was at his side, staring at Hawke triumphantly.

"Commander Frederickson, sorry for the interruption. I was just wondering how long Donovan has been here with you?"

Hawke's breath stuck in his throat and his chest felt constricted. He hoped that nobody could see it on his face but he could feel panic surging upward, the pressure causing the back of his head to start thumping. He'd been unaware that his emotions could have such a strong physical impact. He stared at the Unit Commander, willing him to go along with his agreement or else Hawke would be expelled.

Potentially even fined or sent to juvenile detention for his foray into vandalism. He'd committed a crime, he realised belatedly. A real fucking crime and if Kegsy wanted to be rid of him—this Wanderer kid who'd given him a hard time at the start before treating the Authority soldier with the respect he'd deserved—it would be as easy as one short statement.

Kegan Frederickson hummed thoughtfully and checked his watch. The back of Hawke's legs throbbed like an expression of guilt. He kept his gaze fixed on the Commander, not trusting himself to look at Fielder-Wiley or at Polsen beside him. Mentally, he spoke a mantra not to give himself away. *Just stay calm, nothing's wrong. Just stay calm, nothing's wrong.*

"Oh, I guess about forty five minutes, when our session started."

Hawke felt relief like standing under the spray of a cold shower on a really hot day. At the same time, Polsen exploded with an accusation.

"He's lying!"

Fielder-Wiley glared as he grabbed Polsen by the back of his collar. The Principal's cheeks were red with embarrassment or fury or both.

"How dare you, you piece—" he seethed, dragging Polsen away, not finishing his sentence for whatever reason. Hawke didn't care but he wanted to laugh and yell and jump around and pump the air. Once the gym door was fully closed, he couldn't help but thrust his arms up in the air like an athlete winning a gold medal after years of training.

When he opened his eyes, he found Kegan's intense gaze on him. Hawke felt self-conscious and foolish for his exhibition of victory but he'd had so much energy, he'd had to do *something*.

Hawke anticipated questions. He expected Kegsy would want to know exactly what he was covering up for. To his surprise, they didn't come. Instead, the Unit Commander spoke words that Hawke would recall and consider for a long time.

"I hope it was worth it."

Somehow, Polsen didn't get expelled. His suspension was for two months. There were rumours that Polsen's parents were both top level career Authority officers. Other rumours had the Polsen family as old money who donated a great deal to the Academy. More still painted the Polsens as sue-mongers who would take Willets to court for unjust expulsion if the school went that route.

Hawke didn't care why, none of it was justifiable. The asshole should've been expelled, especially since he wasn't going to follow an Authority career path. He'd decided not to sign up, which had come as a surprise to many except to Hawke, who'd thought it was likely Polsen thought being an Authority would be too much like hard work.

Regardless, Polsen wasn't going to be a problem for a while... or ever again, if Hawke signed up for the Authorities in the meantime. With his fourteenth birthday looming, Hawke felt the need to explore his options; sign up with the Authorities, become a civilian or work for Ellis.

The Authorities promised a logical lifestyle with education and skill sets beyond anything he was likely to achieve for himself. He would be able to see and work in different worlds, find himself a niche that would make him comfortable and secure, have some kind of a normal life. At the same time, he might have to visit the DOME regularly, potentially for his whole life.

He would be obligated to help, perhaps even ordered to give the scientists there whatever they wanted, whenever they wanted. He would be little more than their property.

Remaining as a civilian meant he would be his own man and find his own way in life. Of course Cayden would continue to be his sponsor but what about after his sixteenth birthday, when he was no longer required to be at school? He couldn't rely on Cayden to take him to different worlds or help him out in the private sector. Hawke was likely to get himself a job and then have to work from the bottom up. It sounded tedious, with no guarantees of career advancement. At least with the Authorities there was a career of every type on every world.

Working for Ellis? It would be a betrayal to Cayden—but Hawke had to do what was best for himself. It would be like being a civilian; he would be his own man, live the life he wanted to lead. Ellis would become his new sponsor, educate him and teach him a skill set he might not otherwise learn on his own. Ellis made the idea of working for him sound powerful and fulfilling but he still wasn't sold. Hawke didn't have details and he had the impression—from Kegsy, mostly—that Ellis was a man where the details counted.

Hawke had to talk to Ellis, he had to make contact.

The portal phones were large and clunky but the best part about them was that they had their own private cubicles with a chair to sit on. The portal directory beside the phones had numbers to access each world and then the operator could connect him up to the phone number he nominated. The phone that was called had to be a landline but didn't need to be a portal phone. Hawke admired the intelligence of Authority technicians, to be able to create a two way transmission using an open micro-portal. It was something he might be interested in learning while in the Authorities... except he was average at maths and he was pretty sure stuff like that needed a great deal of expert mathematical comprehension.

He was mentally stalling, thinking about how the portal phones worked instead of picking up the handset and dialling. Hawke made himself look up the world number for Trent, fairly sure the four digit code was 0162. He'd been in a portal phone cubicle a number of times over the past two years with the intention of calling up Howard Ellis but he'd never followed through. Usually he'd look up the world number, think about dialling and then leave without even picking up the handset. Or he'd call Tavi instead. He wasn't sure why he'd never called Ellis; he'd made a lot of excuses and they'd seemed good enough at the time but he sensed there was a deeper reason. Naomi might've been able to suggest what it could be but he couldn't talk to her about it.

Ellis was his secret, a wild card that would change the game. Except it wasn't a game, it was his life, his future. The Authorities would ask for a decision on his fourteenth birthday and he wouldn't be able to stall them. It wasn't like he hadn't seen this decision coming for years.

The number for Trent *was* 0162. Hawke picked up the handset and put it to his ear. Instead of a ringtone, he heard nothing but the echo of air, like a seashell. He dialled the number slowly, pressing each button like it might zap him. There were a number of clicks and peculiar boinging sounds, then an electronic screech that wasn't too loud to bear before he heard the soft sounds of background chatter.

"You have called Auth-net. What's your number?" the male operator asked.

"Um." Hawke fished the note that he'd scrawled Ellis' number onto out of his pocket. He read out the string of numbers and then waited.

"Stay on the line."

Hawke's grip on the handset tightened as he waited through another series of clicks and then there was a ringing. Hawke listened to it purr four times in his ear before it was picked up.

"Ellis speaking."

Hawke hadn't expected Ellis to pick up the phone himself. He momentarily blanked on what he was going to say.

"Um." Hawke pulled a face, annoyed at himself. "It's Hawke."

There was a pause, then: "Ah, it's good to hear from you."

Hawke could hear the smile in Ellis' voice and his grip on the handset relaxed. He sat back in his chair.

"Yeah."

"I've missed having contact with you."

Now Hawke felt guilty. He shifted in the chair again, pulling up one of his feet so he could tuck it beneath himself on the seat. He'd thought Ellis was going to give him a lecture or question him about not contacting him sooner. It didn't seem like Ellis was interested in reprimanding him. It was refreshing to be treated with genuine respect. His memories of meeting Ellis had been nothing less.

While participating in the Junior Oceangate Project, Hawke managed to meet with Ellis six times and each visit had been fascinating and different. Hawke had been shown the city of Gredann and taken places—like to an expensive restaurant that he'd found out Ellis owned, as well as other businesses the man owned and managed—from a top quality hotel to a sub-sectioned house called the Bunker. The latter was the first clue he had that maybe Ellis was potentially a criminal—kids running around picking up satchels of money hadn't seemed entirely lawful.

He'd asked Ellis if he would be doing that, since the runners were about his age. The answer was he could if he wanted to, which had buoyed Hawke's spirits. The idea of his being able to decide for himself was a big advantage in Ellis' favour. It was the thing that the Authorities would never give him.

"Yeah, I've been busy. Studying and... stuff." The excuse was lame. He'd used the portal-phone many times on weekends to call up Tavi.

"Sounds fascinating. I assume you're doing well?"

"Yeah, not too bad." It was getting easier to talk to Ellis because the conversation was being kept pretty light. He anticipated that would change when they started talking about Hawke's upcoming decision. He thought Ellis might be waiting for him to bring it up. "I ended up passing maths okay but I'm better at the sciences. I got the highest score in both World Civics and Authority History." He stopped talking, not knowing what more to say.

"Of course you did, you have an affinity for the worlds that nobody else can appreciate."

Hawke was thoughtful.

"You think so? I'd like to see the different worlds."

He felt like making this declaration was like admitting that he was a selfish, dirty Wanderer after all.

"You deserve to. How are you planning to accomplish that?"

Here it was, they were down to business. Hawke looked up at the ceiling, seeing but not seeing the patterns in the plaster.

"I don't know. It's a big decision. I have more at stake than others."

"Yes, you do, but you also have more opportunities than others."

"You mean with you?"

"Of course. You know exactly what I want to give you."

"Do I?"

"Now you're just being insulting. You're almost fourteen. I assume you're calling me to tell me you've made a decision."

Hawke felt bad for his impulsiveness while speaking with Ellis. He hadn't meant to question what was being offered him—he knew it was worth a great deal, it just wasn't as clear a path as going with the Authorities.

"Sorry, I don't mean to be insulting. It's just more of a risk, being with you. I don't feel like I know enough to make the right call."

Hawke felt vulnerable but he also wanted to be swayed. He was inviting Ellis to win him over. He felt like he could have more freedom on Trent if he chose to work with Ellis; that being a Wanderer would finally give him something positive. He had no powers he could actively use; all his blood had given him was people who wanted to use him for it. Ellis seemed to revere it, and that was a potent drawcard.

"What more do you need to know?"

"You didn't tell me everything," Hawke accused. "I had to hear it from—" he stopped himself, not wanting to mention Kegsy. He felt like he'd given him away regardless.

Silence met him and Hawke let Ellis take the time.

He could hear the open channel between them.

"I'm not sure what you've convinced yourself of, but of course I didn't share everything with you. There is much I expect us to discover together. You are aware that my offer is for freedom and power in your own right. You didn't need any more than that, surely?"

Now it was Hawke's turn to be silent while he thought about Ellis' response. It was true that the details were unlikely to win him over but now that he was trying to compare outcomes, details mattered. Freedom and power; how enticing they were. The Authorities might never let him have either, but he felt like he would have more choices and opportunity for change while working for them. Ellis would be one direction only, though it would be a speedy rise to the top. His life would be interesting and adventurous and his own.

"No, I don't. You're right."

Hawke didn't know what else to say. He wanted to know more but he didn't know how to ask.

"So, you've decided."

"No, I don't know. I don't want to be a civilian." Hawke huffed.

"You don't want to be a civilian," Ellis repeated lightly, as though he was talking to himself more than to Hawke.

"I mean... just a nobody."

"That's impossible. It's not your destiny."

"I don't believe in destiny."

"Then believe in me."

Ellis made it clear that the decision Hawke made wasn't going to be easy. He saw two viable paths. Sign up with the Authorities or go to Ellis. Both of them had advantages and drawbacks. Both of them sounded intriguing and interesting.

"Okay. I'll call again and let you know," Hawke

promised.
    But he never did.

CHAPTER SEVENTEEN

The Hunter And The Hunted

SHE was inside the house. To do things correctly meant he should watch her for at least two weeks but his own impatience for resolution drove him to the back door. His pickup was parked further up the road but his sidearm was tucked in his holster. For this job he carried his own personal weapon, not the Authority issued one.

His heart was beating in his ears, making it hard to concentrate. He was breaking a lot of rules; not just the official ones but also his own. He was unprepared. He wasn't performing at his best. He wasn't waiting for a better chance. He was walking into the unknown. Worst of all, he was being driven by his emotions.

The key was still under the smallest pot beside the door. Careless, he thought, yet it was evidence of a woman no longer running, hiding only because she had to. Because of him. With the key in his palm looking like an accusation, he realised he had a choice. He could put the key back, take his designated leave after meeting his quota and forget that he'd ever found her. Or he could enter the house, finish what was started years ago and get closure.

Closure was appealing. He was haunted by memories that wouldn't rest; memories of her, of their time together. If he put an end to her, he might be able to put an end to that. He might be able to forget what they'd been through together. What she'd put him through.

In spite of his internalisation, it was a barking dog that spurred him into action. How long would he have stood at her back door, deliberating? The noise of the animal next door surprised him. It hadn't barked at him last time. He keyed the lock and opened the laundry door just as the dog's owner growled at it to shut up. The dog quietened.

The Hunter pulled the laundry door closed at his back and put the key on top of the washer. He couldn't hear her moving around and suspected she might've heard something. She was smart and she was paranoid, she'd avoided him for a long time. She hadn't even been sloppy, he'd just been thorough. He pulled his gun out of the holster and removed the safety, pointing it at the floor as he moved forward slowly and carefully. Now that he was doing this—that his decision had been made—his heartbeat steadied and he was calm. His training had taken over.

He kept his back to the wall but the room he was in was narrow and the tiles echoed every movement. Unless she was close, she shouldn't be able to hear him. The house had an open kitchen and dining, a short wall shielding part of the lounge. He faced that direction, peering through the doorway. He saw her in the kitchen wiping down the counters. She was moving in a manner that made him think she was listening to music, but he couldn't hear anything. As he watched, she turned her head and shuffled over to a cupboard where she pulled out a large, colourful book. A recipe book, he supposed. She wore earbuds and danced along as she cleaned the kitchen and thought about what to have for dinner.

The scene before him was so normal. This time the normalcy didn't make him feel guilty. It made him angry. She had the life she wanted. She had a home to go to, a child to look after. What did he have except for a history of rage and regret? He aimed his weapon at her as he approached, not bothering to hide his steps because he knew she wouldn't be able to hear him anyway.

From the lounge, he watched her leaf through the recipe book. From the dining area, he listened to her hum a tune and check the fridge for ingredients. She must've seen movement because she shrieked and jumped back against the counter, her hands swatting at the bud in her ear before she covered her mouth, her eyes wide. His gun had her attention. It seemed to take an eternity before her focus changed from it to him.

Confusion. She had no idea who he was and what he was doing here. As they stared at one another, he watched her expression change. Her eyebrows drew downward and she lowered her hands, her face filled with disbelief. She doubted who she saw, he could see it. After all this time, she recognised him. Was it guilt? Had she thought of him since she'd left him behind? Since they all had?

"You?" she breathed, and fuck her for the pity he thought he saw in her eyes. He cocked the weapon but kept his finger off the trigger. He wanted to growl accusations at her but he didn't trust his voice to behave. The emotion was welling up in him again, surpassing his training, taking control of his head and his heart. He could feel the pounding in his chest, the familiar rage causing his temples to ache. "Hawke Aron?"

He was surprised she remembered his name. The act of her speaking it out loud tapped into his resolve, stripping away the emotionless Hunter that he had become. But it had already been stripped away, hadn't it? He was never the machine he usually was when he was hunting *them*.

"It was you. It was you, wasn't it?" she accused. Was the bitch angry? She didn't fucking deserve to be angry. She'd ruined his life. "You killed them. You killed my husband and my sister! You fucking freak!"

Was she seriously calling him names while he was pointing a gun at her?

"*I'm* the freak? I'm not the one who kidnaps little kids and then leaves them to the enemy! How many lives did you ruin when you Wandered through countless worlds? How many people did you stand by and watch Eddie kill?" He lowered the gun while he seethed at her, not trusting himself to end things before he could say everything he needed to. Everybody else was dead. She was the last person he could do this with. He needed his closure.

"What you've done is a million times worse! We weren't Wandering when you killed them! I had a *baby* at home!" She was edging closer to the knife block. It was possible she knew how to throw them—the sisters had been capable, but the biggest thing he'd remembered about them was the fact they constantly had a book with them. It was the only clue he'd had, other than knowing what they looked like. Armed with this knowledge and the vast resources of the Authorities, he'd found her.

"Perhaps I should've taken your baby and dumped it in another world," he said, feeling the cold settle over him.

She frowned, unable to reply. It had been a long time ago but now she had a child and he thought becoming a mother would make her better at empathy. She'd never been as caring as her sister Carmen.

"Why? Why come after us?" she whispered, edging still closer to the block.

"Stop there, you're not getting a knife," he warned, lifting the gun so he could gesture with it for her to move in the opposite direction. He thought he saw a flash of hatred in her eyes before she did as she was told. Good job.

"You could've just left it alone," she spat.

"What you did deserves punishment and it's justice that I'm the one to give it to you."

"Execution isn't punishment," she argued. "You didn't punish them when you killed them, you punished *me*. You punished my *baby*. You—"

"I'm not fucking justifying myself to you!" he shouted at her, feeling his face redden and frustrated that the conversation wasn't turning out how he wanted. She was supposed to be callous, unreasonable and arrogant. "You ripped me out of my world and put me in fucking limbo!"

She went quiet, staring at him, assessing. He pulled in a breath and let it out slowly. Calm, they were both calm now. He had to keep it together to stay in charge. Emotions were fine as long as they didn't control him. He'd been enslaved to them since entering her house. Not anymore.

"I'm sorry," she said. It wasn't the apology he'd expected. It was spoken plainly, without tears, without fear, without sincerity, he thought. "What happened to you was bullshit and it broke the group up. We left Eddie after that, all of us... except his boyfriend. We left him because of what happened to you. You were supposed to be one of us and he left you behind to save himself."

"I am not! One. Of. You," Hawke seethed. She ignored his words as though he hadn't spoken.

"We decided it wasn't for us, the Wandering. Jerrom hadn't really wanted to for a while already... he stayed because of me. As soon as we found a world that we could be comfortable in, that we could blend into, we stopped. We thought we'd gone through it, the hardship, the single-mindedness of going through world after world, collecting Wanderers as we went. That was Eddie's dream, not ours." She paused, looking up and through him as if from a dream. Hawke felt hypnotised enough by her story that he didn't want it to stop now, he didn't have all the answers yet. "Is Eddie dead?"

"Yes."

"Did you kill him?" she asked.

"No," he said. It was a regret but also fitting that Eddie had been found by Hunters on Alpha Three.

"It took us maybe a dozen more worlds before we found something good. We settled down, living in an apartment together, the three of us. Jerrom and I started a relationship, Carmen moved out and soon after I fell pregnant. We were going to live a normal life, teach our son how to use his talent but not to Wander, that it wasn't safe. And then you found us."

She glared at him accusingly, this part of the story was over because he knew what had happened. She couldn't have known that it was him who'd Hunted them that night outside the restaurant, just like there was no way he could've known that she had a child at home with a babysitter looking after it.

Would it have made a difference? He'd been so angry.

Looking through his scope at the trio as they'd exited the restaurant together, chatting and laughing, had triggered his fury. How dare they have happiness when they'd committed such heinous crimes in their past, uncaring of whose lives they'd torn apart? Jerrom had been the first to go down, blasted into oblivion. The sisters had both reacted the same way, running to him and checking that he was dead. It was pretty obvious he was dead, Hawke thought, since he no longer possessed a head.

One of the sisters had thrown herself on the body and that had been what had saved her. He'd targeted the one standing, looking around.

Carmen.

She haunted him the most. Her face was one that constantly appeared in his dreams, creating havoc with his sleeping pattern, causing him to wake and question his choices.

What you've done is a million times worse, Lyssa had said. Yes, he agreed. Assassinating people was worse than kidnapping them... as long as you were looking just at the action and not at the victim. Killing a kidnapper wasn't as harmful as kidnapping a child. Justifications that he thought she would dismiss, but fuck her. She was the reason he was even here.

"You laughed at my fear. Every time I begged to go home, you laughed," he told her. He remembered it clearly. Her laughter had become more mocking in his memory than he thought might be true but he was sure it had been there.

"I was a fifteen year old idiot!" Lyssa argued. Now her voice was taking on some of the fright that he'd been expecting. To her credit, she wasn't begging for her life. Perhaps she knew there was no point. Her age surprised him and it shouldn't have, he should've figured it out from the look of her now. She didn't seem much older than him. Only seven years' difference and she was better preserved because she hadn't weathered the elements of multiple worlds, like him.

"Why kill her? Why kill *her*? She looked after you."

Hawke glared at Lyssa, furious because he had no response. She'd been 'one of the sisters' when he'd pulled the trigger. It was only afterward that she became Carmen. Maybe, if it had been Lyssa he'd sniped, he might have chosen to let Carmen be. Maybe, maybe. Guessing wasn't doing him favours now.

"I don't belong anywhere. You cheated me out of *belonging.* My world doesn't feel like home anymore. My *family* doesn't feel right to me anymore."

She looked upset and he guessed it was because she thought he was about to kill her. He changed his mind when she apologised again.

"I'm sorry. I'm so sorry. I never forgot what happened to you but I can't take it back. Just like you can't give me back my family."

The laundry door slammed and Hawke aimed the gun towards the intruder, just as there were two consecutive shouts.

"Hey mum! I got a—!"

"Torin, no!"

A dark-haired boy in his early teens stepped into the lounge and froze. He was dressed in a muddy sports uniform of blue and white.

"Please, don't. Please, don't," Lyssa began whimpering, frightened now that her son was in the line of fire.

Hawke didn't want to shoot a child. He didn't want to shoot a mother in front of her child, either. Even without Torin interrupting them, he might not have shot Lyssa.

Maybe, maybe. There was no point thinking about what might be. He was aiming a gun at a thirteen year old while his mother begged for his life in the kitchen, unable to stop what was playing out. He was shielded also, which meant neither of them would know what he was thinking (if the boy had inherited his mother's Intuit powers… he couldn't remember what Jerrom had been). With a hand held up to ward off Lyssa, Hawke took a step backwards to better assess the situation. He looked from one to the other, Lyssa with her tear-filled face, the boy in a state of shock. Neither of them would react in time if he shot them in turn. Bang. Bang.

Instead, he backed up again, bringing himself closer to the front door while they watched. The only sound was Lyssa's intermittent gasps for air as she tried to keep her sobs under control.

Hawke reached back with his free hand and turned the knob of the front door. It was locked. Feeling around, his thumb connected with a latch, which he turned. Trying the knob this time brought success. Stepping through the doorway as he re-holstered his weapon, Hawke shut the front door and decided it would be the end to this madness.

He'd got his closure. As confusing as it had been, he felt like it was finally over.

CHAPTER EIGHTEEN

A Game Of Cards

DAESON found Amethyst and Marcus playing a card game together in the dining room. He paused, trying to figure out what game they were playing. His wistful observation was soon noticed.

"Have a seat," Marcus said, pulling out the chair adjacent to him.

"Thanks," Daeson replied, sitting where he'd been invited to and watching as the cards were gathered together and then shuffled for a new round. "Aren't you on night duty?"

Marcus shook his head as Amethyst dealt Daeson in, giving him thirteen cards to play with. There was only one game Daeson knew that used thirteen cards and it was one of his favourites, Rummage. Jade had taught it to him, explaining that most of the girls liked the game because it was strategic without being difficult to play. The popularity of the game seemed to be spreading to other employees.

"Nah, I'm supposed to be but they're shorthanded right now. Spier woke me up."

Spier was the manager of the Queen when Nick was off-site.

"He doesn't think it'll be busy tonight?" Daeson asked.

"Probably not. All the Authorities won't stray too far from base if there's trouble there."

"Profits will drop," Amethyst said, setting down the remaining pile in the middle of the table and then inspecting her hand, moving cards around within it. "Lots of business from soldiers."

"Yeah," Marcus agreed.

Daeson inspected his hand, seeing that he already had a good run of spades.

They played cards for a while until Spier looked in on them. All three of them paused in their game as the security manager approached stiffly, favouring his right leg. It was an affliction that Daeson couldn't fix, for it had already healed years ago (though badly). Daeson didn't have much to do with the man so he was surprised to be addressed.

"When will Miss Backhouse be back?"

Daeson was unaware Omerri had even gone and he blinked uncomprehendingly at Spier until he realised that she'd done her usual trick of escaping from what she didn't like. In this case, she'd run away from Daeson and his very young age.

"I don't know. I didn't know she was gone," Daeson said grimly.

"She didn't say anything to you?" Spier continued, obviously bothered.

"Miss Backhouse doesn't report to anyone, Spier. What's going on?" Marcus intervened.

"There's a phone call for her, one of those rich guys that are important to her." Spier's gaze flicked to Daeson briefly before he looked at Marcus again. "I know Nick's talked to him too but Nick ain't here either. Fucking shambles."

"Just tell him she'll call back later."

"I don't have a timeframe for him," Spier growled. "I'll sound as fucking useless as a bottomless raft." He turned and moved away quickly, his limp more pronounced because he was rushing back to the phone.

Marcus stared at Daeson questioningly and he felt compelled to respond.

"There's a lot going on." It was vague and truthful and he hoped Marcus wouldn't push it.

"Who's drawing from who?" Amethyst asked, giving her cards a wiggle to remind them that there was a game to play.

"Yeah, me," Marcus said, and drew a card from Daeson's hand before grunting his discontentment. "Somebody's holding onto all the spades."

A few minutes later, Kite sat with them and asked to be dealt in next round. It only took a few more hands for Amethyst to win. She left them shortly after when a new client visited the Queen and she went to greet them. Once Kite's break was over he returned to the kitchen, leaving Marcus and Daeson playing cards together—a simpler game that Marcus was too good at for Daeson to win any hands.

"I know about Synjan," Daeson said, hoping to be given more information. Marcus' expression didn't change.

"I know about her, too," he replied.

"I met her today. We talked a week ago, as well."

Marcus was more interested now but he seemed wary.

"Oh yeah? What about?"

"She was upset with Nick."

"You talked with Synjan about Nick?" Marcus asked dubiously.

It was a direct question and Daeson struggled to answer it. "We know we're being kept apart. Do you know why?"

Marcus was quiet, fingers rubbing his cards pensively. "I don't know why but I'm sure Nick has a good reason."

"You sure it's a *good* reason?" Daeson asked bitterly.

Marcus bristled. "Nick's not dumb, he knows a lot and he can figure out if something will go good or bad. You and Synjan getting together might be something that will go bad."

Daeson pondered Marcus' words. He hadn't considered this outcome and Marcus was certainly giving Nick the benefit of the doubt. However, after dealing with Nick for two years, the man had used up every benefit of the doubt Daeson cared to give him. He didn't think of Nick as unintelligent but he certainly didn't believe the man had Daeson's best interests at heart.

A clattering of pots and shouting erupted in the kitchen, distracting Daeson from both his thoughts and the card game. He looked at Marcus, who was frowning at the kitchen door and then they both heard Nick screaming Daeson's name. They sprang up and ran towards the noise. The kitchen staff met them at the door, rushing out in the opposite direction and making it difficult for Daeson to move through them. Marcus was at his back, propelling him forward.

When they got into the kitchen, Marcus swore and pushed past Daeson because he'd stopped suddenly. When the security guard was able to take in the scene, he swore again. Daeson could only stare uncomprehendingly at the bloodied body Nick had lain on the steel-topped island bench.

"Help me!" Nick cried, his voice hoarse. His front was stained with the blood of the woman he'd carried to the table.

Daeson didn't know what Nick expected him to do. The woman was dead. She wasn't moving, she wasn't breathing and most of her blood appeared to be outside of her body. It wasn't like he could heal it back.

"Daeson, fucking *do* something!" Nick screamed. Marcus had moved forward to hold the body's hand and he looked at Daeson in surprise. It was easy to see he'd made the connection as to who the Healer at the Queen was.

Even though it was too late because she was dead—or so close to it she was beyond help—Daeson had to try. Moving forward on legs that felt stiff and wooden, he placed his hands atop Synjan's chest.

CHAPTER NINETEEN

All Fall Down

WHEN the bullets hit her, it was like she'd been punched from behind and she flew forward, knocked completely off her feet. The three cracks as they left the gun (guns?) seemed to come afterwards; she distinctly heard them as her back lit up with pain and she tumbled helplessly through the air. It was like the world held its breath. She had time to look at the sky—an impulse borne of instinct because her body had arched backwards in response to the slugs entering her kidney, her lung and spine—and marvel at its utterly unremarkable greyness. Then things sped up and she was pitching forwards, staring into a similar banality as the cement rushed towards her.

She could feel her arms flailing, trying to find balance.

She was aware that she would land face first anyway.

The only thing she was able to do was close her eyes.

Synjan crashed hard into the footpath, momentum propelling her almost two metres forward before she came to rest. The skin on her forehead split open and a generous flap of skin was torn down over her eye and ground into the grazed flesh of her cheek and nose. Her hands were also cut, a fingernail torn off and what breath she had left was knocked out of her one working lung. Dirt and stone were embedded in her left eye and her right was gathering blood like it could syphon what was pouring out of her face back into her body and save her.

She wanted to scream but there was no air.

She needed to see but her eyes were stinging, burning, probably closed.

She wanted to move but only her fingers responded.

They tapped out feeble little scratches of bewilderment near her ears, the only thing she could hear. The noise was soon drowned out by the screech of tires and the weird thud of punching metal.

The world became a kaleidoscope of dizzying colour as she was scooped up. Intense pain rushed through her, causing her to gasp and suck air into her lung even as her body was consumed by tearing agony. It was like she was completely encased by a bramble bush, thorns piercing every single pore. They dug deep, scraped along nerves and painted a fire across every synapse so intense that her mind shut down.

When her eyes opened next, she was in the passenger seat and Nick was hunched over the steering wheel, wrenching it violently. It was all Synjan could do to stay in one place and she finally found the ability to speak as they hurtled forwards.

"Hurts," she said and didn't recognise the wet, burbling noise that came out of her throat as her own voice.

"Synjan! You'll be alright! Stay with me, Synjan! Sit up! Stay awake! You've been shot but it's okay. It'll be okay. We just have to get back to the Queen and everything'll be alright, oh Gods, your face, what've we done, fuck," Nick moaned. At first he'd started out yelling but by the end of his sentence he was whimpering. His voice faded in and out as he swapped between looking at the road and looking at Synjan.

The words came at her but they didn't penetrate the bramble barrier of pain and she couldn't concentrate on them anyway. 'Shot' registered and she knew that was why her back was the biggest agony, howling over every other ache in her body

except her legs, oh not her legs, they weren't there

and she wondered about it. The next time she was thrown sideways, she made a conscious effort to move the arm she wasn't leaning on. Slowly, she worked it over her hip and twisted it up to touch her back.

"AH!"

"What're you doing?!" Nick screeched, jumping when she cried out unexpectedly.

"Pressure," she ground out but she was lying. She wanted to put pressure on the wounds, of course, but she couldn't manage it. She was being bounced around too much and the angle was too difficult. Plus, she didn't know where to press because her whole shirt was squelching with blood and just pressing a fingertip to one random part made her simultaneously feel like vomiting and passing out.

"Don't do that, you can't it's... there's too much... I just... you won't be able to... "

Another corner was rounded and Synjan's arm rolled back and landed in her lap. Jerkily, she tilted her head so the one eye that wasn't swollen shut could see it and an immense chasm of despair rose up to swallow her. The blood looked very dark, what did that mean? Had she been shot in an organ? People didn't recover from those.

"It's bad," she mumbled and began to cry. The tears only made the pain in her face worse and her sobs became unsteady wails of anguish.

"Synjan! No! You'll be alright! Sit up maybe, put pressure on it that way!" Nick beseeched and she tried, she really did, but her body wasn't working properly

her legs, she could see them but she couldn't feel them, how could she work without legs?

and she couldn't brace herself long enough to find her balance.

"Can't," she warbled. She swayed forward as he braked suddenly and lost consciousness without warning. When her eye opened next, she was leaning back on the seat and Nick was screaming her name but he was beginning to sound like he was very tiny or far away. The pain seemed to be going with him and for that, she was profoundly grateful.

"I'm sorry," she told him sincerely, finding it too difficult even to hold her head up now. She wasn't sure he'd hear her, but she had to say it anyway. "Tell Ellis I'm sorry. I failed," she admitted and her heart ached with the weight of her impending death.

Strangely, even though she knew what had happened and that she'd likely never open her eyes or speak again, her admission and apology made her feel free. It let her move away from the pain. She thought perhaps she was mapping somehow because she was looking somewhere... over the ocean, into the rising sun. It was so bright she had to squint against it but she couldn't block it out even though she tried.

No, not mapping, she was dreaming.

The longer she looked, the more she saw; the sun was a sliver and soon became a half-circle and there were shapes forming in the centre of it. They became people shapes and warmth washed through her because the shapes were familiar, they were comforting, made her feel it wasn't so bad to have failed after all. She would be okay. The shapes started to solidify and there were three of them; one very tall, one very short and one in between. She decided it was her family.

She was spinning, dizzy, overwhelmed. Her senses were snail antennae, raw and brittle, unsure whether to stretch forward, ready to pull back. Forward was away from the pain, the biting, burning agony she despised, and a promise to walk amongst people she missed terribly. But she wasn't sure she was ready to go yet. It seemed antithetical to give up so easily after she'd been fighting her whole life. Why had she tried so hard with Ellis, endured so much pain? She'd persevered after her entire life had been changed, for what? Nothing? She was seeing shadows with a corona of affinity and she was ready to just... die?

Red! She choked on a gasp. Everything was red and intense again for a moment and then she was bouncing up and down. This time it was black while the red streaked through the space above her, the open space, a vastness she couldn't comprehend. She was on fire and then she wasn't hot anymore, she was freezing and floating, her body threatening to rattle into parts and fly away because it was shivering so hard and

then it came back!

All of it, all of the pain and the flames swarmed around her, stabbing, piercing, detonating huge razor grenades into her skin and

WARMTH

washed through her, taking the pain away.

It didn't happen all at once. It tingled like an electric pulse into her brain, throbbing power around inside her skull before it rolled in an undulating wave through her chest, across her shoulders and down her arms. Her fingers flared as it shot into their tips and rolled back out again. The current infused her heart and bled into her belly, wending its way through her insides like reptilian rays of sunshine. A jolt zigzagged its way down her spine, jumping between vertebrae and every square centimetre of her back before flashing onward. It pooled momentarily at her hips, almost like it was gathering power before it smashed its way down her legs, igniting them. Even her toes vibrated with the potency of the energy before it flowed back over itself, shot up and dispersed through her body like the dying embers of a firebarrel flower.

With a huge intake of breath, Synjan sat up. Colours more vibrant than she'd ever physically seen assaulted her retinas, making her blink. She was on one of the tables in the kitchen of the Queen of Hearts and dazzling light was bouncing off everything she squinted at. She had to look down and contain the impact on her senses because it was too immense to take in all at once. She took a steadying breath, her lips lifting in a grin as she exhaled. It felt like she was floating, adrift on the most delicious bed of life and warmth she'd ever experienced. She had no idea what was happening but she felt fabulous.

Synjan looked at her hands. They were dark red, as if they'd been painted with blood and let dry. One of her nails was gone but it didn't hurt. She gently prodded the pink nail bed with another finger, marvelling at the feeling that squirrelled its way down into her pelvis and shivered across her shoulders when she did. She'd lost nails before and knew this one would grow back.

Her clothes were in a similarly shabby state to her hands. There was a tear in one knee of her pants and her shirt was clinging wetly to her. Perhaps that didn't feel so wonderful but it didn't bother her too greatly. She rolled her shoulders to try and dislodge it but gave up when every movement wafted the heavy, coppery scent of blood up to her, making her wrinkle her nose. It was a monotonous theme, she observed, peering down at her wriggling feet. Even her boots were coated in it.

The good thing was that it didn't hurt. Nothing hurt any more. Even wrapped in blood-soaked clothes, her skin felt highly sensitised and lovely. Alive. Everything felt wonderful and alive and alert in a way she'd never experienced. She couldn't stop smiling.

"He needs water! Fuck, get him some water and when he's awake, meet me in the alley. I need to get her out of here."

Synjan registered that the voice belonged to Nick a few seconds after it penetrated her awed mind, dragging her attention outside of herself at last. She peered over the edge of the table and saw he and Marcus crouching beside... Daeson! The man she'd been thinking about all day. Before she was able to understand why he was sprawled across the floor, Nick noticed her looking and surged up in front of her. He had her attention instantly.

"Come on," he said gently, sliding his hands into her armpits to help her get down off the bench. He was so close, she was overwhelmed with gratitude and love for him and she tried to wrap him up in a passionate embrace that she felt would adequately demonstrate her thanks.

"Ugh, noooo," Nick cringed, holding her at arm's length.

She was bewildered. "What's wrong?"

"You, uh, need a shower and a change of clothes, come on," he muttered, lifting her cleanly off the table before she had any time to think about it. He set her down in the middle of the floor like a small child helped by a parent, her back to the table and the men beside it. Once he was sure she was steady on her feet, Nick led her towards the rear exit. Joy suffused her because he was close and she tried to hug him, pressing her face into the crook of his neck to kiss him. Again, he pushed her away, steering her into the alley with fingers strategically placed on her shoulders and waist.

They hadn't gone very far when he pushed her downwards without warning. What she thought might become some amorous fellatio turned out to be him hiding her between some old furniture and a garbage bin. He shushed her sternly when she started to protest so she relaxed as she'd been instructed to do and leaned back against the wall. He walked away and she heard voices. They sounded vaguely familiar but she couldn't place them. Just as it occurred to her that she could map to see who it was, three loud pops pierced the air.

She flinched and the beautiful serenity she'd been infused with threatened to dissipate as her back tingled with recollection. Determinedly, she held onto the memory of life flowing back into her, not wanting to think about the pain that came before it. She wrapped her hands over her ears and drew her knees up to her chest, resting her chin on them. The energy was still thrumming through her but her heart was a little sadder than it had been.

When Nick returned to her, she found her smile again. She didn't look behind her as he took her hand and led her away.

"Where are we going?" she asked.

"My place," he answered grimly.

CHAPTER TWENTY

This Is Not A Love Story

THE world of Othello was as close to perfection as Hawke could imagine. Filled with cities devoted to specialised subjects and countries that revolved around fields of study, his favourite was the City of Astronomy. It was a small city of steep hills and a narrow, winding valley—terrible for cyclists but great for hikers and perfect for a few observatories to perch at the highest points. There was nothing built up around Astro City (a nickname of endearment that had migrated to other campus-cities on the world), nor would there ever be. Everyone who lived within the city limits observed lights out after eight. Entertainment was limited to indoor activities; nightclubs, bars, theatres and restaurants were established in the basement levels of educational buildings.

There was a spider-webbed network of well-lit underground tunnels. Some tunnels were reserved for the public shuttle system because Astro City was too small to suit a subway. If students wanted to earn extra cash, there were always vacancies for drivers. Pedestrians had their own narrower tunnels or could walk alongside the shuttle system on a designated footpath. Their apartment buildings could be directly accessed, provided they lived in one of the inner city dormitories. Crime was exceptionally low here—though that was to be expected on an Authority designed world with a lofty entry fee and well-armed soldiers to police it.

Every aspect of Astro City was planned, from the

picnic grounds and gardens to the structured township that ensured nobody was too far from a convenience. It didn't matter if some of the businesses weren't turning a profit because they were all Authority run. As long as the city's business takings were successful overall, nothing really changed. A lot of the students found the lack of change boring and eventually tired of living on Othello by the time they were graduating.

To Hawke it was the constant, unchanging face of Astro City that made it feel like home. After moving through so many worlds and unable to cultivate a connection with any of the cities (or even worlds) he passed through, there was comfort in the familiar. It didn't matter if he was away for months at a time or if he didn't visit a particular café for years—he knew it would be there when he returned. Likely not operated by the same people but it would have the same name, same appearance, same menu. There was security in that; of knowing the layout of a city, of knowing how it was run and where he could go to get things. It was this kind of knowledge that people took for granted when they grew up in a single neighbourhood and only appreciated it when they left.

It made sense that he should meet a woman to fall in love with in Astro City. Brita Kate Enervolding came very close. He met her when he was twenty-three.

"If you could follow me into the observation lounge, you'll find that Mount Honourable offers the best views of Astro City. We have two hundred and eighty degrees of uninterrupted scenery from up here and the most spectacular aspect is through the windows to your left."

The young woman ushering the small tour group turned to face the half dozen people shuffling after her and gestured in the direction they should go. Like obedient sheep, they migrated to the window she selected for them and peered out, bleating their approval of the view.

Hawke didn't join them, choosing to approach the window opposite. Instead of seeing buildings made tiny with distance, he admired the row of mountains that lined the city like protective barriers. There were other observatories perched upon them. He knew each mountain like they were his friends; beside Mount Honourable was Mount Caucus, with the Stellar Observatory nestled onto it like a wart. It was an ugly building but functional. Beyond it was Jackson's Peak, so named because some centuries ago a General in the Authorities named Jackson had been an avid mountain-climber and met his death not far from the summit. The mountain had conquered him instead of the other way around so, in honour of the man (or as an unpleasant irony, Hawke couldn't decide which), the mountain bore his name. Huddled on Jackson's Peak was a white domed building called the Bloomfield Observatory. It was the largest of the three and boasted a small theatre that provided a projected space show.

Two uniformed Authority soldiers joined him at the window, one on either side. Hawke looked from one to the other and both met his gaze. They weren't here for the view. He could see a rigidness in their bodies.

"Is there something I can help you with?"

"Why are you carrying weapons openly?"

Hawke blinked. He'd never had trouble walking around with his holster before, a pistol on his hip, clipped in. Citizens here knew him well enough not to bother raising an alarm. He was even acquainted with a lot of the soldiers here, especially those on duty at the observatories. He couldn't know everyone though, and these two were unfamiliar.

"I'm going to take out my ID, is that okay?" Hawke wasn't sure whether to be amused or annoyed at the interruption. Either way, they both looked ready and willing to pounce.

"Slowly," one of them warned. They were doing things by the book and looked younger than him, which was quite a feat when he was only twenty-three. He had an inkling that their training was also a great deal softer than his, especially if they were being assigned locations such as Othello.

He pulled out his ID holder and thumbed his card out. The fellow on his right reached for it and read the details.

"You're a Hunter," he said with reverence before handing back the ID for Hawke to pocket again.

"It's still unfavourable for you to walk around with a gun," the other growled.

Hawke puffed unamused laughter. Both of these reactions were the kind he typically got; usually the younger soldiers romanticised his rank while the older ones considered him nothing more than an assassin for hire. There were exceptions to that rule, but not often.

"Now that you know who I am, you don't have to worry," Hawke said, offering the grim soldier on his left a tight smile. He didn't get a smile back but he hadn't expected one.

"Sorry to bother you," the other soldier said before they both left. Hawke was sure his partner would make him pay for that apology. He turned to watch them go and noticed his tour-guide was surprised by their exit. She glanced over at Hawke and looked guilty for having been noticed.

He'd forgotten her name fairly quickly after she'd introduced herself but now that he was paying attention, he noticed that she was quite a pretty brunette. The worlds were full of pretty brunettes but he noticed this one because of how she'd handled a potential threat. She'd given the tour as though nothing was wrong and then, at the first opportunity, summoned the Authorities. He hadn't noticed her making any calls so she knew how to be discreet. She suddenly seemed a great deal more capable and interesting.

He approached her, reading the name badge pinned high on her left breast. It said 'Brita'.

"Hello," he said as he neared her.

She looked at him and offered him a warm smile. "Hi!"

"Your plan to get rid of me didn't work," he teased with a grin.

"I'll have to try something else, later," she replied.

"You'll have to do it without your security goons."

"Yes, but you'll find I'm very resourceful."

Hawke liked her already.

"So why weren't you arrested?"

"Because my rank is higher than those you sent to arrest me."

She was quiet for a moment and he thought she was trying to figure out who and what he was.

"My name's Hawke," he provided, because he already knew her name. She nodded, her stare assessing. He hoped to change that.

"How about I take you out to lunch?"

"I'm... working." She sounded surprised to be asked.

"They release you in order to eat, don't they?"

"The cafeteria here is a bit ordinary."

"That's not what you said when you walked us past it," he laughed, thinking back to her praise for the small sandwich bar that fed employees and visitors alike.

"You didn't know any better."

"So I'll take you out somewhere else instead."

Brita seemed conflicted. Her gaze shifted off him in order to flit from object to object, landing on everything but him. Funny how she'd kept her composure when she'd considered him suspicious but not when he'd made himself a romantic variable. Brita met his gaze again.

"I can't. I'm sorry."

It was the way she spoke the apology with real regret that made him think something else was going on.

"Boyfriend?"

She made an absurd noise and rolled her eyes. "More like 'Father'."

Hawke hadn't expected that answer. How was her father so great an influence that she couldn't go out with him?

"How old are you?" he asked curiously. She shot him a resentful glare.

"Old enough," she quipped, her tone edgy.

Old enough didn't mean a lot when it came to the Authorities, who viewed fourteen year olds as adults—allowing them to make mature decisions about everything from signing up to serve, driving cars, drinking alcohol and having sexual relationships. Brita didn't look fourteen but behind her makeup Hawke was beginning to think she wasn't so much older.

"Okay," he said with a shrug, then moved to join the herd at the city-view window. Brita stopped him before he got more than three steps away.

"You gave up easily." She sounded disappointed. He turned back to look at her and met her intense gaze. "You know... for a high ranking Authority that walks around with a gun."

He could've shut her down with a single comment

about her age, about how he wasn't attracted to children but it wasn't in him. When he'd first looked at her, he'd thought she was a woman. How she held herself, how she spoke, how she dressed and did her makeup—it all lent to a maturity that a child couldn't imitate. She had a job talking to the public. She had an interest in astronomy (he assumed). Their banter had been light and she'd been witty. Perhaps she was in her late teens? He didn't want to go out with anyone more than five years his junior.

"Nothing to say?" she challenged. Peripherally, he saw the other guests in the tour group begin to shift around the panoramic windows, getting restless.

"You told me no. I'm not going to mess with that." Contrary to his words, he closed in the distance between them, so their conversation could remain just between themselves.

"I said my father won't let me go out on a date. We can still... gather."

"Me and you and your friends?"

"That's usually how a gathering works," she smiled.

It was local slang that Hawke had picked up very recently. There were a few phrases that meant the same thing on other worlds—*get together, chill, hang out*. He'd figured out that 'gather' usually meant more than two people. It might be a parent-approved way of getting to know Brita but it didn't remove the problem of her age. He still didn't know how old she was.

"Where at?"

"Club Lucas. It's at the foot of—"

"Mount Caucus, at the end of the shuttle red line."

"So you're local enough to know that," she said. He thought she sounded pleased and he was glad to have impressed her.

"When?"

"At seven," she said, then stepped away and

clapped her hands twice, attracting everyone's attention. "If everyone could please follow me, I will show you to the observatory itself. In there, you will meet our local hero and head astronomer, Doctor Kenneth Mariandis, who discovered an extra moon around Bodhi - our sixteenth and most far-flung planet."

Mariandis was the reason Hawke had taken the tour, to meet the scientist that had become something of a celebrity. For the rest of the day, however, he thought more of his conversation with Brita than the one he had with Mariandis.

Club Lucas ended up as a bust. Hawke arrived twenty minutes after seven but Brita wasn't there with her friends. He doubted she'd arrived and left in that time. When Brita finally arrived at quarter to eight, she did so full of apologies but didn't offer him an explanation. By the drunken state of one of her friends, he suspected he knew the cause but didn't ask. He liked the fact she didn't blame her friend, it showed loyalty.

The entire night was a babysitting exercise for the drunk girl in the group. He made his excuse after a couple of hours of sitting around and then visited a nearby bar called Twenty, named as such because it was supposed to be frequented by his age group. When he walked in, he saw that the clientele were at least a decade older. It didn't stop him from accompanying a woman back to her place; she was a physics professor and she'd been clear that she didn't want a relationship. She'd mentioned it a few times, enough that he thought her last dalliance might've yielded lovesick results. They had fun and he left early.

A couple of days later Hawke visited his favourite café for breakfast. He was scrolling through the campus news website on his phone, waiting for his food to come, when somebody sat in the booth seat opposite. When he looked up, he was surprised to see Brita smiling at him. She looked fresh and young and makeup free. He thought she was maybe sixteen. He debated the seven year age difference and whether he was intrigued enough with her to disregard it.

"So, you left without getting my number," she said airily. It was perhaps a little too casual, though not forced. He had to remember she talked for a living. The thought of her drawing a wage made him wonder about other details.

"I didn't know whether you or your disapproving father would pick up the phone."

"Is this an indirect way of asking me if I live with my parents?"

"Yeah," he said, even though he thought it was obvious that she did.

She nodded. "I would've given you my mobile number."

"So you can hide phone calls from strange men but you can't hide a dinner date?"

Brita's eyes widened and she leaned across the table to stare intently at him.

"Are you a strange man, Hawke?"

"Strange enough that you tried to get rid of me."

"Speaking of, where are your guns? Do you not need them while breakfasting?"

"I only carry the one," Hawke said, wondering how she'd noticed that he wasn't wearing his holster when the table should've hidden it. Had she scoped him out? Why hadn't he noticed?

"So what is it you do for the Authorities then?"

He hesitated answering, not because it was classified but because of the reaction he anticipated she would have.

"I work for the Hunter Division."

Now it was her turn to pause as it occurred to her what such a thing meant.

"I take it you're a Hunter and not in a clerical position there," she replied, keeping her voice light. He didn't trust it because she looked serious.

"That's right," he said, searching her face. He watched her schooled expression, the thoughtfulness in her eyes as her mind turned over the information.

"How do you end up getting a job like that?"

"It helps if your sponsor is the Hunter Division Overseer," Hawke explained.

"Your sponsor?"

He'd given away more of himself than he'd intended to.

"Yeah. I... I grew up as an Authority Ward so I was assigned a sponsor. He's more like a father to me, though."

He expected her to make a bit of small talk, think of an excuse and leave. He'd literally told her he was an orphan assassin. Not really boyfriend material there.

"That's nice, that you have that bond," she said. He nodded, waiting for the crunch.

"How long ago did you order? The pancakes here sometimes take a while to come but they're *so good*!"

"I didn't order the pancakes."

"You should! They're delicious here."

He smiled and nodded, wondering if she was being exceptionally diplomatic or if she wasn't intending on leaving. He could give her an excuse, he supposed, and see if she would take it.

"Are you working today?"

"Not today." Brita tilted her head as she regarded

him, almost expectant of what would come next. When he kept silent, she prompted him. "Were you hoping I'd be free?" she grinned.

She was flirting without self-consciousness, making her agenda clear. In that moment he ached to mean something to her. He wanted to know everything about her; her secrets, her body, her soul. He'd never wanted to possess such intimate things from another person before and he couldn't speak from the force of it.

She must've seen something in his expression because she sat back and made a noise of affirmation, as though he'd verbally replied. A plate of poached eggs on toast was set down in front of him, along with a tomato juice. Brita stared at the red juice.

"Healthy, if not tasty," she said.

"I like it," Hawke replied. To prove how much he liked it, he took a long sip.

Brita screwed up her nose.

"You drink up, I've just got to make a phone call."

He watched her leave the café and stand outside on the corner, dialling someone and then chatting with them. The waitress returned with a small plate filled with butter patties and individual jam squares.

"You're brave," she said cryptically. Hawke looked up at her, an ageing woman with faded red hair who looked positively eager to share the reason why.

"I already know about her father," he said, hoping to take some of the power out of the woman's statement. He didn't like petty gossips who enjoyed ruining a good moment.

The waitress scoffed. "Her *father* isn't the problem, ducky. It's her mother you should be worried about."

"Because?" he asked, already bored.

"Because she's the daughter of General Katrin Enervolding."

Hawke could read the rest of her unspoken

sentence on her face: *And you're not good enough*. It was a sentiment he'd learned to rebel against. The waitress didn't get a tip and his pursuit of Brita was decided. He couldn't walk away even after he found out she was fifteen. He justified it to himself, reasoning that they would take things slowly. There might be career consequences for dating a General's daughter but he could deal with that later.

CHAPTER TWENTY-ONE

Stacked Deck

EVERY muscle in Daeson's body felt like it was cramping. The intensity of the pain and restriction of movement was so complete that he thought he might be dying, exchanging his life for Synjan's. Beneath his hands he'd felt her heartbeat pulse within her chest, as though he'd recharged her. He'd given her too much; he'd somehow left nothing for himself. The agony was so great that he wished for the mercy of death.

Daeson's throat was abruptly clogged with water and he coughed up what went down his windpipe, otherwise it was relief. His chest loosened and his jaw was able to work. He managed to put his lips around the bottle that was held for him, like he was a suckling babe, and he drank deeply and greedily.

His muscles relaxed a little at a time. His legs were the last to recover. Once he was able to hold the bottle of water on his own, he did so, sitting up and taking sips. In front of him was Marcus in a crouch, watching him intently.

"Incredible," he said before reaching out and touching Daeson reverently on the shoulder. Daeson didn't trust himself to say anything in reply. He was only vaguely aware when Marcus stood up and left him. He wondered if the security guard was going to get him some more water—he didn't think he needed anymore, his belly felt full to sloshing. Daeson waited patiently, listening to the murmur of voices outside.

Two rapid gunshots close by had him cringing against the kitchen cabinets, followed by a delayed third. They sounded like they'd been fired directly outside, in the alley. Daeson held his breath and listened but couldn't hear anything else. The silence seemed to mock him and he wondered if he'd really heard what he had.

He waited for someone to join him in the kitchen but nobody did.

He waited for someone to go outside or come back inside but nobody did.

He wondered where Marcus had got to and could feel the first tendrils of worry curling around his heart.

Daeson stood, seeing immediately that Synjan's body was no longer on the counter. He'd vaguely been aware of her heart beating beneath his hands. Still, she shouldn't have been able to get up and walk away. Daeson was struck by the amount of blood that was atop the island counter and had trickled onto the floor. The practical kitchen-hand in him noted that it would be easy to clean because there was a drain in the floor, but there was *so much* of it. How had he managed to heal Synjan at all? He looked at his hands to see if they held the answer and was taken aback by the blood that covered them—it looked like he was wearing red gloves.

He moved to the sink and looked out the kitchen window as he scrubbed his hands clean. Through the glass he saw more of the building opposite than the floor of the alley between. He rose on his tiptoes and thought he could see something lying on the ground. Trepidation filled his core. He heard someone groaning but when he turned around to look who it was, the noise stopped and he was alone. The groaning must have come from him.

Daeson took a step towards the door, kicking a pot and causing it to clatter across the tiled kitchen floor. He flinched from the noise, surprised by it and annoyed at himself. Looking down, he counted a half dozen pots and pans—and a colander—on the floor. One of them rested on a puddle of blood near the base of the island.

He forced his gaze away and headed for the door, drawn to it even though he knew he wasn't going to like what he was about to see. As he opened the door, the wind wrenched it out of his hold and slammed it against the wall. When he stepped outside and saw the two men lying on the ground, their clothes rippling in the wind, he was unsurprised but stricken. When he got closer, he saw they were both dead; one shot twice in the back, the other in the head.

Hammond. Marcus.

He imagined the scenario. Nick and Synjan exited the Queen together and met with Hammond and Marcus, who either witnessed or worked out that Synjan had been healed. Marcus certainly knew who the Healer was, perhaps he'd mentioned it to Hammond or the door guard had been surprised to see Synjan up and walking around. In order to keep them quiet about Synjan (or Daeson), Nick had shot them.

Daeson went to Marcus even though Hammond was closer and knelt beside his friend. They hadn't been close but close enough for Daeson to mourn him. Had it really been a few minutes ago when Marcus had been defending Nick, his soon to be murderer? Both men were long-term employees at the Queen, they shouldn't have been disposed of so thoughtlessly, left in the street disrespectfully.

Daeson laid his hands on Marcus' chest. He'd thought Synjan lost so he wouldn't make any more assumptions. He thought about healing. He thought about living. He thought about Marcus telling him that if he got together with Synjan, things might go bad.

Nothing worked.

Daeson stayed as he was, hands on a man whose

body was still warm, ignoring the sound of the opening door at his back and the sharply drawn in breath that followed. He didn't react until Ladd tried to pull him away.

"Come on back inside," Ladd said, his voice soothing yet strange—no doubt the man who guarded the front door was affected, seeing what had happened to his colleague. "We'll make everything okay."

There was nothing Ladd could do that would make this okay.

"What are you going to do?" Daeson shouted at him, fighting off Ladd's tentative hold and standing up to face him. "You're not going to call the Authorities, are you? So what are you going to do?"

Ladd glanced away and Daeson followed the look, seeing they weren't alone. There were two other other daytime security guards circled around the bodies. Spier was there as well, holding one of Hammond's legs. He looked guiltily at Daeson and dropped the leg, where it landed with a hollow thunk on the concrete.

Ladd became more insistent. "Daeson, get inside. We'll handle this. This isn't the place for you."

Ladd was right. This was entirely the wrong place for him. There was no point saying anything more to anybody here, they were all blind. Even Hammond and Marcus, who'd seen everything that had gone on and did nothing but their jobs. He was sure that Spier and Ladd and the others would get rid of the bodies— bodies of people who used to be their workmates and friends—and then continue on as though nothing had happened.

Daeson couldn't bring himself to look at Marcus' corpse again. He walked to the Queen's back door, feeling as though he could no longer ignore what was happening around him. When it affected those outside the Queen, he could pretend that they were only criminals and deserved their afflictions. He couldn't pretend that Marcus and Hammond had deserved what had happened to them.

Daeson walked aimlessly through the building—or so he thought, until he found himself in Marcus' room downstairs. He shut the door, wanting privacy before he looked around. He saw a jacket draped over the back of a chair at a desk. There was writing paper on the desk's surface but nothing was written on it. Farther around was a narrow wardrobe that could only hold a modest supply of clothes. A double bed filled most of the room. On the bedside table sat a lamp (that was currently turned on, for Marcus' room was underground and had no windows) and a figurine of a sparrow made out of fireglass. The figurine reminded Daeson that Marcus had been fond of small birds and had often spoken about wanting to keep an aviary, but he hadn't the funds or the space. Marcus would never be able to do that now.

He'd expected to be overwhelmed by grief and sadness but Daeson found himself lamenting the pointlessness of the situation instead. Everybody at the Queen of Hearts knew what they were doing was wrong, yet most of them weren't bad people. Nick certainly was, and likely Xenik was too, since he had the stomach for extracting information out of unwilling captives, but the rest of them were just hardworking people, their loyalty misplaced.

Did Omerri know? She'd created the Queen, with its brothel and nightclub and gambling rooms... but Nick was in charge of the details. He reported to her but did he report everything? What would she say if Daeson told her that Nick killed two employees? Would she recoil in horror and comfort him for what he'd been through? Would she justify that Nick was only doing what was needed, because someone had to? Or would she say nothing at all, damning herself further because she knew that Daeson would see the truth?

He crawled onto the double bed and lay on his side, staring at the wall and finding a smudge on the paint. He imagined Marcus might have gone to sleep staring at that smudge, but of course the idea was irrational because the light would be turned off.

Daeson rolled over and reached for the lamp. When he found the button that turned it off and clicked it, the darkness was complete.

"Daeson."

His eyelids fluttered open. A soft amber glow filled the room and he rolled onto his back to see the source. Omerri held a lantern between them, the light inside borne of battery power rather than of flame. He made a sound that was garbled even to his own ears. He didn't know how many hours had passed because he was still tired. He realised his exhaustion was because the heal took so much out of him. Grief did the rest.

"Daeson, darling, come to bed. All is forgiven."

All is forgiven? Was she serious? She'd run off because she hadn't known he was eighteen years old, it wasn't something he'd done to her. He needed to talk to her about everything that had happened after she'd gone but his sleep-addled brain wouldn't allow him to get it all straight in his head.

"No. I'll see you in the morning," he told her. He didn't miss the frown that flitted across her brow before she smiled again.

"Darling, you can see me when we wake up together. Don't you want things to go back to normal?"

Daeson didn't think their versions of normality were the same.

"No, I want us to spend the day together tomorrow. No interruptions."

She blinked her surprise.

"You don't want to spend the night together, first?" she asked through a light smile, though her voice had hardened. They both knew she didn't believe he would join her.

"I need to be on my own right now," he admitted.

"Then on your own you'll be," Omerri agreed. She left, taking the lantern's light with her, darkness shrouding the room in her wake.

Daeson went back to sleep.

CHAPTER TWENTY-TWO

Afterglow

VEN though she wasn't entirely sure why they were going to Nick's place in Portside, Synjan had more pressing questions to ask.

"He healed me, didn't he?"

Nick spared her a glance, pressed his lips together and continued to look out the windscreen. He was driving a car she didn't know, at a vastly reduced speed to the last time he'd been behind the wheel.

"Daeson," she offered helpfully, in case he wasn't saying anything because he wasn't sure who she was talking about.

It took a while but he eventually answered. "Yes."

A zing of unadulterated pleasure shot through her and she grinned broadly at her companion's profile. "I knew it. Does Omerri know?"

"That he healed you? Fuck, no!" Nick exclaimed. "Though I s'pose she'll have to," he added despondently. "You can't tell Ellis about him."

"Oh."

"I mean it! Not a word or Omerri'll kill us both!"

Synjan didn't like the idea of that so she veered away from the topic.

"He's been living with you for a long time," she hinted.

Nick refused to take the bait.

"Why did you tell him to stay away from me?" she asked, her voice cracking. Without warning, her lower lip trembled and she was fighting off tears. She ached with the knowledge that there'd been another Wanderer so close to her yet the man she loved and trusted had kept him from her. Deliberately.

"Hey," Nick crooned, reaching over to touch her cheek briefly. "Don't cry."

The words had no effect as her sobs increased. Even the tears felt good and cleansing, in a way. "But you kept him a secret. Another Wanderer! Why didn't you tell me?"

"Synjan, think about it," Nick encouraged, his voice gentle and patient.

She was quiet for the rest of the drive, overwhelmed by conflicting emotions. The answer to her question came to her as they rode the elevator up to Nick's penthouse. Ellis. If Nick had introduced her to Daeson two years ago, it would only have been a matter of time before Ellis found out. Ellis loved Wanderers. When he'd first met Synjan, he'd told her of his fascination and worship of beings who were more than normal humans. They had powers and could do extraordinary, inspirational things. He'd always doted on Synjan because of her power, wanting to know every nuance of how it worked and what she could do, rejoicing with her as she grew older and stronger with her Navigating.

Ellis had always done his best to keep her dealings with the Authorities to a minimum. She was certain that was why he was so disapproving of her spending recreational time at the Queen or doing jobs for Nick. Ellis knew how the Authorities treated Wanderers and he didn't like her brushing shoulders with them by choice. Over the years he'd bribed the Authorities for every bit of Wanderer information they'd ever recorded. He'd presented it to Synjan one year for her birthday but she'd been so saddened by the collection of torture stories that she hadn't read much of it and the whole situation had become miserable. Still, he'd proved his adoration to her with that act.

If Ellis had found out that Omerri was in a relationship with a Wanderer Healer, he would have done everything in his power to steal Daeson away from her. Ellis and Omerri at odds was not a good thing for anyone and Synjan and Nick would be the ones to bear the brunt of it. Nick had kept Daeson a secret from her in order to avoid complications with and between their respective bosses. Even though she regretted it, Synjan understood.

"Can I get to know him now?" she asked as the elevator doors opened directly into the foyer of Nick's luxurious apartment.

"I'm still not sure it's a good idea," he admitted, leading her through the open living space towards his bedroom ensuite.

"But he saved my life!"

"I know."

"I need to at *least* thank him."

"We'll see."

"You won't let me because of Omerri," she sighed, waiting obediently by the shower stall as he leaned in and turned it on for her.

Nick gave her an assessing stare. "She's in charge," he shrugged and there was enough of a warning in his tone that Synjan decided not to continue arguing. They were very alike. Both of them loyal to their bosses—to a fault.

"I think... just get in," Nick advised, looking her over.

She'd been deliberately avoiding looking in the mirrors in the large bathroom so she didn't know how bad it really was. She merely nodded and followed his instruction. Stepping under the hot spray fully clothed felt weird but liberating and she laughed jubilantly as she closed her eyes and the water pelted her upturned face. The external warmth didn't match the power of the heal but it was almost as lovely as it washed over her. The delicious sensation of life and energy flowing through her veins was revitalising and held her immobile with joy.

When she felt a presence beside her, she opened her eyes and found Nick had stepped into the spacious stall with her. His clothes were on the floor on the other side of the glass and she suddenly wished to be as naked as he was. She began hurriedly undoing buttons as he reached up to release her hair from the pins she'd tied it up with that morning. A lifetime ago.

"I thought you were dead," he whispered, his expression raw and his voice tight. His fingers worked into her hair, arousing tingles across her scalp and down her neck.

She nodded, her heart swelling with the love she felt for him. His pain was affirmation. She toed her boots off and threw her shirt into the corner. It slapped loudly against the tiles, leaving a bloody watermark that was soon washed away. Her bra followed.

While she worked on her pants, Nick unexpectedly gripped her shoulders and turned her around. At first she thought he was reassuring himself that there weren't any bullet holes in her back—and wasn't that something she wanted to see for herself?—but then he was working shampoo through her hair. She did her best to keep her head level as she bobbed down to take her pants and socks off but he didn't seem to mind. As he progressed to conditioning, she used soap to wash her body, finding she had to scrape bits of dried blood away but most of it came off quickly. For that she was glad. He combed her hair through and then she rinsed off.

"Have I missed any?" she asked huskily, holding the soap above her shoulder.

He took it without a word and she could hear it

squelch as he rolled it between his hands, gathering suds.

At first, he was focussed and efficient. He moved her long hair aside and washed her nape with a vigour that told her there was blood she'd missed. He rubbed his thumb over her left elbow and wiped diligently behind both knees. When he gently spun her to face him, his gaze was scrutinising as he washed her ear lobe and ran a finger inside the shell as well. He then took a step back, leaving her in the spray alone while he looked her over, making sure all vestiges of her near-death were gone.

His fingers traced her body and she smiled as she closed her eyes. Down her neck and across her collar bone, his touch drew shivers. Her nipple hardened against his palm as he tried to wrap his hand around one breast, brush-squeezing it before moving lower. His fingertips across her ribs had her catching a shaky breath, released in a whimper when his hand slid between her legs. She began to tremble with a need more ravenous than she'd ever experienced when he drew circles on her inner thigh, the slippery mixture of warm water and soap making her entire body feel slick and tingly.

He moved in to embrace her with unexpected fervour, pressing his lips to her forehead and talking against it while he squeezed her to him. "I don't know what I would have done if I'd lost you," he admitted thickly.

She could hear tears in his voice and her heart joined the song already throbbing inside her. She was alive, whole, and every cell was infused with love and a lust so overpowering it left her spinning. She clung to him, her anchor. "You didn't," she whispered back, curling her arms around his shoulders and lifting herself upwards. Her legs wrapped around him and she ground against him, his hardness growing against her softness. "I'm still here," she told him, elated when he dropped the soap in order to support her. "See?" she hissed, shuddering as his fingers slid into her, testing to see how ready she was. She had to bite her lip to keep from crying out as he brushed the centre of her arousal.

Wordlessly, he carried her out of the bathroom and took his time reassuring them both about how very alive she was.

CHAPTER TWENTY-THREE

Yacht

HAWKE made his way up the stairs to the bow deck, where he'd intended to do some stargazing. He'd left Brita and Tavi in the saloon, which could potentially end in disaster but he could tell they were both making an effort to be civil to one another. He'd brought his glass of red wine with him, which he held aloft, careful not to spill it onto the deck. He still wasn't used to the yacht's movement, even though he'd been on it for three days and right now they were anchored. He'd thought he would be the only one on the bow deck but he could see the unmistakeable silhouette of a man already there.

"Kegs," Hawke greeted before leaning against the railing beside his mentor. Kegan had a bottle of beer in one hand and he lifted it to acknowledge Hawke's arrival. "Thought you'd gone back to your cabin already."

"Clearly you were wrong," Kegan replied jovially.

"Still celebrating, then," Hawke said, sipping his wine. The yacht belonged to the Unit Commander. Many Authorities who lived on Ulsa Maya ended up purchasing large watercraft and living on them because it was cheaper than buying a house. Ulsa Mayan property was difficult to purchase, since it was in high demand within a world of archipelagos.

In celebration of Kegan Frederickson's fifty-second birthday, he'd invited the Cayden family for a jaunt on his yacht. Hawke had been included in that invitation and then Hawke extended it to Brita. It was their first off-world holiday together.

"The night is young," Kegan noted.

Hawke checked his watch. "Yeah, it's still your birthday. Just."

"Another year gone."

Hawke fell silent and the pair of them looked out over the dark water together. In the distance Hawke could see the flashing light of a buoy.

"What's that light?" Hawke asked, pointing it out.

Kegan looked in that direction. "A shipping buoy. Cargo ships run through here." He looked sideways at Hawke. "Thought you preferred to look up."

Hawke took a sip of his wine and nodded. "The zodiac constellations are the most common," he said. "I know them well."

"Is that right?" Hawke didn't know if Kegan was genuinely interested or merely indulging him. "Never noticed. Been through a lot of worlds." Kegan took another sip of his beer.

"Bet I've been through more, even with your head start."

Kegan turned so he could face Hawke directly. "I've heard you can portal in and out, same day."

Hawke was coy. "That's against the rules, isn't it?" he smiled.

Kegan made a dismissive noise. "It's against the body's limits," he clarified. "How do you do it? Is it the blood?"

Hawke watched as he swilled the wine in his glass, thinking about how to reply. Kegan had never treated him negatively and the question from anybody else would've felt invasive. Not from Kegan though, who Hawke trusted more than every other person in his life because he'd never asked for anything.

"It seems that way, doesn't it? Haven't you noticed that you can tolerate it better the more you do it? I know some people go backwards but most build a resistance. I certainly did."

Kegan nodded thoughtfully.

"Yeah, the lucky ones. The talented ones," he added, sounding amused.

Hawke wasn't sure what the joke was but he smiled along anyway.

"Has there been trouble at Oceangate lately?" Hawke prompted, curious about whether Kegan still made contact with Ellis. He assumed so but they hadn't discussed it for a few years.

"All was quiet when I was there last week."

Hawke expected more but that seemed to be the end of that sentence.

"How's Tiln doing?" Hawke asked. He'd never met the woman who'd captivated Kegan during one of his many visits to Trent.

"I almost invited her tonight."

"Oh? Why didn't you?"

"She's not a big fan of the Authorities."

"Neither is Brita."

Kegan made a thoughtful noise. "Well, they obviously made the wrong decision, didn't they, these women? Being with the likes of us. Maybe they'll come to their senses one day."

"I keep waiting for it to happen," Hawke admitted, a fear of his rising to the surface.

"Maybe it's our responsibility."

"To do what?" Hawke prompted, unsure what Kegan was implying.

"To let them go and find someone they deserve."

Hawke thought about and lifted his glass to Kegan. "I say, fuck that."

"I'll drink to that," Kegan said, clinking his bottle of beer against Hawke's wine glass. They both drank.

"What are you boys drinking to?" Brita asked from behind them. Hawke turned guiltily to face her, relieved that she'd only just climbed the last stair onto deck and probably hadn't heard any of their conversation.

"About the women in our lives," he answered truthfully. Brita smiled widely. She was still in her sparkling cocktail dress, a choice she'd worn for Kegan's birthday dinner in the galley. With her hair elegantly twisted to one side and draped over her shoulder, she was both sophisticated and sexy. Hawke couldn't help but admire her. When she joined him, he placed an arm around her waist and she pecked him on the lips before looking at Kegan brightly.

"And that's my cue," Kegan said, standing straight.

"Oh, don't leave because of me," Brita reached out to touch his arm.

Kegan chuckled and left without replying. Brita took his place at the railing, facing Hawke.

"It's a beautiful night," she said, not looking at the stars or the ocean. Hawke hummed his agreement and looked up. He could see the Pisces constellation and he pointed it out to Brita, who cuddled in close.

"How are you feeling? Bit better?" he asked softly, turning his head and looking at her. Their lips were close enough that it was easy for her to capture his and they kissed for a while. She tasted a little of mint.

"Mmm, much better," she replied with a smile.

She'd been queasy the first day out but that had quickly passed. He didn't think she'd thrown up but he also doubted she'd tell him if she had. Looking at her now, she certainly seemed much better. Her eyes were bright and she looked exceptionally happy. Obviously she and Tavi hadn't argued before she'd decided to join him.

Hawke took a sip of his wine. It was almost finished now and Brita was watching him closely.

"Something on your mind?" he asked.

"Not at all. Just reflecting on our time together."

It was unusual for her to be so melancholy. Perhaps she was feeling the romance of being out under the stars on a fancy yacht and wanted him to come to bed with her.

"We could do some celebrating of our own," Hawke said, his hand caressing Brita's back. He could feel the zipper of her dress but no doubt it would have some kind of hook or button at the top. He thought about how best to tackle it.

"Ten years deserves some celebration, certainly."

The comment was enough for Hawke to pause. He hadn't realised they'd been together for ten years... she was twenty-five now and he was thirty-three. She must've misconstrued his desire for sex as a marker of their ten year anniversary together. Shit, had she bought him something? He could always play off the holiday as his gift to her.

"So serious," Brita jested, poking him playfully in the ribs. He flinched and she cuddled him—in apology, he supposed. She spoke while her head was nuzzled beneath his chin. "This is almost perfect."

Almost? He knew Brita, knew that she was hinting at something. Perhaps she thought he was planning something. He'd talked about celebrating and she'd talked about ten years together.

Oh fuck.

She was expecting him to *propose*. Of course she was, everything had lined up for it. Ten years together plus first off-world holiday together plus romantic trip on a yacht plus standing under the stars. If he'd had a fucking clue (and if he'd wanted to get married), he would have a ring-box in his pocket right now.

Panic set in. How he handled this moment could destroy their relationship. If he mentioned it—even if just to joke about it—he could lose her. He was selfish enough to not want that, he'd even drunk to it moments ago. The best way to get around this was to be clueless. She would be disappointed or frustrated with him—exasperated, perhaps even angry at him... but she couldn't blame him for being... well, dumb.

"I know what can make it perfect," he began, knowing that this also fed into her hypothetical proposal, but he didn't know how else to get around it. "I can take you back to our cabin, get you out of that dress and worship your body. *Multiple* times," he promised, giving her what he thought might be a lecherous grin and hoping to get away with it.

Brita looked up at him, searching his face with an expression on her own that he didn't recognise. The longer she looked, the more his grin faded.

"What?" he asked, playing the fool and feeling as though his thumping heart would give him away. Brita shook her head and laughed softly.

"That sounds like a promise I'll hold you to," she said, reaching down to cup him. He shifted beneath her hand, surprised that she was playing along. He was sorry to see some of the sparkle leave her eyes but also pleased that he wouldn't be missing out on anything, either.

CHAPTER TWENTY-FOUR

The House Always Wins

DAESON awoke in darkness. He felt as though it was morning, even though there was no light. Momentarily disoriented, he reached across the bed, expecting to find Omerri and feeling only cold sheets. The events of the previous day returned and he recalled that he was in Marcus' room. With a heaviness in his chest, Daeson fumbled for the lamp and turned it on, casting a harsh circle of light in the corner.

He squinted against it and rose. He felt crumpled and uncomfortable from sleeping fully-clothed, on top of the covers. He wanted to change clothes... jobs, souls. There was a funny taste in his mouth that he didn't recognise. He needed water.

Daeson found the shared bathroom and entered the toilet stall first before approaching the sink. He washed his hands while looking around for a cup—perhaps one that held toothbrushes or razors—but there weren't any. He bent and drank from the tap as best he was able, turning it off and straightening once the taste was washed away and his thirst quenched. With his hands braced on the lip of the sink, he stared at himself in the water-spotted mirror. There was a soft sprinkling of whiskers on his face, indicating he needed a shave. His brown hair was neatly cut, for he routinely had a visit from a barber, arranged by Omerri for the Queen's live-in staff. His blue eyes registered nothing of the shock or age he expected to see in them, which was both a relief and a puzzle. He'd heard many times that eyes reflect a life lived. He felt like yesterday morning should have left its mark on him.

He left the bathroom and headed upstairs to the

ground floor, exiting out of a sitting room into the corridor close to the dining room. He pushed away the thought that he and Marcus had sat there playing cards yesterday. Before he was murdered. Daeson paused at the landing of the next set of stairs however, trying to remember the last thing Marcus had said to him. Was it 'wonderful' or 'amazing'? It seemed neither of those things and yet both of them.

He moved on, taking the next set of stairs to the top floor. It was later than sunrise but earlier than Omerri usually awoke. Daeson thought he could sit on the chaise and think about the things they needed to discuss while he waited for her to wake up. He thought she might like that and he wanted to start the day well, considering there was a good chance the day would end poorly.

He opened the bedroom door and entered, seeing the rumpled bedcovers even before he closed the door behind him. The shower was running in the ensuite; he heard splashes of water as Omerri cleaned herself. Daeson wanted to join her, prompted further by the desire to strip out of his clothes, but he thought it would only distract him. Their nakedness together could only serve to lessen the tragedy. He sat on the chaise and waited.

The bathroom door opened, which baffled him because the shower was still running. His confusion took a different form as a naked man stepped out, rubbing his head with a towel. Once the towel was lowered, Nick got all the way to one side of Omerri's bed before he noticed Daeson and jolted, surprised at being watched. Daeson stared at him, expecting Nick to yell some kind of protest at walking in on him, but he merely dressed hurriedly instead. The shower shut off but Daeson's eyes were still fixed on Nick, who pointedly ignored him.

Omerri emerged next, one towel wrapped around her body and another around her hair. Unlike Nick, she noticed Daeson the moment she entered the room. When they made eye contact, a torrent of emotions battered his already fragile state and he stood up, unable to remain seated. Out of the corner of his eye, he saw that his movement had captured Nick's attention.

"How long have you been with him?" Daeson accused, his question based on the assumption that this was not the first time. Even though he was speaking well enough, he felt out of breath, like he'd been winded. Perhaps that was why such things were described as 'a blow'. Daeson felt like he'd been dealt just that.

Nick picked up his shoes and left the room.

"What are you talking about, darling?" Omerri asked once the door closed at Nick's back.

"How long have you been cheating on me with Nick?"

"Don't be so dramatic. You rejected me last night when I needed you."

"So you went to Nick?" he asked incredulously. "Do you even know what he did?"

"He told me! He told me everything, about how you almost spoiled things for us, for yourself. He told me that he had to sacrifice his friends for you." Her arms spread wide to demonstrate how magnificently Daeson had ruined everything.

"So he kills two people and it's my fault?" he asked, hearing his voice rise an octave. It made him feel like he wasn't going to be taken seriously. He had to calm down and say what needed to be said. She knew about the murders. That knowledge begged for another question to be asked. "So he tells you he's a murderer and you decide to sleep with him?"

Omerri huffed. "It wasn't like that. He was upset."

"*I* was upset! *He's* the one that pulled the trigger! He doesn't get to be upset!"

"Daeson, calm down. What's done is done."

Her words were so flippant that he could only goggle at her, his mouth open as he struggled to connect the woman he loved to the person he was looking at now.

"Did you not even think of me? Of us?" he asked.

"I went to you, I needed *you*. You turned your back on me. Did you think of *me*, then?" The towel on her head unwrapped and fell to one side. She caught it and pulled it the rest of the way off, her long black hair falling in wet strands over one shoulder. She looked beautiful, wrapped in a towel with glistening long, black hair, her stare intense. But she was ugly, too.

"It's always about you," Daeson replied. "You don't care about anyone else. You use everyone around you. Me. The girls... Nick."

Omerri rolled her eyes and stood near her dressing table. She dropped her towel onto the floor and twisted her hair with her hands so that excess water would drip upon the towel at her feet. She checked her appearance in the mirror and adjusted how her hair fell over her shoulder. Once she was satisfied that she was tidier, she turned back to face him.

"Don't be jealous. I don't care about Nick the way I care about you," she said. Her voice was soft, her expression matter-of-fact. She was telling him to behave.

"That doesn't make it better."

Her hands went to her hips and she looked away. He thought she was gathering herself to apologise, that there might be tears and she would throw herself at his mercy. She'd hinted that she'd felt rejected and it was possible that Nick—who always managed to talk women into his bed—had taken advantage of her fragile state. He knew Omerri didn't take rejection well, that she needed constant love and admiration.

"It's not like we did anything," she said.

Daeson struggled to understand what she was talking about. Whatever her words were indicating, they were a lie, so he was confused about why she would even bother.

"What?" he asked, thinking she couldn't possibly be talking about herself and Nick.

It was exactly what she was talking about.

"You walked in at the right moment and stopped us from getting into bed together." This was a combination of truth and lies and Daeson stared at her, queasy and concerned. "I know you're upset, that there was intent for me to... to be with him, but I was vulnerable and it's not like we actually did anything."

"Omerri, are you serious? I saw you both come out of the shower."

He didn't remind her that he could feel every lie that she told, squirming in that inside-place of his.

"Yes, I know," she huffed, appearing to lament her decision to shower with Nick. Omerri took a couple of steps closer to Daeson, in appeal. "That was wrong, I know. I'm sorry and it won't happen again. At least we didn't go through with it."

"Go through with what?" he asked, though he thought he knew. He needed to hear her say it, to see where this path of madness was truly headed.

"Do you really want to shame me, to make me admit it?" she pouted. When he didn't reply, she continued. "Alright then. At least we didn't have sex."

Incredibly, she lied. She knew about his talent and she lied anyway.

"Nick's clothes were lying on the floor beside the bed," Daeson said.

"I'm not responsible for where he puts his clothes,"

she scoffed.

How could she deny everything as though he was too stupid to see what was happening? Though really, he couldn't believe what was happening, it was too bizarre for him to comprehend.

"You admitted to me just moments ago that you slept with him."

"I did no such thing!" she said, but she didn't look sure. Finally there was truth but he thought it curious that she was uncertain.

"I don't need to catch you in the act to know it happened," he told her.

"Daeson! Why won't you believe me? You know I can't lie to you."

"You *can* lie. You're lying quite a lot, actually."

It was the reminder she needed because she looked away again. He recognised it for what it was, this time. She was thinking up another tactic. This was what she did; she thought up ways to manipulate him. Not just him, he was sure, but everyone in her life. This was why she was sitting up in the penthouse and everyone else was running around doing her bidding.

Somehow, it helped him to deal with the pain inside his chest—it didn't lessen it, but he thought he could survive it.

"How long have you been fooling me?"

"I haven't been fooling anyone, Daeson," she replied, her tone cool when she turned to face him. He thought he might be talking to the real Omerri Backhouse now, the one that hadn't a chance to think up a new tactic because he wasn't falling for any of them and had stalled her next idea.

Her words sat in that peculiar place in his stomach where metaphors lay. It was ironic that this was the statement that was caught between truth and lie, considering it depended on whether someone could be fooled... or wanted to be fooled. Had he *wanted* to be fooled by her?

"Did you ever love me?" he asked quietly, suddenly vulnerable and doubtful.

"Of course I love you!" Omerri said. She closed in the distance between them, enough so that they could reach out and touch one another, but she must've seen enough of his hurt and anger not to try. "Daeson, I love you."

It made it harder on him, that this statement was real. She loved him, yes, but did she love him like a child loves their favourite toy? He didn't think it was genuine, anymore.

"Do you love Nick?" he asked.

"Stop talking about Nick," she said, sounding annoyed. "I didn't do anything with him."

Daeson had nothing to say in return. He couldn't. He was too shocked to reply. Somehow, in the middle of their argument, in between statements of truth, lies and half-lies, she'd started to believe her own lie. Somehow, her lie had become the truth. He didn't know that this was something that could even *happen*. She'd lied about being with Nick and then lied about lying, he'd seen it, he'd felt it, and now she was making a declaration that he absolutely knew wasn't truth, and yet it didn't affect him anymore.

"How can that be?" he asked himself. Omerri answered, thinking he meant her.

"Because you don't know what you saw. You misinterpreted."

Truth. Truth and more truth. How was she doing this? Was his talent broken? No. It wasn't him, it was *her*. There was something wrong with her, to be able to twist the lies in her head and make herself believe it. When they might've had a chance before, to work through this, there was nothing left for them now. He couldn't stay with someone he didn't trust. He couldn't stay with someone after such a revelation. It didn't matter if she loved him because he couldn't know if she'd merely convinced herself of it. He doubted it would take her long to convince herself out of it, either.

This was how she did it, how she lived with herself, how she justified the terrible things Nick did... that she asked him to do. Daeson saw it now. He'd heard it throughout his time at the Queen. She was the boss. She was responsible for everything that happened here. Nick was only her puppet, the one she had the tightest hold on.

Daeson turned and headed for the door.

"I thought you wanted to talk things out," she said scathingly. He didn't respond.

There was nothing more to say.

As he headed downstairs, he thought it made sense now, why Nick hadn't liked him from the very start. Nick had been with Omerri for years before Daeson had come along. It made sense that Nick had shared Omerri's bed many times during his time here. Daeson had always dismissed his ruthless antics as being borne from a thirst for power and control. He understood now that it was because of love, devotion and loyalty to Omerri. She'd taken another man—Daeson—into her bed and Nick had remained her loyal subject while watching from afar. No wonder Nick had hated Daeson from the start.

Nick and Omerri deserved one another. Thinking about everything they'd done, about the illegal activities and underhanded dealings and how Omerri paraded around in front of the Authorities who wouldn't touch her because she knew too many of their secrets... he could believe in such a thing as evil. He'd thought the cleric on his home world was bad but he was nothing in comparison to the crowd Daeson had fallen in with.

He walked past the open door of the white room, the first room he'd stayed in. If he was going to leave this place, he would need to take a change of clothes with him. At least some underwear. He wasn't going to go back upstairs to get it. There was a chance that he still had some of his clothes in this room. With a two year gap, he hoped they would still fit him. He didn't think he'd grown much between then and now, but the clothes wouldn't lie.

The wardrobe offered him not only a couple of shirts, but also a small bag to put them in. He found three pairs of underpants in a drawer and put them in too. There were no socks so he would have to make do with what he had on for now. His property deed and pouch of coins were long gone, thrown out to hide evidence of his Wandering. They hadn't been worth much in this world anyway.

He went down the next set of stairs and knocked on the door between the Queen and the neighbouring house where the girls lived. Jade wasn't rostered to work today so he had to call on her at home instead. It was early enough in the morning that she might not have gone out.

Ruby answered his knock. She was barefoot and dressed in denim cut-off shorts and a white t-shirt. He'd never seen her in anything so normal. She looked like she'd been crying. When she saw who was at the door, she didn't say anything but she did open the door wider to let him in.

Daeson thanked her and moved past. He'd been in this house only twice, which was enough for him to remember where Jade's room was on the ground floor, close to the back. He headed in that direction and knocked on her open door. Inside he could see her brushing her hair. She was dressed up nicely, like she might be going out to the shops. When their gazes met, her expression changed to concern and she put down the brush. Daeson stepped inside at her invitation and she hurried to close the door behind him.

"I walked in on Omerri and Nick," he said before she could question him. There was no point delaying the news.

There was a large winged chair facing the bed that he sat in, and Jade sank to the edge of the bed.

"Oh, Daeson. I'm so sorry."

She didn't look surprised.

"Did you know about them?"

"Kind of. I'd heard rumours but I didn't know for sure."

"You had to have an opinion," Daeson challenged, angry to be the last to know. Jade tilted her head.

"I wasn't going to make trouble between the two of you because of rumours, Daeson."

He slumped in his chair, defeated. Why was he trying to pick a fight with Jade? He'd come here for comfort, not to make enemies.

"This place is poisonous."

"I know. It doesn't deserve you," Jade agreed.

"Or you."

She laughed hollowly, like he'd made a bad joke.

"I'm serious. When I met you, you were saving up to leave."

"You know about my mother."

Like a good daughter, Jade had given up half her savings to stop her mother from losing her house. Daeson was surprised that Jade would extend herself in such a way, considering the abuse she'd suffered at the woman's hand.

"That was a while ago, don't you have more saved up?"

"Not enough to get out of Gredann," she said with a

shrug.

"What about Portside?"

"Only if I don't want furniture," she smiled.

"Then stay in Dockside on your own terms, with a different job. It's still an escape."

"I don't see it that way," Jade explained sadly, as though she was letting him down. In a way, she was.

"I hope you change your mind. If you do not leave soon, I fear you never will."

They both fell quiet, staring at one another before Jade broke the silence.

"Do you have a plan?"

"There are a lot of farms outside of Gredann. I should be able to pick up work at one of those."

Jade nodded, then stood and extended her hands to him. Daeson stood and they embraced. He felt like he was abandoning her but she wanted to stay. In spite of everything, she wanted to stay.

"This house doesn't have a back door, buddy, but if you leave out the front here, nobody will see you go."

"Thank you."

There was little else to say. On the way out, Jade ducked into the kitchen and supplied Daeson with a couple of small water bottles and some packaged food, which he dropped into his bag. It was full but not brimming.

"Do you have enough money?" Jade asked.

Omerri had always controlled Daeson's money. He'd thought it was a convenience but now he realised it was just another way for her to control him.

"I can get by with what I have," he said. He wasn't going to take Jade's money when it was connected to her ability to escape.

She was satisfied with his answer even though he hadn't replied directly. How many times had Omerri fooled him this way, replying to questions that sounded like answers but were really trickery or distractions? How many times had she phrased herself just so and he wouldn't question her? How many times had her words felt not quite right in his gut and he'd justified to himself that her lies were only to protect him? How blind in love had he been?

"What kind of blessing should I give?" Jade asked, pulling him out of his reverie.

"What?" he asked, confused.

"For your travels. What kind of blessing? I want to wish you well."

He'd told her that the Gods here were the same as on his world. His world had been full of blessings and well wishes connected to the Gods, he'd even told her some of the Lessons that the stories of the Gods held. She'd called them morals, which made sense to him and he found quaint.

"Portos," he said, instinctively. "May Portos be your guide."

"Then may Portos be your guide and rain down blessings all over your ass."

"Thank you, Livia," he said, using her name because he wanted them to part honestly. He kissed the top of her head when she hugged him again, tightly.

Daeson stepped through the front door and down onto the footpath. The morning was still cool but it held the promise of a hot summer's day. He hoped to catch a ride before noon.

CHAPTER TWENTY-FIVE

Broken Rhythms

FTER three hours of impassioned and fulfilling sex, Synjan was forced to leave Nick's bed. And his apartment. They showered again, he produced some clothes that fitted her and then she was hurried out the door before she fully comprehended what was happening. Certainly before she rallied an objection. The sunlight was fading, Nick had another night at the Queen to oversee, there were things he couldn't put off any longer—she understood, right?

Synjan said she did but she was lying. When he left her outside the Office and drove off, she was swallowed by a feeling of solitude so intense it muted her senses. Staring up at the familiar walls of her home stirred no emotion. She couldn't bring herself to go inside but there was no impetus to be anywhere else. She turned away and started walking.

The curfew siren sounded its first warning and she observed her neighbours hastening to shut themselves inside their homes. A bicycle squealed to a stop and was carried up the stairs and inside as she passed, children were called home and someone kindly asked if she'd heard the siren as they bustled in the opposite direction. She nodded to acknowledge that she had but they were already behind her. None of it seemed to have any substance.

It was curious. She'd gone from feeling *everything* when she was healed to feeling nothing in a short amount of time. It was like she'd used up her year's quota of emotions in just one day and what remained was a hollow shell. She was looking at the world—her home—but not understanding any of it because she couldn't connect with it.

What finally spurred her back to the Office was the roar of an Authority vehicle as the night patrols started. Sour emotions rose like bile but she turned and ran, suppressing them. Mapping was a reflex, the grid a solace and the rhythm of her feet striking the cobblestones soothing. Her mind burrowed in on itself as she made her way through the streets. Everything from the broken bits of gutter she leapt over to the way the shadows shimmered over the warehouse walls was known to her. She'd run routes, dodged detection and lapped this town more times than she could count, yet tonight it was different.

Tonight, it didn't feel like her home, just a place she lived. And it wasn't so special.

She emerged from the internal stairs in the Office to find Ellis sitting at the dining table. Most of the lights in the living area were turned low, except for the ones glowing brilliantly above his head. He was seated at the end of the table, half turned towards the stairwell with one leg crossed over the other. His right arm was draped elegantly across his lap, the other curled around the book on the table.

The whole scene struck her like she was watching an inexplicable stage production. Ellis was the star. She was his understudy but it occurred to her in that moment that their roles would never be reversed. How could they? She wasn't in control of any aspect of her own life, let alone on the verge of controlling Ellis or his business. He'd never surrender his power willingly. She was the one who followed orders. She helped out when Nick asked her to. She did everything she was told and even asked for more aggravation, in order to please them. Her blind acceptance assured that it would always be this way but where did that leave her?

Today, it had almost killed her.

"Synjan," he smiled, her name on his lips part exclamation, part reprimand. "Where have you been?"

Dying. She blanched and searched for a better answer. "Walking."

"All day?"

"Oh. No, I was... doing stuff for Nick for a while."

"I see. Did you hear about the base?"

"Yeah." He was frowning at her like she was a puzzle he couldn't decipher and she was compelled to add something else, to deflect his scrutiny. "Can't believe it got bombed."

His expression didn't change. "Are you feeling alright?"

I almost died today. "No!" she exclaimed, probably too exuberantly.

Ellis blinked, his fingers starting to tap thoughtfully against the edge of the book.

"I, um, feel a bit... queasy," she qualified.

"Something you ate?" he asked mildly.

She realised she hadn't eaten all day, yet she didn't feel hungry. "Probably. I might go to bed and see if it passes."

Pointing in the direction of her bedroom was unnecessary but she did it, feeling like a small child asking to be dismissed by a parent. Ellis nodding his assent only fed into the hyper reality of the situation as she scurried away.

Taking off the foreign clothes didn't abate the feeling of disconnection like she expected it would, nor did being surrounded by her own belongings. She crawled into bed naked, rolling her wooden kitten between her fingers. She clasped it close to her nose, able to make out only the shadow of it in the darkness.

I almost died today. She clenched her eyes shut, expecting the thought to resonate as it had when she'd been with Ellis but she just felt... empty. If she concentrated, she could recall the glorious feeling of being alive after she was healed but no details of the horror that necessitated it. She knew it had happened, could recall the facts but was unable to embrace the near-death on anything but a superficial level. Perhaps it was her mind trying to protect her. No doubt its toxicity would infuse her slumber by delivering vile nightmares... if she managed to sleep.

It was her last conscious thought. When she awoke the next morning, it took her a few moments to process that she really *was* awake. She'd slept soundly and by the time she'd completed her morning routine, she found it was after ten of the clock. She'd even slept in!

Dressed in casual clothes, she padded out to the kitchen. She still wasn't overly hungry but she had some toast, cleaned up after herself and walked into the living area. There were things she needed to do today; she was fairly certain she had a meeting that evening but she couldn't be bothered looking at her appointment book. Everything seemed so trivial and unimportant. From her vantage point in the middle of the room the house was filled with cheerful sunlight and cosy furniture, homely and comfortable.

With renewed eyes, she recognised it for what it was. Not hers. They were Ellis' belongings, pristinely arranged in Ellis' home. A variety of circumstances had led to her being welcomed here but as she looked around, it was apparent to her just how little impact she'd had. She'd claimed a bedroom and an office, most of which were filled with the things she needed to do her job. Nothing here nourished her soul and she was bereft in the wake of that realisation.

The day became a protracted event with Synjan moving listlessly from room to room, occasionally crossing paths with Urvasi. They shared friendly smiles but no conversation. At dusk she walked up to Whale Lookout but watching the sun sink into the ocean failed to revitalise her. She was soon faced with the realisation that it was also just another place now. The sanctuary she'd visited when she'd needed to be made whole in the past no longer had the cure she sought. She'd been propelled beyond it; the veil woven of comforting things and places had been torn away and it wasn't able to cover the void inside her anymore.

She returned to the Office before the sun was gone, admiring the way the sky burned with colour. It seemed an excessive tribute to such a lacklustre day and it made her feel inadequate. There was beauty and untold treasure to marvel at in the world around her, yet she spent every day focussed on the mundane, the negative, the lethal. She was loyal to Ellis, thankful and obliged to him, but she wasn't doing justice to herself.

Ellis found her a short time later in his office. She was sitting at his desk reading the Wanderer files he'd gathered. Once, he'd told her they were for her, because of her blood, but he'd added to the collection. Since she hadn't returned to it in the years between, he was obviously accumulating information for his own purposes. With a more mature perspective, she could now appreciate the resource for what it was. It was reassuring that the Authorities still didn't know what all twelve powers were.

"Looking for something?" he asked tersely.

Synjan lifted her head and gazed blankly at him. Standing in the doorway, he looked austere in his fancy black suit and she realised she was supposed to be going with him. He was rightly annoyed that she wasn't ready to attend the business meeting he was about to host at his restaurant, Elfremi's, but she couldn't muster the usual guilt to please him.

"No. I was just looking over your Wanderer

information."

"*Your* Wanderer information," he scowled, tugging at his shirt sleeves as he stepped into the room. "Why aren't you ready?"

The light refracted on his glasses, momentarily shielding his eyes until he stopped directly in front of her. He looked disgruntled but still as vital as ever. She thought he would remain that way and possibly never die. A man so invincible didn't need someone like her, who had more frailties than she cared to admit.

"I'm still not feeling well."

"You could have let me know sooner."

"I'm sorry. I forgot."

His expression shifted through a range of emotions that she could name easily by now; exasperation, anger, sympathy, frustration. She was a problem and he didn't approve that she wasn't solved yet.

"You're not yourself. You should see a doctor, there's obviously something serious going on. You're never sick."

She nodded, feeling like she was able to concede to his demands—even though they weren't really fighting. The need to oppose him was an instinct. "You're right. I'll make an appointment tomorrow," she agreed.

His shoulders relaxed. A solution had been offered and accepted. "Good," he pronounced and stepped around the desk to kiss her goodbye. He paused to frown at her before his lips connected. "Where are your glasses?"

She tilted her head up at him and frowned back. A glance down at the papers she'd been reading confirmed what she suspected; she could read everything perfectly. She'd done it automatically, her thoughts distracted. Now she realised the truth. Daeson had healed life back into her and healed her poor eyesight. Wonder opened inside her like a flower to the sun. It was all she could do to muster a response. "In my office. I don't need them yet."

Ellis' expression was disapproving but he kissed the top of her head anyway. He sighed as he straightened, already looking around for something. "Enjoy your evening and get to bed early. I'll let you know how it goes in the morning. First thing," he told her dismissively.

Synjan murmured her assent, watching as he found the paperwork he sought, shuffled it into a sleeve in his briefcase and left. He didn't look back and she remained at his desk thinking about that for far longer than was warranted.

CHAPTER TWENTY-SIX

A Formal Affair

WITH the business on Baxter finished, Hawke returned to Othello. Standing outside in the portal pick-up zone, he zipped up his jacket. He'd come during spring but the chill of winter remained like an uninvited relative. He'd sent a portal-gram to Brita yesterday, with his arrival date and time. There was always a chance she might not show up but he recognised her little green car when it pulled in.

He jogged over and tossed his carry bag into the back, dropping into the passenger seat and meeting the peck on the lips Brita offered as greeting.

"My place?" she prompted, pulling out in front of another car that beeped. She waved a vague apology through the back window and accelerated. Hawke secured his seatbelt and marvelled once again at her driving behaviour. He'd forget that she was impatient and aggressive on the roads until each time he got in the car with her.

"Sure. Aren't you working?"

"I took the day. Have to welcome my sweetheart home," she said, reaching over to squeeze his thigh. Hawke grinned, happy that they were back on the same path. He wasn't looking forward to the day when she told him there was someone else in her life.

"That sounds promising," he said, covering her hand with his own so it would stay where it was.

"So how many weeks are you here for? Twelve?" she guessed.

"Maybe. Official word hasn't come through but it should be about that." With ten months on the job, it was likely he would have a full three month break. If a hunt went over the six month deadline, the bureaucrats started scrutinising their validity. Hawke usually ignored whatever they had to say but he would always accept their compounded leave. It was rare for him to be called back to work earlier, but it had happened. Enough to make Brita cranky whenever their time together was cut short.

"It better be," Brita said through her teeth before she turned a glimpse of a bright smile his way, caught between looking at him and the road. "I have plans. Boo-ha-ha."

"What the hell is that?" Hawke teased.

"It's an evil laugh!"

"You're supposed to laugh it, not *say* it."

She giggled and smiled as she drove, passing cars and braking hard at lights that she couldn't charge through.

Hawke stared at her profile, knowing she was turning thirty soon and wondering if she was worried about it. When he'd turned thirty, he hadn't much cared, but approaching forty made him uneasy. She'd teased him about his sensitivity but his insecurity was borne from his lack of achievements rather than the impact of time on his body and face. She seemed as young and vivacious as ever, her light blue eyes still held that twinkle of mischief and intelligence that had captured him early on. While he'd been away, she'd had her hair cut fashionably messy. It was still long enough for him to run his fingers through.

Indecent thoughts followed and he shifted her hand a little higher on his thigh.

"You'll have to wait, I'm not doing that *now*," Brita admonished. Her cheeks had pinked but he didn't think she was embarrassed. More like excited.

Hawke said nothing but moved his gaze from Brita

to the windshield, where the scenery of his favourite world—a world he'd made his home—passed in a blur.

Hawke lay replete in bed with Brita pressed against his side, her head resting on his shoulder. There was a large black and white photograph on the opposite wall that was new since last time he'd come here. Half of it was filled with a section of ferris wheel while the other half had nothing but sky. It intrigued him, that she would choose something that he found banal.

"I should mention we're going out to dinner with some of my friends," Brita said.

Inwardly, Hawke cringed. He hated most of her friends.

"Do I know them?" he asked.

"You know one couple, Tina and Gregory, and you know Janine as well, but she's got another man in her life now."

"I don't know a Janine," Hawke said as Brita rolled away. His body felt cold where she'd been.

"Yes, you do. I work with her at Shuttle Operations. You met her last time you were here." Hawke said nothing and Brita looked over her shoulder at him when she sat up. "Brown hair, freckles, bit shorter than me." When he remained quiet, she rolled her eyes. "Big breasts."

"Oh, yeah," Hawke said, even though he still didn't have a clue.

"Perv," Brita said. She grabbed her pillow and threw it at his head as he laughed. She headed for the bathroom but her mobile phone rang and she detoured to it. Hawke watched her look at the screen before she answered it, then she sat at the foot of the bed, solving whatever problem had arisen at her work. He reasoned that after hours calls on her days off were the price of being the boss.

He thought to beat her to the shower, hoping she'd join him. It had been quite a few days since he'd last shaved and he was developing a light beard. He knew Brita usually kept a few disposable razors in one of the sink cabinets. He opened the top drawer and found a pack at the back, though it was the rectangular box near the front that caught his attention. A silver foil packet had fallen halfway out. Within the foil's blister pack he could see there were a few rows of blue pills and a single row of pink pills.

He knew there were multiple reasons why a woman would use birth control, and Brita choosing to use it was certainly none of his business. Early on in their relationship when she'd mentioned she might like to be a mother one day, he'd been forced to admit that he would never be able to do that for her, his sperm count was low to the point of non-existence. The DOME had discovered this during their tests throughout the years. Impregnation would be nothing short of a miracle. Initially it had been a relief but on reflection it became a disappointment. He and Brita ended up having unprotected sex and years later there were still no consequences.

The birth control was a reminder that he'd promised her nothing, that they'd never spoken about exclusivity and his fear that she might end up with someone else while he was on mission was a possible reality. Still, she'd come for him at the portal terminal and taken him home and into her bed. They were still together. They had a 'don't ask/don't tell' understanding—not that they'd actually discussed it outright. He used protection with other women and assumed Brita did the same with other men.

Before he could be discovered searching through her bathroom items, Hawke closed the drawer and hopped into the shower. When she eventually joined him, he kept his discovery to himself.

Tina and Gregory were a married couple, both of them friends with Brita before they fell into their own romance. Hawke had known them for some years and didn't mind them, though they were both braggarts, touting their achievements and material possessions at every opportunity. Janine was someone he only vaguely remembered, she was too insecure to make an impact on him the first few times he'd met her. Her new boyfriend Evan had enough confidence for them both and was the kind of man that Hawke wished he'd met under different circumstances—like being his quarry.

Evan was a passive aggressive bully that reminded him of Polsen, only with more charm and diplomacy... not that it made him charming, more like a sleaze, forcing his opinions on others. Brita appeared not to notice, though this was not her first time going out with the new couple. She laughed at Evan's jokes even though they weren't funny.

"I heard a rumour," Evan began when the desserts arrived and were set down before everyone.

"I don't listen to rumours myself, but go on," Hawke interjected, wanting to swat the bastard down at every opportunity. Unfortunately, Evan's eyes sparkled in a way that reminded Hawke of a time long ago, when he'd faced down a foe over bread rolls.

"Oh, this rumour is exceptional. It's about *you*. When Brita mentioned your name, I was *positive* I'd heard it before. It took me a while to make the connection, *Hunter* Hawke Donovan," Evan said, leaning back in his chair and ignoring the slice of cheesecake in front of him.

"You're in the Authorities," Hawke stated. It was the only way someone could know his rank, though Evan would have to be fairly high up to have access to the names of the Hunters. Hawke didn't bother to see if surprise registered on the faces of Brita's friends though he did notice Evan looking around the table. His words wouldn't have had impact, Brita had already told her friends years ago. Not to be outdone, Evan revealed more about what he knew.

"Do you realise how many times the Nakhari Base have requested your assistance?" Evan addressed his girlfriend and the others around the table. "Nakhari Base is the biggest Authority Base on the world of Femme," he explained. "City of Ning, I believe, a city which is a *sight* to behold, or so I've been told. Myself, I've never been there."

"Femme?" Tina squealed. "I've always wanted to go there, but I can't because they'd treat my poor Gregory so badly," she pouted at her husband who shrugged.

"I'm not a fan of slavery," Hawke countered, not feeling guilty for his jab at Tina. Femme might be considered a tourist world because it was pretty and technologically advanced, but any world that enslaved its citizens was fucking backward in his book. Femme wasn't the only one, either. He doubted Tina would speak so fondly of the four slavery worlds that treated women as possessions.

"But they wouldn't have you there to *enslave* you, Hawke." Evan leaned forward and picked up his fork, slicing into his cheesecake as he spoke. "Quite the opposite, in fact. I heard they want you because of your special abilities. Wouldn't *that* be empowering?"

Brita's hand not only found Hawke's knee, she gave it a warning squeeze. Hawke did the calculations in his head about who might have this kind of knowledge about him and he didn't like the answer.

"That kind of information is classified," Hawke bluffed, hoping Evan was lower down in rank than he expected and had somehow come across the paperwork because of his job. "I'd hate to have you arrested."

Evan stared at Hawke for a brief moment before breaking into laughter. To Hawke's ears it felt forced but everybody laughed along with him except for Hawke and Brita.

"You're a *delight*, Hawke. Brita told me you were witty." Evan winked at Hawke before eating his forkful of cheesecake. Hawke thought that would be the end of it. Evan thought differently.

"I do wonder though, how a man who dislikes slavery so much as to not be a fan of it," Evan began, capturing everyone's attention once more, "justifies killing those of his own kind."

Rage bubbled up from Hawke's chest and lodged in his throat.

"Evan! That's too far, even for you," Brita replied, speaking for Hawke. Their table had grown quiet, wide stares focussed on Evan, Brita and Hawke.

Evan lifted his hands in a gesture of surrender, his fork still held in one.

"Oh, I meant no insult by it. I've let my interest eclipse my manners and for that I do apologise. The Hunter Division does valuable work protecting the worlds from those defiant criminals who shift worlds willy-nilly." Evan turned a shark-toothed smile to Hawke. He lowered his hands, dropping his fork onto his plate before extending his hand for Hawke to shake. "Forgiven?"

The rage was still coiled in his throat but he was aware of being watched. A sideways glance at Brita revealed tension in her shoulders and expression. He didn't want to make a scene. Evan's behaviour would be a reflection on him, not on Hawke. It was difficult to shake Evan's hand so he consoled himself with a jab of his own while he did it.

"As much as a Spy can be forgiven."

Evan's eyebrows shot up in genuine surprise and he laughed off Hawke's comment as yet another joke. Hawke relished the sound of its forced quality.

"If I was as petty as him, I would report him but guys like that don't pay for their actions, that's why they end up that way," Hawke said, his tirade not slowing down even though they were fifteen minutes into their trip away from the restaurant. "Fucking Spies, they think they're better than every other Division because their training touches on a lot of different skill sets. They don't get that this makes them masters of nothing. Except lying," he spat.

He glared out the window.

"He thinks he knows everything about me because he saw my file. It's a big fucking file but he doesn't know *me*. It's the whole 'sum of my parts' argument, don't you think?" Hawke looked at Brita, who was driving serenely. He supposed she wasn't in a rush to be anywhere. "I am not the fucking sum of my parts. You can't know me by the shit you read on a page. I know that's what Spies do, but it's all fucking trickery, you with me? A con-man doesn't know who you are just because they can get close to you."

She said nothing. He thought she was letting him vent, so he took advantage.

"And it's the same old fucking bias, isn't it? Like what he does is somehow more ethical than what I do. Like getting close to someone before he slits their throat is better than putting them out of their misery at a distance." A glance at Brita revealed a frown and he retreated from discussing the killing. "He's got fucking balls, going at me across the dinner table like I don't matter enough to treat with respect. It's the same old shit, Brita, they're happy to use me to their advantage but they only tolerate me. Like I'm some fucking secret to keep in the corner. And the ridiculous thing is, it's because of my *blood*, not because of what I do."

He fell silent, listening to the purr of the engine of her little car. They were only five minutes away from her place now and he could feel himself calming. Brita didn't say anything in response, focussed intently on driving.

It wasn't like her not to ask questions. He'd anticipated some difficult ones. Like how he'd figured out Evan was a Spy. Or if Hawke had ever seen his own file, to know how large it was. Or why he'd chosen to become a Hunter in the first place. Or how he felt about his bloodline (though she might've made assumptions about that already).

It took him a moment to realise what was bothering him about her silence.

He knew Brita well enough to know that she avoided conflict by not talking about things she didn't like. She'd explained a few times that there was no point continually discussing subjects that caused her heartache. This both inspired and frustrated him. He could understand her point but she would never be able to resolve anything should they disagree—not that arguing ever fixed anything anyway.

Her silence was what made him understand why he'd never fallen in love with her... and never would. He loved her; he loved her so much it hurt to be away from her but it wasn't the same as being *in* love with her. He should've asked her, should've prompted her to tell him what was on her mind, but he already knew.

She never talked about his being a Hunter. He'd thought that her dislike of his position was understandable.

It wasn't until that moment in the car coming home from the dinner, that he realised she never talked about his being a Wanderer, either.

CHAPTER TWENTY-SEVEN

Rescue Mission

ELLIS had been gone more than an hour when Synjan received an unexpected visitor. She was sitting at the dining table eating the supper that Urvasi had insisted she needed when Omerri erupted from the stairwell. Synjan froze, her lips closed around her forkful of food and eyes widening at the petite tornado that barrelled into the room. She'd never seen the elegant madame in such an unkempt state; her eyes were red, her cheeks were stained with tears, her hair was a mess and her mouth was the most perfect proclamation of tragedy that Synjan had ever seen.

"Thank the Gods, *Synjan!*" Omerri wailed, hurrying around the table and falling into the chair beside her. Perfectly-manicured talons clutched at Synjan's arm as Omerri made a show of looking furtively around them. "Are we alone?"

Synjan was forced to chew quickly and swallow in order to answer. It was enough time for her to develop three strong hypotheses about what had rent Omerri's world asunder. All of them centred around Daeson, which aroused a welcome spark of interest in Synjan.

"Ellis is out. Urvasi is downstairs."

"Good. I need your help!"

"*My* help?" Synjan asked, her voice going up an octave with surprise.

"Yes! Daeson's *gone* and I need you to tell me where he is! I can't find him and I... I can't live without him," she declared, flapping her hands frantically. She was soon clutching at Synjan again, her sodden blue eyes wide with appeal. "*Please.* I need you to...use your talent and… tell me where he is. I've looked everywhere! You can do that, can't you? Find him? Please, you're my only hope!"

Synjan put down her cutlery and moved to detach Omerri from her arm. "Okay. I'll look, but you need to calm down, alright?"

"Yes! Yes, I can do that!" the onyx-haired diva assured hastily, scrabbling at Synjan's fingers as they tried to pry her loose. The two of them worked at odds for a few seconds, one trying to shake the other off, one trying to cling desperately.

"Let go of me!" Synjan ordered sternly, wrenching away.

Meekly, Omerri withdrew, busying her fingers with combing through her long tresses instead. "I'm sorry," she whispered raggedly, trying to find a more refined pose on the chair. "I'm beside myself with worry."

"Where do you think he might be?" Synjan asked, abandoning her food. She turned to face Omerri more squarely.

"How would I know?!" Omerri cried and Synjan realised her mistake.

"I mean have you checked through the Queen?"

"Yes! All three buildings. I had the entire staff searching. He's not there."

Synjan mapped and confirmed she was correct. Daeson's lovely blue pattern wasn't in any of the familiar places she'd seen it for the past two years. She'd have to widen her search.

"How long has he been gone?" If she had a time frame, she might be able to guess how far away he was. She was trying to avoid searching the whole city pattern by pattern. Her question had unexpected consequences.

"I don't know! Hours!" Omerri howled, losing all the composure she'd been harnessing. "We had a fight this morning — he didn't understand though, he thought I was with Nick but I'm *not*, he's wrong, he just— I couldn't make him *understand* so we had words and he went off and I thought he'd just gone to sulk like he usually does but then this afternoon I went looking for him and I couldn't find him *anywhere* so I started looking in earnest and I realised he's gone, he's really *gone*! I knew I had to come to you because you'd be the only one who could find him now, oh please, Synjan, help me bring him back home!"

Synjan took a breath before she responded, determined to stay calm. There was no point arguing with most of the story that had just been vomited at her (even though there was a great deal she could side with Daeson on and rebut), she just had to extract the important parts.

"You had a fight this morning?"

Omerri nodded, her lips arranged in a pretty pout of despair.

"And you didn't look for him until this afternoon?"

Another nod.

"Okay." Daeson could have been gone all day and Omerri wouldn't have any idea. Following a hunch, Synjan took a drink of water and sat back in her chair. Closing her eyes to concentrate better, she opened her mind. She lifted up, away from all the details of the thousands of patterns in the city and oriented herself towards the Portal. It beckoned her from beyond Gredann's outskirts and she moved slowly towards it, searching. She remembered her mother telling her that even though she was an Intuit she, like every Wanderer, had *some* instinct about the Portal.

It only took a minute for Sorrell Walker to be proved correct. Daeson had indeed left Gredann and was travelling south, in the general direction he needed to go to get to the Portal.

Synjan opened her eyes and stared at Omerri. There must have been something in her expression that alerted the older woman to what she'd found because her eyes lit up.

"Did you find him?!"

"Daeson Wandered into this world, didn't he?" she asked, ignoring the question asked of her.

Omerri went still. "I... don't see how that is relevant."

"I need to know."

"Yes. He did," came the reluctant reply.

Synjan nodded. "Then he knows what the Portal looks like."

Light blue eyes widened fearfully. "He's travelling towards the Portal?"

"Looks like it. He's well south of Gredann. I'd say he's been walking all day." There was a special kind of relish with which she delivered this message and she was rewarded with an appropriately horrified response.

"He can't leave!"

"He has."

"It's not safe!"

"He survived here. I'm sure he'll be fine."

"With my help! Synjan, you have to go and get him!"

"Do I?"

"Yes!"

"Why?"

"Because he's all alone! The Authorities are far more likely to find him than someone trustworthy, especially now he's travelling at night! Besides, I love him and I can't live without him!"

The words rolled off Omerri's tongue effortlessly enough to be true but Synjan still didn't trust her. "And having a Healer around full time is certainly comforting, I suppose," she goaded.

For the first time since she'd swarmed in, Omerri's disdain surfaced. Synjan could see the effort it took to suppress her true feelings in the way the brightly-painted lips thinned. "Daeson is more than just a Healer to *me*," she said stoically.

Synjan sighed, no longer interested in scoring points. Daeson was travelling towards the Portal and she was the only one who could reach him before he got there.

"Was Ellis' vehicle downstairs?"

It took Omerri a moment to follow the conversational turn. "I… no. I was able to drive in."

"I'll need a vehicle to go and get Daeson."

"Take mine!"

"How will you get home?"

"Nick will come and get me."

Of course he would. Synjan nodded. "Telephone him while I go and get some things together." She drank the last of her water and left the table without waiting for a response.

When she entered her bedroom, Synjan wasn't really sure what she needed to take but she was motivated by the notion that she might be away for a while. She had no idea what she was going to say to Daeson to get him to come back but she didn't anticipate it would be a quick conversation. They'd spend at least the night working it out.

The disconnection that had been so prevalent in the last twenty-four hours returned to swathe her as she hastened around the room. Into her camping backpack (it had a foam bedroll attached to it that she might end up needing) she packed far more than she probably needed but time was pressing and she didn't stop to debate. She gave over to instinct. All her ammunition supplies, guns, holsters, makeup, toiletries and a few changes of clothes were followed by the family keepsakes she treasured and as many bottles of water as she could squeeze on top.

As she was about to leave the room, the Wanderer files she'd brought upstairs caught her eye. After a brief hesitation, she sacrificed some water to work them in, along with a pencil case of stationery. Maybe Daeson could be tempted by the information in a way she initially hadn't been.

Back out in the living room, Omerri had finished talking to Nick by the time Synjan returned. The doll-like woman was pacing the floor despondently, hugging her elbows. She frowned as Synjan brushed past and set her backpack down on the kitchen floor.

"What's that for?"

"Supplies," Synjan said shortly, rifling through the pantry to find as much packaged food to take with her as she could.

"What for?"

"Doubt we'll be back tonight."

"Oh," Omerri breathed, no longer objecting as the food was shoved in wherever Synjan could manage.

"Is Nick coming?" Synjan asked, straightening up and hefting the pack. It was heavier than it looked.

"Yes, he's on his way."

"Where are your keys?"

Omerri withdrew a single key from her pocket and approached Synjan. Instead of just dropping it in Synjan's outstretched hand, she placed it on her palm and wrapped both of hers around it. Drawing it to her chest as she stepped close, she looked earnestly into Synjan's eyes. "Bring him back safely," she beseeched.

Synjan raised her eyebrows. "I'll do what I can." Her words didn't seem to reassure Omerri but Synjan didn't give her time to object. "What are you going to tell Ellis?"

Omerri looked like she'd been slapped.

When an answer wasn't forthcoming, Synjan persisted. "I'm supposed to be in bed and here early in the morning to talk to him. I'm already in trouble for hiding your secrets. You need to make this right with him."

"I don't want him to know about Daeson!"

"I know that. But have you got a better story to explain what I'm doing—other than the truth, I mean?"

"You're as bad as him," Omerri muttered beneath her breath and Synjan wasn't sure she enjoyed being likened to Ellis. Especially since she couldn't deny it.

"I'm doing *you* the favour."

"I know, it's just—"

"Look, I don't want to be a bitch but this isn't my mess to clean up. It's yours. You owe me."

Again, Omerri's true feelings for Synjan surfaced in her expression but she made a conscious effort to keep things civil. "Fine. I'll think of something to tell Ellis."

"Excellent. You should head downstairs. Nick's here."

"Alright," the older woman sighed and reluctantly pulled away. At the head of the stairs, she turned and delivered her parting shot. "I look forward to seeing you soon."

Synjan nodded, mapping Omerri's descent and answering in her head. Something in her argued that 'soon' wasn't likely but she wasn't interested in defining it.

Once Omerri and Nick had left, Synjan tidied up; it didn't seem right to walk out leaving a half-eaten meal on the table and all the lights on. Once she was satisfied everything was in order, she pulled on the backpack, grabbed her house keys and went down one floor to the business level. Bypassing the offices, she unlocked the heavy door to the vault. Ellis had stacks of thousands of Authoritan dollars in there and she took a few bundles. Daeson wouldn't be the first person to be persuaded to do something he didn't want to do because of wads of money waved in his face.

After she crammed the money down one side, she shouldered the pack and locked up as she trotted down to the garage. Bizarrely, Omerri had driven over in her limousine but Synjan didn't have time to waste. It would already be a challenge to get out of the city without being pulled over; perhaps the grandeur of it would be a deterrent. She could only hope.

She placed the large backpack in the passenger seat beside her, aware of it in her peripheral vision as she reversed out of the garage. Part of her knew that she wouldn't need all the things she'd taken but she was studiously ignoring that inner voice. She had a Wanderer to find by whatever means necessary.

As she drove away from the Office, she didn't look back.

CHAPTER TWENTY-EIGHT

Always A Choice

DAESON lifted his gaze from watching the small puffs of dust his feet kicked up and frowned at the sky. All morning it had been a wide open blue but early afternoon brought fat grey clouds that amplified the humidity. He felt smothered by it as he walked to the beat of an endless chorus of crickets. A bead of sweat rolled between his shoulder blades and he turned at the unmistakeable sound of an approaching wagon.

He was struck by a familiar memory, watching a horse and cart approaching him from behind... but it wasn't quite right. On his world, on Kharltae, the merchants had all been heading in a different direction, travelling away from Stonehearth, where he wanted to go. This time the wagon travelled in the same direction, its load full of hay bales instead of wares, the driver clearly a farmer, not a trader.

Daeson lifted a hand, gesturing that he wanted to catch a ride, not expecting the horse and cart to stop. He was surprised and pleased when it did.

"I'm looking for work," he said.

"You worked on a farm before?" the farmer asked, his gaze travelling over Daeson's form. His strength was being assessed, he was sure, but his clothes were light city-clothes, not the kind that would survive a day's hard work without tearing at the stitching.

"Yes sir. I grew up on a farm."

"Get on up, then."

Daeson climbed onto the driver's bench beside the farmer and thanked him.

"What do I call you?" the farmer asked.

"Daeson."

"Right. You can call me Nick."

Daeson blinked his surprise and looked forward when the farmer flicked the reins to get his horse pulling again. In spite of the invitation, Daeson couldn't call the farmer 'Nick'. He couldn't even think of him as 'Nick'.

A fair distance of ground was covered before the farmer turned the wagon off the main road, leaving compact dirt for loose dirt instead. Small grooves lined the driveway and the cartwheels fell into them—the ride smoothed out but Daeson thought this might be a task he was called on to help with. The driveway would need levelling soon.

"It's too late in the day for you to start work," the farmer said, "so we'll feed you and give you a bed. We can begin fresh on the morrow. I hope you still rise with the sun."

"I do," Daeson promised.

The farmer grunted.

He was fed dinner at the family table along with another farmhand. The farmer and his wife had two very young daughters. Over the meal, Daeson was briefly quizzed about his experience driving a tractor which he replied in the negative. He fell silent when no more questions were directed his way and allowed the conversation to flow around and over him, lost in his thoughts. When it was time to sleep, the other farmhand showed Daeson to their shared bedroom, which was just big enough to hold two beds and a wardrobe. He showered first and returned to the room to find the farmhand already snoring. Dressed in fresh underwear, Daeson crawled into the second bed and stared at the ceiling for what felt like a long time before sleep finally took him.

He was woken by the other farmhand moving around the room, getting dressed. Daeson hurriedly pulled on pants and a fresh shirt before following him downstairs to the kitchen table where a large helping of oatmeal was spooned onto a plate for him. It was still dark outside, though the sky had a mild streak of the sun's rays upon it, casting the world into an inky blue.

Pinks and oranges streaked the bottom of the horizon as Daeson and the two farmers headed out of the house towards the first field. Daeson was supposed to watch and mimic once they got out there, but he was distracted by the long black car parked at the end of the drive, on the opposite side of the road.

Anxiety flooded into him. How had he been found here, already? Was it Omerri or Nick sitting in the car, waiting for him? If he ignored them, no doubt someone would be sent over to talk with him.

"Look at that, you don't see too many of those around," the farmer commented. He looked at Daeson and his eyebrows rose in inquiry. He'd guessed correctly that a strange car was here because of the new farmhand.

"I'll be right back," Daeson said, intending to send the car away. He jogged down the long drive, careful not to put his foot into a wheel rut. He could see the limo door opening in the back

Not Omerri, I can't look at her again

and a blonde woman got out.

Synjan.

Daeson slowed down to a walk, confused as to what Synjan was doing here and why she was in Omerri's car. Was Omerri in the back with her? Who was driving? Was Nick here too? Synjan crossed the road and started down the long driveway to meet Daeson. They both approached one another but once there was enough space between them to talk, Daeson stopped. His arms were loose at his sides as he stared at her.

"Hello, Daeson," Synjan greeted him with a polite smile. She looked like something was on her mind.

"Hello. How are you feeling?" he asked. She looked better than the last time he'd seen her.

"Alive, thanks to you."

Daeson shrugged, uncomfortable with her gratitude. He'd saved her but she was still a stranger. He understood that, to her, it would be personal. To him... she could've been anyone. He glanced behind her at the limousine.

"Who's with you?" he asked.

"Nobody, it's just me. Omerri asked me to come."

Daeson visibly relaxed. He scoffed at Synjan, amazed that Omerri would think he would ever go back, after all that had happened. She truly was an expert at lying to herself.

"You don't want to go back?"

"Would you?" he asked, wondering if she was fooling herself too. Synjan hesitated in her response, clearly unprepared for his question. "I don't know why we do it, why we close our eyes to what's in front of us. Is it easier to pretend everything's okay? You, especially, after what happened?"

He watched as Synjan shook her head, the pain in her eyes clear. She wasn't oblivious to what she was doing in her life then, but was she like Jade, who would set herself so lofty a goal that she would never achieve it, hoping for the impossible and doing what was easy? Or was she like him, who had finally looked at the harsh reality of his existence and chosen to walk away?

"It's not easy. I've never found it easy but I've also never been able to close my eyes." She paused, choosing her words carefully, no doubt. "Do you know what a Navigator is?"

The question was unusual and he wondered why she would ask it. The only navigator he knew about was the kind that worked on ships. She couldn't be asking about that. He felt like he was missing information.

"Tell me."

"I'm a Wanderer, like you. I'm a Navigator, I can find the Portal and I have the ability to see people in my mind—"

"That's how you found me," he said, annoyed and impressed at the same time.

"Yes. Every person has a different—well, I call it a pattern. So I can tell people apart. And you're right, it's not easy to watch bad things happen. I find it even harder than you."

"Do you know he killed Marcus? Nick, I mean. Nick killed Marcus," Daeson said, needing someone else to know, to mourn him. It was because of her, even though it wasn't her fault. Maybe it was even because of him, but it wasn't his fault either. It was Nick's fault. As to who or how or why Nick had done it, Daeson didn't need to know. The reason didn't matter.

"To protect us."

"I don't want protection like that," Daeson said firmly.

Her expression shifted at his words but he didn't know her well enough to identify it.

"I understand. You may not want it but you need it. They know that and—"

"Don't tell me what I need. I don't need it anymore. I've left that behind and I'm done with it. I don't need you lecturing me," he told her, drawing himself up and placing his hands on his hips. He didn't want to hear Nick's and Omerri's words coming out of this blonde woman's mouth.

"Hey! I ended up where I was yesterday because I was on the base protecting *you!*" She threw up her hands in a plea. "Nick asked me to do it so the Authorities wouldn't find you."

Daeson took his hands off his hips, dangling them at his sides again. He hadn't known she'd sacrificed herself to protect him. It made him look at her differently; Nick did things unto others but Synjan did things unto herself. He didn't know her well enough to trust that she wasn't the enemy.

"Is that the kind of work you do? Putting yourself in danger?" he asked her, his tone calm.

"Let's just say that yesterday was not the first time I've been shot."

He looked at her, curious as to why she would put herself in harm's way for someone like Nick. Daeson supposed the interrogations and healing tasks he'd done for Nick were much the same, only he wasn't in danger when he did it. This world seemed to take advantage of Wanderers and their powers.

"Why do you stay?" he asked.

She struggled to answer. "Lately, I'm not sure. Are you going to stay?"

"What are you talking about? I've already left," he said, gesturing at the fields on either side of them.

"You've left Gredann, I mean Trent."

He'd left Gredann, the city... but she meant Trent, the world. It took him longer than it should've for him to comprehend the implication. She was asking him if he was going to leave the world, this time on purpose.

"I know it's dangerous to Wander," she continued, "but if you stay here, they'll find you."

He didn't ask who they were because it didn't

matter who she was referring to. Nick or Omerri or the Authorities. His powers were useful to all of them.

"With your talent, they'll never stop looking."

"Which one?"

"Omerri, Nick, the Authorities... Ellis. They'll all want you."

"No, I mean... because of the healing?"

"You're a Healer," she agreed, looking confused.

"Oh, you don't know," he said. He'd thought Synjan would have been told because she'd spoken nothing but truth throughout their entire conversation. He'd thought she'd been prepared by Nick or Omerri, knowing how averse he was to liars. If she hadn't known about his ability to detect a lie, honesty was part of her character. His opinion of her elevated a great deal—out of everyone he'd met, only Jade had spoken nothing but truth. "I also know when people are lying."

She frowned deeply.

"You've got... *two* powers?"

"Omerri said it was unusual," Daeson said, admitting he knew this much.

"Not unusual. Unheard of."

He shrugged.

"Daeson!" a distant voice called. Daeson turned to see the farmer staring at them and holding up his hands. He looked impatient.

"Look, I have to go. I don't want to lose my job," Daeson said thoughtlessly, instinctively wanting to please his new employer.

"Don't be ridiculous," Synjan admonished. "If you want money, I've got money. If you want to leave, I can help you. You can't stay here."

Daeson opened his mouth to protest but nothing came out. She was right, he couldn't stay here. They'd discussed how he wouldn't ever be left alone—but the farmer had shown him kindness and it didn't feel right to not pay him back.

"I'll have some money then. I should pay these people for food and board."

Synjan frowned but then it disappeared and she nodded emphatically. She dug into her pants pocket and pulled out a wallet. Daeson was given a handful of bills. He took them from her and jogged over to the farmer. The man looked surprised when Daeson handed over all of the cash.

"Thank you for taking me in. I'm doing something else now," Daeson said. The farmer stared blankly and Daeson had to turn away without a response. He and Synjan walked up the driveway together and as they got closer to the parked limousine, Daeson saw a huge dent and a long scrape along the side of the car.

"What happened to it?" Daeson asked.

"Oh, I've never driven a vehicle this long."

Daeson rounded the car to the passenger side, only to find another long and jagged scrape down that end as well. He didn't mention it and got in. This road didn't have many corners so he might be safe. He adjusted his seatbelt as Synjan settled herself behind the wheel.

"You didn't want to get your stuff?" she asked.

"I didn't have much, anyway."

"You shouldn't Wander without supplies."

Her comment brought to the fore what she'd assumed he was doing. He supposed he'd decided that as well, since he was in the car with her.

"It didn't do me much good last time," he said, thinking about his property deed and the coins he'd brought from Kharltae and how worthless they'd ended up being. "A tent might be nice."

"We'll get you sorted," Synjan promised before starting the car.

CHAPTER TWENTY-NINE

Driven

BY the time they arrived at the Portal, Synjan's senses were in overdrive. She felt like she was being pulled in a thousand different directions at once. When she reached the limits of the limousine's ability to drive off-road and switched it off in the open paddock, she could finally relax the focus she'd been forced to maintain to get them there. Balling her hands into fists while stretching, she rolled her shoulders with a sigh and turned to look at Daeson.

"We're here!" she enthused.

He gave her a look that told her she was being too loud or too obvious and pushed his door open, ready to fight the pending storm.

While they'd travelled, the weather had worsened. Summer's humidity had compounded and the whole region was on the brink of pandemonium. What was normally a broad grassy field surrounded by tall, leafy trees had become a writhing mass of shifting greenery pelted by strong, erratic winds. Greenish black clouds roiled above them, rumbling discontentedly as lightning randomly fired across their swollen underbellies. The air hummed with static electricity and, when Daeson opened his door, the smell of imminent rain (and probably hail) invaded the vehicle's cabin, promising a downpour soon to be unleashed.

Synjan fought her way out of the driver's side, squinting against the flying sticks, stones and leaves swirling around her. The door was wrenched from her hands and slammed closed as soon as she stepped clear and she made her way around to Daeson's side as quickly as she was able, the wind tugging viciously at her hair and clothing, her steps unsteady.

"Quite a send off!" she yelled at him, grinning as she gestured at the sky.

Daeson nodded and opened the back door of the limousine, leaning in to pull out her backpack so he could get to his.

After the last six and half hours driving with him, she didn't expect a great deal more. Daeson had proven very difficult to engage in conversation. She'd thought, when they first pulled away from the farm, that they had infinite conversation options, just considering discussing their talents, but she'd been wrong. Synjan had done most of the talking, telling him how she'd been born in Gredann to Wanderer parents. When she realised he wasn't asking questions and seemed more interested in what they were driving past, she'd switched tactics.

Asking him about his life hadn't improved the situation like she'd hoped it would. It had begun a little more positively—he'd been willing to talk about his world and he told her about how rural his life had been—but when she'd asked what had spurred him to Wander, it changed. He'd made some bitter comments about how it had been an accident, told her some of the event's details and become tight-lipped once he talked about waking up in the park in Gredann.

She was terribly disappointed. She wanted to know what Wandering had been like. She wanted to hear his thoughts on Gredann and the life he'd fallen into. She wanted to know how he'd endured a relationship with Omerri for so long. She wanted to hear what he hoped to find in the next world.

Most of all, she wanted to apologise because she knew (without asking) that everything past had broken his heart and he was now walking away because there were no better options available to him. Synjan wasn't responsible for his negative mindset or his shattered feelings but that didn't change the fact that she spent the rest of the drive lost in her own thoughts, trying to think of ways she could make his two years in Trent up to him.

Was leading him to a new world enough? She doubted it.

Their time in Poworth was relatively brief—they were there under an hour—but productive. Synjan took Daeson to a well-equipped store that sold travelling and camping supplies. When he offered no opinion either way on colours, styles or types of gear, she gave up asking and just shopped for him. He followed her obediently and watched as she gathered everything he'd need, from compact cooking equipment to all-weather clothing. The tent he'd spoken of wanting was designed to attach to the outside of his large backpack and she thought he looked quite satisfied with its pop up and easy pack away style. She believed he almost smiled.

At the register, Daeson's eyes widened at the amount Synjan paid for his gear but she justified it by saying she'd only bought the best quality equipment. Plus, Ellis wouldn't miss the money.

While they ate lunch at a local eatery, she went through everything, removing price tags and packing for him—including the rest of the cash. He tried to object but that died when she pointed out that Authoritan dollars would travel far better than the coins from his world had. Wherever the Authorities were known, their currency counted. It might buy him a night of comfort in a hotel when he needed it most, or even new supplies. If he could afford the space, he was better off taking it.

Now that it was time for him to gather his belongings and leave, she wasn't sure how to feel. Part of her wished he would stay but she knew, logically, that he couldn't. Of course, there were untold dangers ahead of him and she wished she could help him. He would be fine, she was sure, but...

When Daeson dropped her pack in front of her, Synjan took it and put it on, not wanting to lose it to the wind. Daeson was still organising his gear so she moved out of his way, drawn automatically towards the Portal. They were parked about twenty metres away from it and it was *magnificent*. She couldn't help but smile as she gazed at it, enraptured. She was closer than she'd ever dared go and she was dazzled by the shifting rainbow of colours that swirled and flashed within it. They were like dancing foil wrappers folded around a blinding pillar of light, its intense whiteness shining through the gaps as the beautiful array of colours exploded in endless, dizzying flares that shifted and swirled along its length.

Its song was hypnotic and deafening. Even louder than the gathering storm was the sound of her blood rushing through her veins, her heartbeat twice as strong and rapid as it pulsed in her ears, tingled along her limbs, burst in her chest. She was a part of this creature, this light that throbbed with life as surely as she did, and it echoed through her. As she stood there staring at it, she got the distinct impression it was looking back at her... and it approved her presence.

"Well, thanks for... everything!"

The words, shouted from beside her to be heard over the storm, startled her out of her reverie. She stared at Daeson, wanting to say so much to him, needing to warn him yet knowing it would do no good. He would be alone, beyond her protection, beyond her help. All he had were instincts and his abilities to rely on. She hoped it would be enough.

Synjan nodded and reached out to shake his hand, holding it while she bestowed on him the last he would know of her world—a traditional Dockside blessing. "May the wind always fill your sails, the sun shine fair upon your face and the channel home run deep and swift," she bade earnestly.

He inclined his head to acknowledge her words then pulled away from her. He walked towards the Portal, his steps as sure as they could be in the wild weather, his course unerring. He had no reason to look back.

Like a switch had been flicked, the rain began falling, blocking her view. Panic fluttered in her chest like a trapped insect, wild and fearful. She wanted to see him go, *needed* to watch him disappear into the Portal! She had to be sure he was safe, beyond the reach of everyone here, so she ran after him. He was a dark shadow falling between her and the light and she chased him with everything she had.

The storm's rage battered her. The Portal's song enticed her. She surrendered to the chaos.

Daeson's left hand lifted towards the prismatic splendour of the light and she was close enough to see it! To touch him. Her hand slid into his right and, just as he turned to look at her, he took the last step needed for his outstretched hand to be coated in light. Like a welcoming embrace, it surrounded them and they were gone.

AUTHOR'S NOTE

Here you are at the end of the second book this time. Thank you for coming along on the Wanderer journey with us.

The third instalment, titled Transition, is due for release in May 2016. It's going to have quite the change of scenery (plus a few more surprises).

Synjan, Daeson and Hawke will continue to travel from world to world, discovering not only each other but also their own true selves. We look forward to you getting to know and love them as much as we do.

—D & L

P.S. We would be extremely grateful if you could rate this book where you purchased it. If you really wanted to make us sing and dance with joy, you could rate it on Goodreads, too.

OTHER BOOKS BY THE AUTHORS

By Delia Strange

Femme: A Wanderer of Worlds Novel
Blue Shift

By Linda Conlon & Delia Strange

Axiom: Wanderer of Worlds 1

ABOUT THE AUTHORS

Delia Strange

I have always been addicted to strange and unusual stories. They call it speculative fiction nowadays. I was also enchanted by all manner of fantasy—from dark to epic to contemporary. I remember fondly those black and white TV episodes of The Twilight Zone.

Once I discovered that not only could I read such stories but also write them...! I haven't looked back since.

In my private life I'm married and have a young daughter, and have adopted two cuddly cats.

Linda Conlon

As a child, I was a voracious reader. Whether I was on one of our numerous family holidays, travelling to my younger brother's incessant sporting events or just lazing around at home, I was reading. It was a running joke in our family, that I never had my nose out of a book. My parents eventually learned not to pester me about the life I was 'missing' beyond those beloved pages; I didn't care. I was living hundreds of lives vicariously.

When I met Delia, that changed. She opened the world of writing for me and I experienced for the first time the wonder of creating, rather than just experiencing.

Now, I don't read nearly as much as I write and I'm very much looking forward to publishing the stories Delia and I began together as seventeen year old ingénues. It's time we told them to someone besides each other.